WARRIOR SAINTS - DESTROYER

STONEHAVEN ACADEMY SAINTS BOOK 2

CARLA THORNE

Copyright © 2020 by Carla Thorne

All rights reserved.

No part of this book may be reproduced in any form or by any electronic or mechanical means, including information storage and retrieval systems, without written permission from the author, except for the use of brief quotations in a book review.

Cover Design - Najla Qamber Designs

❧ Created with Vellum

CHAPTER 1

Sebastian

The boy had died.

Grief both crippled and propelled me into vast emptiness. My spiritual form churned in the depths of pain as anger and compassion warred in my supernatural psyche.

My presence shook with the burden of Mary's tears until the weight of it split the natural sky in a thunderous clap of utter despair. I soared until I could soar no more, and still could not escape the earthly desolation of the lost human.

I had done everything the Creator expected of me, yet the Warriors faltered.

Choices spiraled out of control, and the Destroyer took every opportunity to decimate the brilliant and gifted souls in my care.

And now those left in the wake of a staggering blow crashed against the rocks, all but defeated, and withered beneath a tidal wave of guilt.

My Creator loved me, of that I was sure, but how was I to reconcile my assignment and my failure and ever be worthy again?

I gathered Mary's tears and counted each one. I saved them to remind me of her anguish and of my own inability to help.

There would be no comfort. Nothing we had established carried us through the torrent of the loss, and I could only wait for the Warriors to trust me again.

I hovered in their atmosphere and lingered with them in their personal space.

They'd lost faith in the Creator, and they'd lost faith in their abilities.

And all I could do was suffer in their midst and contemplate the horror.

How had it happened?

How had we gone from that promising time in the garden to the end of a life?

Where did the Destroyer gain ground?

The days, weeks, and months of the Warriors passed in human time, and I vacillated in the spiritual realm—in the past, the present, and future—and waited…

And wondered…

And grieved…

I contemplated their series of moves and their battles. I retraced the steps, but the end was the same.

We'd lost him.

The boy had died.

CHAPTER 2

S cout

I went back to that garden every week for months after we'd met Sebastian.

Spring came, our finals blurred by, and I went to that garden regularly, and I sat on that hot bench in hopes of finding answers.

I'd all but given up on the thought of a god-like supreme being until that night we'd met the apparent angel. How was it possible there was an omnipotent ruler somewhere who loved us and wanted the best for us when so many people suffered and died?

Where was the Creator when a mass shooting was being planned?

Where were the Enforcers, Guardians, Protectors, and Warriors when children in other countries faced atrocities I couldn't comprehend?

And where was the Creator in the death of my family?

I wanted to talk to the man-angel-holograph-something-or-other who landed in the reflection garden that night and spoke all kinds of unbelievable things to us. If anyone knew where my family was, or how I could talk to them, wouldn't it be *that* guy?

"Umm... Scout?"

Ivy approached in my favorite pair of white shorts. Well, not *my* white shorts, but the pair of white shorts of hers that were my favorites when she wore them.

I forced my eyes off her shorts. "Just sittin'."

She shoved her hands into her back pockets. "Well, it's really hot out here and we have work to do, so..."

"It really happened, right? We were in this garden this past December and we met a freakin' angel, right?"

Ivy's shoulders sagged as she slid onto her usual large rock. "All right. We've been over and over this, Scout, and it's so hot I could cook fajitas on this rock, so can we go inside and finish what we came for and talk about this later?"

"Fajitas sound good."

She frowned.

"OK, OK, I know." I tossed my stick on the ground. "I need to get out of my own head and back into the real world and stop dwelling on all this."

"I've never said that. There is no rush on your grief. I know you want answers about your family, and everyone has to grieve in their own way and time—"

"Yes, I know." I stood. "You think what happened here with Sebastian was a special, isolated occurrence, and that his appearance doesn't mean he knows anything about my family."

"I didn't say that either. I understand you think if there's an angel there might be a heaven, and it would bring you comfort to know more, but what happened to us is so unbelievable and..."

"And even if he knew exactly where my family was, it

wouldn't change a thing because they're not coming back the way I knew them."

"Oh Scout, I also never said any of that. This is you being you and talking your own self into your own logical conclusion."

"Fine, then. Maybe a better question for Sebastian is where the heck was he and *my* Warrior helper when everyone died? Huh?" I looked to the sky. "What's the answer to that, angel? And why don't you answer? You said you'd be here when we needed you!"

Ivy stood and adjusted the big buckle on the belt she wore with those white shorts. "All right. We need to get out of this heat." She pulled me toward the path. "Remember. The visit that night was about our assignments, and about how Sebastian would be there when we needed him with our jobs. I don't know if you'll ever get all the other answers you want, Scout, but I'm here for you."

And I was there for her, but I'd been a mass of confusion since December and couldn't seem to pull myself out of the tangled mess. I was gonna have to get my brain straight if I was ever going to help anyone. Thankfully, there'd been no sign of any so-called assignments since that night. We were all still loosely bound together by our angel sighting, but it all seemed to fade—like everything did—with time.

"To recap," I said. "You're still on board with the whole Warrior thing."

"Oddly enough, I am. I don't know what it's all about, but I'm rollin' with it. I don't feel like I have a choice."

"And you think I'm putting too much thought into it."

"You put too much thought into everything, but that's what makes you *you*. Look. You have to do your grief journey on your own schedule. As for all the other stuff, you'll have to remember how much you already know. Seriously. You knew more of what was going on in the garden that night than anybody."

"Yeah, I felt pretty confident back then. Now? Not so much."

She pulled close beside me and bumped me off the path. "You'll be back."

"Hey, have you heard from Corey since our visit last week?"

"No, and it's weird. I know her parents have her on lockdown and she's getting better as fast as she can, but it's so messed up. She doesn't act like she used to. I mean the good parts. Not the sad parts."

"I know what you mean. The music and favorite subjects and stuff. But her parents explained how they're balancing her meds and she's in therapy all the time."

"Yeah, but the Corey I know doesn't seem to be there. You know? My mom's gone through medication adjustments and it's never looked like that."

"No two cases are the same."

Ivy stopped cold. "She's not in there, Scout."

Her tone sent chills up my arm. It would have felt good if it wasn't so scary. Ivy'd been right about the heat. I was sweating in places I know no creator ever meant for people to sweat.

"She'll be back too," I said. "It takes time."

Ivy didn't seem convinced. It took a moment for her to shake off her intense expression—and for me to shake off the chills.

"Anyway," she finally said and skipped down the path. "Do you know what day this is?"

Oh boy.

I didn't know much, but what I did know was that question never ended well for a guy. "Not gonna lie. I do not know." Then I braced for the blast.

"I guess you wouldn't really know it... But this is near the same day last year that I came to Stonehaven Academy. This very ice cream social we're setting up for was the day I met Paige and some of the other student ambassadors and club sponsors."

"And it wasn't long after that we met over the snake in the garden."

"Yep," she said. "The first part of September. And here we are. About to start school again…"

I wiped dripping sweat from my forehead. "…and about to die from the heat…"

She laughed. "That's your fault. Honestly, I don't know how you kept your lawn care business going all summer in this misery. And believe me, I didn't want to hike down to that garden."

"All right. I get it. I'll get a hold of myself before school starts."

"I know you will," she said. "Now go cool down and get into your school shirt for this meet-n-greet. We're representing Stonehaven."

"Hey Ivy?"

She turned and I couldn't speak. That hopeful expression and warm smile was the reason I got up every morning.

"Yes?"

"It's going to be a great year."

Her expression changed. "Sure it is, Scout."

But I'd seen that look before.

Ivy already knew something wasn't right.

CHAPTER 3

S hanar

Everything had been going as planned—for a while.

The Agent I'd fought for and won from his parents seemed to do exactly what I wanted, but there'd been an utter disaster.

I cornered the kid in my supernatural form as he walked home. "What happened with the Corey situation? She's still alive."

The kid didn't even blink anymore when I surprised him. He glanced over each shoulder and didn't slow down. "I'm not talking to you out loud. There's always a camera somewhere. I won't be caught looking like I'm talking to myself on the street."

I hovered near him as he went. *"Fine. What about Corey?"*

"I don't know. Paige had everything under control, but something went wrong."

"Don't pretend you don't know what went wrong, boy. You have competition, and you failed."

He picked up the pace as he trotted across the street. "You

don't need to remind me of my competition. Believe me. I have a front row seat to keep an eye on them."

"And yet, you cannot handle them."

He made an abrupt stop on the corner. "What's your point?"

"My point is, you have a responsibility to me. Now that the Warriors are aware of their strengths, you must get stronger also." I shifted my position. "I thought you didn't want to talk out loud. I'm sure there's a camera at this intersection."

He rushed toward his house. "Why don't you go talk to my parents? Isn't this more of their problem? Aren't they the ones who have an alliance with you?"

Ah, yes. The alliance. It'd been easy to trick them when he was a sick child. There was no better mark than a weepy father and mother whose son's disease-ridden blood was about to kill their baby.

Boo. Hoo.

It was even easier when the father's natural and inherent instinct was to lean into the darkness for help, rather than into the light.

And that's exactly what happened.

Generations of his family drew strength from my side of the fence. It was as if their slant toward wickedness ran through the bloodline.

I knocked the kid around a bit on the sidewalk and caused him to stumble. *"Is that what they told you? It's not the whole truth, you know. Bargains were made, but you grew. You could've made some of your own choices."*

"Fine. I choose to not listen to you anymore."

Rage engulfed the dark matter of my presence. I channeled it toward the boy and used the sudden appearance of a stone on the pavement to thrash him to the ground, face first. *"It's a little late for that. You've already made choices and completed tasks I set before you—and I have rewarded you with gifts and favor you've chosen to keep and use."*

The boy lifted his head from the steaming pavement. Blood pooled as drops fell from his smashed face. *"Then take them back."* He spit on the sidewalk and tried to stem the red flow from his nose as he stood. *"Take it all back."*

"Really? Everything?" My laughter rocked our atmosphere. *"You have no idea what that truly means. You should talk more to your parents. They've left out a couple of details."*

"What details?"

I glanced at the sticky blood on the ground. *"The most important details."*

The boy charged ahead. "I'm done here."

I let him go.

He couldn't get far anyway.

CHAPTER 4

M^{ary}

The ice cream social could not have gone worse—and that wasn't even the biggest disaster of the day.

The Saints Café wasn't cool enough to be comfortable, let alone serve ice cream. Student Council wasn't putting scoops into paper bowls so much as it was pouring melted goo and then topping it with sticky sprinkles.

Ivy wandered over from the fine arts table. "What's with the heat? I can hear the air conditioning humming at full blast, but it's not getting any cooler."

"Mr. Silva came by a bit ago and told the sponsors there's an issue. He's called for help, but it won't likely get better while this event is going on."

"Terrific. Who would plan this thing during August in Texas anyway?"

"It's tradition," I said and pointed to a melting bowl of chocolate chips. "Want a spoon of chocolate?"

"Normally, I'd be all over that, but it's too hot and I need to get back to discussing drama and choir with new students. At least the air is moving around."

And with that, a loud clanking sound signaled the shutdown of the entire system.

A collective sigh swept across the room as attendees rushed to get around to all the clubs they were interested in so they could get out.

Scout grabbed a handful of cookies from under the table and joined us. "What's with the heat?"

"Stay out of the cookies," I said. "Those are to crumble up on top of the ice cream."

"Yeah. No." He popped one in his mouth and paused while he chewed. "No one's eating the ice cream puddles. Dibs on the cookies."

I glanced over the tops of bobbing, sweaty heads. "What's Deacon doing here? He doesn't actually participate in a club that I know of."

Deacon waved us over when he saw us. I checked my table. "I'll be back to help you clean up," I told the StuCo president.

She gave me a *save yourself* kind of look and dropped her spoon.

Ivy jumped to see over the crowd. "Who's that with Deacon?"

"Uh… The one guy's his brother," I said. "I don't know who the other guy is."

She tugged on my sleeve and leaned in. "We need to find out because…*wow*."

"Right? It's like Wonder Woman and Aquaman had a baby."

"And popped out a Thor—because he's so fair and all. Or another J.J. Watt."

"Yeah, Wonder Woman and Aquaman's baby would be darker. He can't be a student here. He's so big and seems older."

Ivy put a finger to her lips. "Shhhh… Let's just look at him in all his blond-hair-blue-eyed sexiness."

Scout scooted closer. "What's going on?"

"Nothing," I said and pulled my gaze away.

Ivy fanned her face. "We're trying to get over to Deacon and his brother and that other guy. Can you believe more people are pouring in here?"

"They don't know the AC is out."

"Hurry up!" Deacon squealed and waved harder like it'd help us get there.

"*What?*" We piled behind him in line. "Why are we standing here?"

Scout nodded toward the guys. "Hey, Marcus. Hi, uh…" He extended his hand.

The big guy took it. "Jacob."

"Oh yeah," Deacon said. "If you don't already know, this is my brother, Marcus. And this is Jacob. He moved in one neighborhood over from me."

I met his intense blue gaze. "You're a new student here? A…senior?"

He grinned and looked away. "Nope. Junior."

Deacon slung his arm around the big guy and poked him in the chest. "This dude's a beast on the football field. The Stonehaven Saints might actually win a few games."

"Nice," I said. "And they'll let you play? I mean, all those weird rules about changing schools when you're an athlete."

"We're working it out. I didn't come here just to play for the Saints. It was more of a family business decision. And because my parents hate each other."

"Oh."

He blushed and turned away. "Sorry. You all didn't need to know that."

We all took a step forward with the line.

"Doesn't bother us," Scout said. "You can't say much that would shock us."

Ivy pushed Scout forward. "Hey, Marcus, what are you doing here? Are you a new student too?"

"Nah… I graduated from the public school down the street. I'm only here because this guy doesn't have a car."

"Yep," Deacon said. "My big bro is off to college in central Texas to play baseball."

"Wait. You're brothers and you went to different high schools?"

"Yeah. True story," Deacon said. "There are five of us and we're all adopted. Our parents got us at different times, so we went to whatever school was best at the time. In Marcus's case, he was already at the other school and wanted to stay."

I'd liked Marcus from the day I met him. His bright smile, deep dimples, and sweet personality made him my favorite of Deacon's brothers. I hugged him. "Congratulations, Marcus. You're gonna be great."

"Thanks. You too, killer. No mercy on the field."

"No mercy."

"I'm goin' out," Marcus said. "Hurry up, bro. I have to be somewhere."

Jacob smiled my way. "Soccer?"

"Yeah, but I don't think any college is looking for me."

"Me either. Your friend Deacon exaggerates."

"Ya think?" I laughed. "And that's only one of his charming personality traits."

At that moment, as mine and Jacob's eyes met in that hot and crowded room, something happened. It wasn't big and dramatic and colorful. It wasn't earth-shattering. My heart didn't thump and my knees didn't buckle.

It was like a soft little white-capped wave that surprised us. Its curling water came from behind, splashed around us, and pushed us toward each other in a quiet surf.

Jacob was easy. Jacob was significant. Jacob was…something I couldn't see clearly. But as with everything those days, I tucked the feeling away to question it later.

Scout broke the spell. "What are we in line for?"

Deacon took another step forward. "OK. Brace yourselves. Three words. Colorado. Ski. Trip."

"Oh c'mon." Ivy turned to leave. "Can any of us even ski? And I don't have the money for any trips."

"No wait," Deacon said. "Put your name on the list while there's still space. You can always remove it later. Take the info home and think about it."

"When is this trip?" I asked.

"It's the week between Christmas and New Year's. Two nights, three full days. Telluride, Winter Park, or somewhere in Colorado. Doesn't matter."

"And how are we getting there? Holiday airfare? Packed airports? No, thank you."

"Fifteen-passenger vans. We sleep and listen to music. Some adult sponsors drive."

"And how many hours is that?" Ivy rubbed her forehead. "All of us in a claustrophobic van on icy, mountain roads with a bunch of gear? Also, *I have no gear.*"

Deacon raised his index finger. "OK, you guys are not nearly as excited about this as I thought you'd be."

Another step forward.

"Who wouldn't love Colorado in the winter?" I asked. "We never get to play in snow. But really, none of us ski."

"Yes, but we do love to drink hot chocolate with baby marshmallows and cuddle around a fire."

"Ewww," Ivy said.

"Not necessarily with each other," Deacon snapped.

"I get it," I said. "This is about Claire Cannon. I bet she's on that list. Anybody wanna bet?"

"No," Scout said. "I think we all know Claire Cannon's on that list."

"Just sign up while there's room," Deacon begged. "We'll sort it out later."

"I don't have the money," Ivy said. "And I don't know how many of our parents will want to pay for this."

Deacon smirked. "You all worked all summer. Didn't you save your money?"

I pinned him with an irritated glare. "Seriously? This, ladies and gentlemen, is from the guy who did nothing all summer but play video games."

"It's been a hot summer," he whined. "And you have no idea how many things my mom can find for me to do when I'm not in school. Me and Marcus took out our old deck and hauled off the wood to save money on the new one my mom wants."

"Congratulations," I said. "You pulled out some nails and moved wood around. Hope you didn't get a splinter."

"Very funny. What did *you* do?"

"I lifeguarded all summer at my community pool."

Scout, Ivy, and Deacon looked at me funny.

"What's wrong?"

Deacon's look of disbelief was comical. "You were serious about that?"

"Yes. It's great money and I've guarded every day, and didn't see you once. Plus, they have competitions with the guards at other pools. It's fun."

They all looked away as we took another step.

"All right," I said. "I can see the irony. Leave it alone."

Jacob remained quiet and followed along.

"Speaking of pools," Deacon said. "I understand Scout's giant hot tub and pool is up and running. I suggest a pool party this weekend to get this school year started right."

"Agreed," Ivy said. "Scout, you should post something. Everyone will show up and bring snacks."

"I don't know…"

"It's OK," Ivy said. She slipped her arm in his. "It'll be fun. We'll all be there."

"Yeah… Let me check with my grandma."

Deacon arrived at the table. "What's it gonna be?"

"Sure. We can put our names down." I glanced at the others and knew it wasn't likely to actually happen.

"Yep. Claire Cannon. Right here at the top," Scout said.

Scout passed Jacob the pen, but he passed it to me. "Go ahead."

"Are you going?"

"Oh yeah, I love to ski."

"All right," I announced to the others. "We have a real skier in our midst."

"Why do we need a real skier?" Gavin's voice tickled my ear from behind.

"Oh, hey! I thought you were at practice."

"I was. I am." He swiped a massive amount of sweat from across his face. "Sorry. I won't come any closer. I had a quick sec to come and share some news."

"What's that?"

"Movin' up to varsity."

"That's great, Gavin, but I am not one bit surprised." I bent to sign my name and pick up a packet. "Let me introduce you to Jacob."

But he and Jacob were already in the midst of the Stonehaven Saints football handshake.

"I guess you've already met."

"Yeah. Coach brought him around last week. But this week, I'll actually get to outrun him in drills."

"You think," Jacob said.

"I *know*. I'll see you out there later?"

"Yeah, I'll have all my paperwork in Coach's office by evening practice."

Gavin gave me one of his sly little winks. He did that when he wanted to kiss me but knew he shouldn't. "I have to get back."

"OK. Do you want me to put your name on this list?"

"Did it earlier before I headed to practice. I thought we could talk about it tonight."

Yep. There we were looking like an old married couple while our friends stood and watched. "C'mon, you guys, it's not that bad."

"It's pretty bad," Ivy said.

"Forget it," Deac said. "We're all signed up."

A cool puff of air landed on my neck as we stepped away from the table. I jerked around because I thought maybe Gavin had come back.

He was long gone.

"Hold on a sec," I said.

Scout stopped. "What is it? Oh…"

We all looked to Deacon, who studied his hands. "Yep. Something's up." He shoved them in his pockets as we looked around.

I tried to whisper above the crowd noise and so the big new guy couldn't hear. "It could be anything, and God forbid it's something big like an atta—"

"Don't even think that," Ivy said.

"I'm heating up," Deacon said.

Jacob nudged his way into our circle. "I don't want to alarm anyone, but look."

He nodded to the vents across the top of the cafe. Smoke curled from each one.

Scout snapped his fingers. "OK, how's this? Jacob and Deacon go to the back and calmly and quietly make people aware and start pushing them out. That *might* prevent a stampede when they start smelling smoke. Ivy, you and Mary go to the front and herd people toward the parking lot and watch for people who might fall or try to go back in. Flag down the fire truck when you hear it coming."

"What about you?" I asked.

"I'm going to find Mr. Silva and pull the fire alarm."

"Sounds like a great plan," Deacon said. "Let's do it."

Of course it *sounded* like a great plan. Though Scout had spouted the instructions in mere seconds, it took less than that for all hell to break loose. Why did we think there wouldn't be mass chaos?

Ivy and I grabbed a couple of teachers and parents on the way out. One was supposed to head toward athletics and make sure they didn't come running from the safety of the practice field and into a burning building. No such luck. She screamed and started crying and then took her own kid and ran for the main road.

I guess I understood the panic in a world of active shooters and mass casualties, but didn't somebody have to stay and help?

Ivy's guy bolted around to the front of the school to make sure no one entered.

In less than a minute, the wail of sirens sounded in the distance. Scout, Deacon, Jacob, and Mr. Silva headed out behind the last of the crowd. They were dang heroes, that's what they were, stridin' out of the café after everyone was safe, like wind-blown, slow-motion characters in a comic book movie.

"Get away from the building," Mr. Silva said. "I have to lock a few more doors."

"Hurry," Scout said. "I'll wait here and make sure no one tries to get in." Then he put a cookie in his mouth.

Ivy smacked the rest out of his hand. "Did you seriously stop for more cookies during a real smoke evacuation?"

"Yes, there was smoke, but it's unclear if there is a fire. Mr. Silva is convinced it's an electrical incident with that stupid AC system."

"Yeah, duh. That doesn't mean there's not a fire behind that wall or that there could be any second."

We found a tree and collapsed in the shade as firefighters converged on the area. "You should text your rides and let them know we'll walk to the road or something. There's no getting in or out of here."

Scout grabbed his phone from his pocket. "I guess there'll be an info blast later about when to come back and get belongings and clean up our tables."

Ivy poked her hair behind her ears. "That's going to be a literal hot mess."

I glanced at my fellow Warriors—and Jacob. I wanted to talk about it, compare notes, evaluate our actions… But Jacob was there.

Mr. Parrington passed by and slowed to take a good look at us. "I can't even with you four today."

Mrs. Thomas dropped her purse under another tree nearby. "They did a good job," she said. "Deacon was as cool as a cucumber when he started telling the adults there was a problem. I saw Scout grab Mr. Silva and pull the alarm."

Mr. Parrington nodded. "Thanks for letting me know." He seemed to be trying so hard to put the pieces together. It had to be frustrating by that point to never know exactly what was happening with us. "We'll talk soon," he said and walked away.

Marcus jogged toward us. "C'mon. I can get us out. I parked back by the tree line to be in the shade."

Deacon grabbed the ski trip packet he'd managed to hold on to. "Yessss! You comin', Jacob?"

The big, new, apparent football star had continued to be eerily silent. "No. I have to get to Coach's office and make sure some paperwork has come in so I can practice."

"Mary?"

"No thanks. My mom is coming because we have something else to do. I told her I'd head out to the road."

As the others left, I waited for Jacob to say something. What, I didn't know, but somehow I thought the guy who spotted the smoke and was so completely chill about it all might have something to say—especially after slipping into our group like an unidentified Warrior.

Was he? A Warrior?

I'd sensed something about him, but then wondered if what I felt was real. Whose side was he on?

Jacob smiled and stood to leave. "It was nice to meet you, Mary."

I stood too. "Wait a minute." I yanked the front of his sweaty shirt and pulled him so hard and so close he barely got his hand out to brace himself against the tree trunk.

"Take it easy," he said and lifted his hands. "I don't know what's happening here."

"Don't you?"

"Mary, I really don't understand. Have I done something to offend you?"

"Have you?"

His gaze narrowed, but nothing about him said anything more than that he was confused. He took a long look at my face —my whole face, centimeter by centimeter—to the point of it being uncomfortable.

I released him with a shove. "I have a question for you."

"OK."

"What are you?"

CHAPTER 5

Scout

The pool party finally happened, but it wasn't until Labor Day weekend.

School had started with its usual bangs and thuds, and everyone jockeyed for position on the social ladder—especially since Paige was gone.

The fried cooling system had to be replaced, but it was done in record time because of the heat. The *small electrical incident*—the school didn't call it a fire—was investigated and settled, and we were once again dragged into Mr. Parrington's office for a couple of questions. We didn't know why. It wasn't that big of a deal, and what difference did it make?

The new guy, Jacob, didn't help us stay under the radar.

Mr. Parrington looked him straight in the eye. "And you were the first one to see smoke?"

Jacob considered the question. "I guess, but all I did was say I thought I saw something, and these four jumped into action. I happened to be there to help out."

Thanks, Jacob. Way to point the heat away from us.

But after a while it all died down again, and I sat cross-legged on the edge of the hot tub while a bunch of people I didn't know ate my snacks.

Ivy relaxed in the water nearby. "Scout, you really need to get in here."

"Nah…"

"Do you want to go sit on the steps of the pool? You don't have to get all the way in. Just sit there. I'll sit with you. We can judge the chicken fights."

Nothing sounded lamer than that, but I still couldn't do it. The thought of watching people have their heads forced under water either on purpose or by accident was too much. To be honest, I didn't even look at the pool while there were people in it. It had all become one big nightmarish blur, and I didn't think I'd ever be comfortable around a big cement hole full of water some people seemed to find amusing.

"No, I'm good, but Ivy, look. Don't let me stop you from having fun. You don't have to babysit me. I'm fine. I don't know if I'll ever be a pool person."

"But we agree it's fine if I'm a newly-converted pool person and I can be a pool person here any time I want, right?"

"Right. Open and unlimited pool privileges."

"Good, because the pool at my apartment complex is creepy and dirty."

"My pool is your pool," I said and then felt my face catch fire.

"Oh brother."

"What?"

Ivy scooted closer. "Mary and Gavin are headed this way."

"Have you ever figured out what it is about him you don't like?"

She grimaced. "I don't trust him."

"You hardly know him because you haven't tried."

"And that's fine by me."

"How is that fine? I know you don't run to everyone with open arms and make fast friends, but you don't shut people out when they try either. Mary's one of your closest friends. How do you not know Gavin after this long?"

"I don't like the way he treats her, OK? He doesn't give her any space. He's everywhere, checking up on her... If he thinks they're alone in the hall he's sucking her face off." Ivy paused and shuddered. "Gross. You don't think they're... Ewww. No."

"I am the last person who would know anything about that."

She thrashed around in the water to face me and then laughed. "I'm sorry, Scout. Your face is so red."

"Yeah, hangin' around you keeps me in a constant state of some kind of embarrassment."

She smacked the water. "Well, I'm sorry I'm so embarrassing to you."

"You know that's not what I meant."

"What did you mean?"

"C'mon, Ivy. You're beautiful and talented... I don't know what I'm doin' here. I don't have pool parties where friends as cool as Jacob show up. I mean, look over there. That's a herd of leftover Arrows who don't know what to do without Paige. My grandma called those swimsuits scandalous and threatened to send one of them home. She gave her a pink, sequined breast cancer t-shirt and told her to wear it." I paused to catch a breath and should have stopped talking. I didn't. "This is truly not my life. Ever since we all got together, I'm completely out of my league. And you... The time I spend with you..."

Ivy blinked water off her lashes and stared at me.

I'd been trying to dig myself out of a hole and I only slipped in deeper. I was a teenaged boy. I had little to no control over how my body acted or reacted to anything. I was a mess. A mess with a supersized zit growing in the middle of my forehead right that very moment.

Ivy touched my knee and another swarm of hormones attacked from nowhere.

"I know what you meant, Scout. We're fine."

Easy for her to say.

In her mind, we were back where we started—our Scout and Ivy groove that everyone knew and recognized.

All my mind could see was her bobbin' in the water in a yellow swimsuit top and tiny swim shorts. I figured I would have to jump in the cold, deep end whether I was ready or not. We were more than friends but not quite anything else, and one day I was gonna grab that girl and kiss her. She was either going to kiss me back or beat the crap out of me.

I wouldn't survive it either way.

CHAPTER 6

I^{vy}

So… Scout was having a weird night at his own pool party.

I assumed it was because it was at his pool.

Nowhere in my most horrible nightmares, imaginations, or visions could I see being in the car one minute with my family, and the next under water, fighting for my life—and watching my family float away, disappear, and die.

I wanted to be there when he conquered his fear and dislike of socially acceptable water events.

It wasn't going to be that night.

And then Mary and Gavin showed up.

Gavin held her hand as they walked toward the hot tub. She clearly wanted to let go and fix the tie at her waist that held her striped wrap in place. The guy held on when she tried to pull away. It eventually dropped from her body and he scooped it up.

Possessive much?

Mary dropped her bag by a chair and rushed over. "Great party, Scout."

"Thanks. I think."

"C'mon in," I said. "There's room."

Gavin was at her heels. "Hey guys." He bent to nudge Mary's arm. "I thought we were going to see Jacob and the guys and start a volleyball game."

"We are. Go ahead. I want to talk to Ivy a sec."

Gavin seemed annoyed as he attempted to crowd in beside her. "I'll wait with you."

"No, go ahead. I'll be there in a minute."

I shot Scout an *I told you so* glance.

"Yeah," Scout said. "It's all set up. Just pull the net across."

Mary settled in as Gavin skulked away. "Where's Deac?"

Scout pointed toward the house. "He's in there charming my grandma out of another plate of brownies."

Mary laughed. "That would explain why Claire Cannon is over there with two other guys. He's going to lose his homecoming date two years in a row."

"Do you think she has any idea she's the object of his affection and the subject of so many of our conversations?" Scout asked.

It was kinda funny when I thought about it. We had at least one Claire Cannon conversation every time we were together and I doubted she knew Deacon existed.

Mary moved closer as another person dropped in. "What else is new? Have you heard from Corey?"

"No. I don't hear from her much. I wish she'd text me… Hope she's OK."

"What was the last word on when she'd come back to school?"

I reached for my Dr Pepper. "I don't know, but hey, check it out." I took a drink and pointed. "Cassidy is totally into Jacob and I think it's mutual."

Mary turned her gaze toward the couple and watched every move they made for longer than seemed necessary.

"Uh… Mary? Is there something you want to talk about?"

"What? No. Of course not."

I bit back a laugh. "Have you talked to him any more since the small electrical incident? Remember, it wasn't a fire."

"No. We don't see each other during the day, but he and Gavin have apparently been tearing it up on the football field. Half the time I don't know if they really don't like each other or if they're playing."

"Jacob is older and twice his size. They better be goofin' or Gavin might get his butt handed to him."

As we spoke, the two prepared for volleyball. Jacob stretched his long, muscular arms to snap the net into place while Gavin flapped in the water nearby and tried to help.

"I better get over there. It's time to pick sides."

"You just got here. C'mon, we have more people to talk about."

Mary hopped out. "No, I told Gavin I'd be there for the big game. We're a pretty good team at the net."

I wanted to roll my eyes but I didn't. "You athletes are pretty competitive."

"No, this is for fun. Come and play."

"I'm good. I'm waiting for Deacon to arrive with more brownies and we're going to watch and add commentary from over here."

"OK. See you in a bit."

Mary skipped off to stand in the group of people who waited to be chosen. Jacob won the coin toss and got to pick first.

He picked Mary.

Wait. *He picked Mary?*

Deacon returned and sat beside Scout with a bunch of snacks. "What'd I miss?"

Scout took a brownie. "Uh... You could say pool volleyball got a whole lot more interesting."

"How?"

"Captain Jacob had first pick and took Mary."

I laughed. "Yeah. Right out from under Gavin's control of her every movement."

Deacon waved it away. "He's messin' with his head. Classic psych move, and Mary's a good sport so she'll play along because she's also competitive."

"That's a pretty big move," I said. "He didn't even pick one of his own big football guys to dominate at the net." I dropped a bar-b-que chip and chased it around the swirling water to fish it out. "That's the words, right? You want tall people at the net to block and hit it back?"

Deacon shrugged. "Sure... But this is pool volleyball. These guys are more interested in whose bikini top is going to slide off."

"Don't be a pig." I tossed the wet chip and it stuck to his chest.

"And don't forget," Scout added. "You rotate to serve, so it's not like they'll be in the same place all the time."

"But Jacob's got Mary right beside him," Deacon said.

"Duh." I tipped the bag for dry chips. "Because she's a good athlete. She'll set him up for that spike thing or whatever. That's how you get points, right?"

Scout rubbed his eyes and laughed. "We are some amazing armchair quarterbacks over here. How has ESPN not called us to give us our own show?"

We watched a while, then it got more crowded.

Deacon changed position as the game heated up and the cheering got louder. "Why does Mary look so aggravated?"

"That could be anything," I said. "I don't think she's a big fan of Jacob. Ever since the fire—"

"Small electrical incident," Scout and Deacon said together.

"Sorry. Forgot. Since the small electrical incident, she's steered clear of Jacob. Maybe his move to pick her for his team made her mad. Or maybe she's mad at Gavin because he keeps making ugly faces across the net. You know he's not happy about Jacob picking his girl." I held my hand up for Scout. "C'mon. Pull me out. Let's get a better spot to watch the fireworks."

Those fireworks didn't take long to start.

I didn't know the score, but Deacon said that game was to win the set. OK, sure. What did interest me was Jacob and Mary at the net—directly across from Gavin. Mary looked like she was trying to have fun. Gavin, not so much. "Gavin should be careful," I whispered to Scout. "His claws are showing."

As expected, Mary tipped the ball to Jacob. I was unfamiliar with the rules, but I understood the stretch of his arm and that the explosive strike he executed was a game winner. The speeding ball dropped right behind Gavin and into the water for a flawless score.

The expected celebration was a mass of slippery hugging arms, splashes, and high fives—topped off by one spontaneous and joyful embrace between two not-quite friends—Mary and Jacob.

And Gavin lost his mind.

Rather than a sportsmanlike congratulatory handshake across the net, Gavin stalked forward, chest first, at the net, and bumped them apart. In one swift move, he dove down and shot up from underneath the barrier and took a swing. Gavin had some meat on him, but he had nothing on Jacob, who avoided the punch and pushed Mary out of the way.

Deacon jumped in to possibly... I have no idea what he was going to do.

"Aw crap, Scout," I said. "I'll go get your grandparents."

"No need. Between the security cameras and their stations by the window... Three... Two... One."

"Knock it off! Out of the pool!" Scout's grandpa was right on time.

Sadly, Gavin was slow to listen. When Mary made the mistake of stepping back in, she took one of Gavin's raging elbows dead-center to her face.

The blood came as though someone turned a faucet on at her nose.

Jacob scooped her up and had her on the side of the pool in only a couple of strides.

Scout tipped out an ice chest and gathered what he could in a towel.

Gavin hovered nearby like a near-feral cat that wanted to come closer but was afraid.

But Jacob...

Like a protective papa bear or big brother, he leaned against the wall, sat down, and propped her against his chest. "Lean forward. Breathe through your mouth." He held the wad of ice and blood-soaked towels and regularly switched them out with Deacon's help. "I got you," he said more than once and peeled her wet hair away from her face.

Scout's grandma rushed over with her phone. "Did she lose consciousness?"

"I saw black for a second," Mary said. "But I didn't pass out."

"Good. How's the bleeding?"

"Hasn't slowed yet," Jacob said.

"All right. Your mom's on her way to take you to the ER."

"Seriously? It's a nose bleed."

Deacon handed Jacob a fresh towel. "Uh... No. Looks—and sounded—more like a nose crack."

"Just being cautious," Scout's grandma said. "Don't want a crooked nose on that beautiful face."

"Tell your friends to head home," Scout's grandpa said.

"I need to be with Mary," he said and glanced around the pool. "I think they know the party's over."

"All right. I'll see everyone out."

Scout and I dropped to the ground near Deacon, Mary, and Jacob.

Gavin tried to slip into our protective circle. "Mary, I—"

"Dude." Deacon raised his hand. "This is not the time."

"I'm sorry, Mary," he persisted. "You know that was an accident."

She nodded. "Go home, Gavin. We'll talk later."

He didn't stay, but he didn't exactly leave either. Jacob shot him a withering glare that sent him shrinking to the corner of the house. I got madder with each burst of blood that spread on every towel we could reach, and wished Jacob would've used one of his grizzly-sized paws to smack the crap out of Gavin.

Scout's grandma stayed close. "How's the pain?"

"Between rolling an ankle on the field and takin' a cleat upside the head, well… I'm past all that."

"Dizzy?"

"No." She leaned her head back against Jacob's chest. "Why won't the blood stop?"

"Because it's probably broken," he said. He gently pushed her head forward again. "I know you want to lay back and rest, but stay this way so you don't choke or swallow too much blood. That'll only make you queasy."

I scooted closer. "Here. I'll hold your forehead in my hand so you can relax."

Deacon glanced at his hands. "No. Let me." He shrugged. "Worth a try, right?"

"Great idea. Now you're thinking like a…" I looked around. "Great idea."

The fast clip of Mary's mom's sandals screeched around the corner.

"I'm guessing that's your mom," Jacob said.

"Yeah. Let me stand up."

"No."

In one smooth move, Jacob stood and once again had her in his arms. He headed around the house. "Which one's your car?"

Mrs. Hunter pointed. They strapped her in with fresh ice and towels.

"Let us know," Scout's grandma called after the car.

Gavin still hovered in the periphery of the chaos and didn't say a word, and Jacob slipped off with his friends without a backward glance.

Deacon slapped his arm around Scout's shoulders. "Well, for someone who didn't want to have a party and didn't even get wet in his own pool, I'd say you'll be a legend within an hour."

"Yeah, that's exactly what I wanted." He tore away from Deacon's grasp.

I rushed to comfort him. "It's OK, Scout. None of this is your fault. Who knew Gavin had such a violent streak?"

"You did, didn't you?"

"Look. Just because I don't trust the guy doesn't mean I knew he was capable of decking his own girlfriend during a game of volleyball."

"And what about Jacob?" Deacon asked. "He instigated that whole thing by messing with Gavin's girl."

"That's one way to look at it," I said. "But it's no excuse for that kind of reckless outburst."

Scout narrowed his gaze. "But you yourself would have ripped Gavin in two if you could have reached him."

"So what? I'm not perfect. Never mind that now. Let's help your grandma clean up and get into some dry clothes so we can go by the ER."

"Yeah." Deacon rolled a whole plastic-wrapped tray of Rice Krispie treats into his dry towel.

"Really?"

"Yes. Really. Who knows how long we'll be at the hospital?"

I picked up a trash bag and gathered paper plates. I scanned the area for stragglers and was surprised to find Gavin still hanging out around the side of the house—with a girl.

But not just any girl.

Corey?

CHAPTER 7

Mary

My head bobbed against the seat as my mom took a turn too fast. "I don't teed ta hopital."

"Yes, Mary, you need the hospital. We have to be sure. It looks like a crime scene back there. What happened? Scout's grandma said Gavin hit you?"

"It was as assident."

"I'm sure it was, honey. Stop talking and rest."

"Then top assin testions."

She smiled and held my hand. "Sorry, baby. It's too swollen for you to make sense. You can tell me all about it after they get an x-ray, get the bleeding stopped, get the swelling down, get the pain under control… Honestly. How could Gavin be so careless?"

"Dats a testion."

"Sorry."

I squeezed my mom's arm with one hand and kept the ice

pressed hard against my nose with the other. The pain thrummed through my face like the beat of a thousand bass drums. My eyes blurred as the swelling spread upward, and it became harder to get a breath.

And boy, was I mad.

And hurt—not just physically.

And completely confused.

Why did Jacob pick me? I was flattered at first. Everyone talked about what an amazing athlete he was. Even Gavin admitted that. I thought it was about the game... About strategy. But why do something that would so obviously cause tension at a friendly pool party volleyball game?

And I couldn't even begin to explore the depths of my sadness about Gavin.

The rage in his eyes and anger that was so focused on Jacob, he'd forgotten me.

He didn't pause. He lunged.

It wasn't fun anymore with Gavin. None of it was. Not the scene in the park near Scout's house earlier on the way to the party, not the discussions about our friends and plans, and not the time and attention—*all the time and attention*—he demanded of me.

Nobody knew and nobody asked, but close friendships seemed to be sliding away, and more and more of my time was spent telling Gavin how happy I was with him but how I wasn't ready...

I glanced at my mom. I wanted to talk to her and it would probably be OK, but I literally couldn't form words and it wasn't the time.

And my dad... He was totally going to lose his sh—

"You OK, baby? Almost there."

I nodded as I thought about my dad's head popping off when he got off the plane from his work trip and heard about my nose. God help Gavin.

As for the other stuff, he'd *never* know about that.

Time got fuzzy later on as I rested in a curtained room and waited for what they'd do next.

One by one, my friends snuck in and waved. Ivy blew me a kiss. Deacon had somehow found a yellow gown, a blue shower cap looking thingy, and green latex gloves.

I laughed and it hurt.

My mother sent Gavin home.

And I thought I saw Jacob poke his head in. He'd rescued me... I was wet and bloody in his arms and he held me. He whispered in my ear *you'll be all right,* and I was as safe and comforted as I'd ever been.

A masked face hovered over mine. "OK," he said. "Let's get this nose straightened out and get you home to rest."

I thought I nodded, but I don't think I actually moved.

"Not gonna lie, Mary." The doctor held his gloved hands near my face. "This is gonna hurt."

CHAPTER 8

Mary

Ivy toed open my bedroom door and heaved another large flower arrangement into my room. "Well, this one is the most interesting yet."

I focused on the pointy, orangey-bluish top of a long green stem and shook my head. "What *is* that?"

She set the wooden square on my dresser. "Believe it or not, I know this one. That's a bird of paradise." She twisted the container. "See? No wait." She twisted again. "See? It's a flower. A flower that looks like a bird."

My cat got up from her perch at the end of the bed and stretched. "Look at that. Paisley heard bird and got interested."

"Well, it is interesting, I guess."

"I don't know how I feel about that one. Does it seem obnoxious to you?"

Ivy snorted. "Obnoxiously expensive. How many does that make?"

I held up my hand. "One for every day since the broken nose. So three. I'm just glad I've only missed one day of school because of the long weekend."

Ivy crawled onto my bed beside me as Paisley made a circle and stretched out the other way to flick her tail at the bird. "You get to come back tomorrow?"

"I could have come back today, but I had to see the doctor to make sure everything was in place and healing, and my parents didn't want me to get hit again trying to get to class."

"Does it hurt bad?"

"Not really. But it's gross and looks horrible with these two black eyes and all the bruising. This bandage is atrocious. And you don't want to know what was stuck up my nostrils or running down my throat…"

"Yeah, thanks for that."

I tilted my head and studied the bird flower again. "I guess it's kind of pretty in an exotic way. Like it's from the jungle or the tropical exhibits at the zoo. You know, like where the toucans live."

"Is that the pain meds talking?"

"Nah. Don't need them. Just need to let all this heal. Slowly."

Ivy uncapped her soda and offered to do the same for me. "All right. Who are we going to talk about first? Gavin, Jacob, or Corey?"

I didn't want to talk about any of them.

"C'mon, Mary, Gavin is beside himself. All these flowers, all the gossip… Word is, you haven't let him visit, and you haven't talked much."

I grabbed my phone and scrolled. "Look at this. I now know the true meaning of one person blowing up a phone. I think it might actually be a thing. It's going to explode. I can't get a word or text in edgewise."

"I heard some of the guys on the football team gave him an extra butt-kicking at practice because he hit a girl."

"Aw, c'mon, is that true? He didn't do it on purpose."

Ivy took a long drink and set it aside. "Stupid hormonal guy stuff." She fluffed pillows and settled in. "Now really. Your boyfriend hit you. Accident or not, it wasn't like you were all having a good time and the ball slipped or you collided at the net and he tried to stop. Everyone saw, Mary. He was mad. Like out of control. Jacob put his whole body in front of you as soon as he realized Gavin was coming under that net and it still didn't help in the end. You could have lost some teeth or got knocked out or had a concus—"

"Stop. I know." Her descriptive words rattled me to the core. My stomach roiled into a queasy mess. "I know." The hard shock of that lightning bolt to the face kept coming back to me. That second of blackness. That instant recognition that someone I loved had hit me in anger... I'd never experienced that before. And coupled with all the other stuff, I was at a loss.

"Say something, Mary."

"I don't know what to say because I don't know what to think."

"I'm sorry for what I said a second ago, that was too much."

"You're fine. But I'm having some problems with the whole thing."

Ivy pulled a box of chocolates off my nightstand. "All right, let's talk it through." She picked through crinkly paper. "OK if I eat one?"

"Sure. Scout's grandma brought those by. She felt so bad about this happening at her house."

"She's a sweet lady. So, what's your gut telling you?"

That was the hardest part. Saying it out loud. "Gavin was angry at both of us, Ivy. I've been over and over it in my head. If we'd been at a party and some guy flirted with me, I don't know for sure what Gavin would have done. But that night I hugged Jacob because we'd won. It was a spontaneous thing. It's what you do when you win and when you're comfortable with people. We were all celebrating. I would have turned around and hugged someone else too if I hadn't been hit."

"What are you saying?"

"Gavin wasn't just coming after Jacob. He was coming after me because of Jacob."

Ivy dropped her piece of chocolate back in the box. "OK, wait a sec. It's no secret I'm not the president of Gavin's fan club, but you're saying he had a burst of anger so violent that he knew and didn't care you might be collateral damage?"

"I guess I am. He came across that net to hit us both."

"Mary!" She hopped off the bed and rushed to close my door. "No. There's got to be more to this. What aren't you telling me?"

I tucked my bare toes under the throw at the end of the bed. Paisley's warm body heated them. "I love Gavin, but I have to break up with him."

Ivy slid back on the bed. "O-K."

"I don't want him to think it's this. He seems really sorry and I don't think he did it on purpose."

"But… You just said you think he knew exactly what he was doing."

"Yes, but I don't know if he can control it. So, does that make it on purpose if he has a problem and couldn't help himself?"

"That depends on the problem, doesn't it? It's not like he has a physical condition that makes him flail his arms. What he did was start a fight. What do you think he can't control?"

"Umm… Anger maybe? Aggression?"

Ivy froze in her spot. "What else has Gavin done to you, Mary? Are you afraid of him?"

"No. Not afraid. Just cautious."

"Why?"

"He's possessive. And pushy. And he puts pressure on me to—"

"Oh, thank God." Ivy flopped on her back in a bouncy heap and scared the cat. "Thank you! I thought I was the only one who saw that and thought everyone else thought I was crazy." She sat up when I didn't respond. "Wait. I'm sorry. I'm just so relieved to hear you say it. Please. I promise I won't overreact again. Tell me. Tell me everything."

"Everything was fine for a long time. We texted every day and saw each other at school and on weekends if we could. He wanted to do more things together. He wants me to come by football practice, and he wants to run laps with me on the track, but that's something I always do myself or with soccer friends. He's over here way too much. My mom automatically set a plate for him for dinner the other night because it was Tuesday. My dad put it back in the cabinet and wanted to know why we didn't eat as a family anymore."

"Why Tuesday?"

"Because Tuesday is the day his parents do something with one of their clubs or some group. I don't know."

"And your parents aren't a part of that one? I thought you said your parents and his parents are pretty tight. Like they do all the snooty foursome stuff at the country club and all."

"Not so much anymore. I don't know what's happening there, but they're not as close as they used to be."

"Well, the football team was on two-a-days a while, and all they do is meet and practice. I wouldn't think Gavin has the time for anything. With Jacob in the lineup, the coach seems to think we could go all the way this year."

I would have snickered if I could have. "All the way where? The funny home video show? Last year someone ran the wrong way with the ball."

"Fine. But Jacob has college recruiters snooping around so it's apparently a whole big thing. But back to you and Gavin."

"He makes the time to come by. He leaves gifts in our mailbox. Before school started, he talked about when and where we would meet before school to walk in together."

"That's creepy."

"He always tries to sign up to be in the same car as me for driver's ed." I pulled my hair back and rested my head on the pillow. "As if I want my boyfriend watching me learn to drive and giving me pointers later."

"That would be awkward. Can you imagine Scout and Deacon in the driver's ed car together?"

We laughed until Ivy got serious again.

"Is it true you haven't seen Gavin since the party?"

"Yes."

"Are you going to have him come over so you can talk and tell him you guys should take a break?"

I gestured at the growing floral department in my bedroom. "I guess I should do it here, but as you can see from all this stuff sitting around, he's trying to make up. I don't know how he'll take it."

"But you'll be downstairs with your parents around…"

"Yeah, but… Can I ask you something personal?"

"Of course. Ask me anything."

"Umm… How do you handle all the physical stuff with Scout?"

"What physical stuff?"

"You know, the kissing. The making out and all that."

"Yeeeaaah, that… I don't handle it because there isn't any. And if some guy ever asked me to *handle* anything, I'd probably bust out laughing or run away or something. After I punched him in the face."

"Come on, Ivy. You know what I mean. You and Scout are joined at the hip, and it looks like more than friendship."

She shrugged. "I guess, but we don't do all that. Yet, at least."

"Never?"

"Never."

"As in he's never even kissed you?"

"No, he hasn't kissed me." She grabbed a chenille pillow and punched it before she gave it a hug. "He looks like he wants to most of the time, but it's not happened. I don't want to make the first move. You know Scout. He probably has a diagram on his white board of how the whole thing is supposed to go. I wouldn't want to mess up his plans. He might not recover."

"You're probably right about that. What are you guys doing during all that time you spend together?"

"We talk, and we study. I visit with his grandma a lot when I'm over there. That's nice, you know, to watch a day in the life of an average woman who doesn't have odd habits like my mom does."

"But your mom is doin' OK, right?"

"Yeah, but when I'm with Scout's grandma I don't have to roll up any pills in a piece of cheese and hope she eats it."

I hurt myself when I tried not to laugh. "Ouch!" Ivy could be dang funny when she wanted to be, but everything still hurt inside and out.

"Sorry," she said. "Can I get you a fresh ice bag?"

"No, thanks."

"Good. Now don't change the subject to my mom. Back to you and Gavin. Apparently, something's going on over here. How are you two wearin' out your parents' couch?"

Again, I wanted to laugh at her joking question, but it wasn't funny anymore. Maybe it had been at one time. "Like everything else, it was all fine for a while. It was fun. He's my first serious boyfriend, so we had all the awkward first kisses and stuff. Then..."

"Then..."

"Then he got aggressive. One time he grabbed my wrist when we were kissing and tried to shove my hand uh... you know." I pointed.

"Pig!" Ivy spat out. "I know you're trying not to say it, Mary, but that doesn't make it more innocent than it was. He tried to force *your* hand into *his* pants. That's not OK."

"No, it isn't," I agreed. "Especially since we'd already had this whole discussion about sex. And he tried the whole argument about how us touching each other wasn't technically intercourse—yes, he used that word."

"Gross."

"Right? I thought I was in health class."

"Intercourse," Ivy repeated. "What a weird word. Scout might use it, but I doubt even he would say it at a time like that. Intercourse..."

"Stop saying that. It's getting worse."

"Sorry. What happened next?"

"We had a huge fight because he squeezed my wrist and wouldn't let go. It hurt."

Ivy looked like she was about to chew through her bottom lip.

"Ivy, you can't repeat this to anyone."

"I know. I'm just so mad right now. How long ago was this?"

"It's been several weeks."

"You took him back after that?"

"Yes, and he promised to never try anything like that again. And he didn't. He was a perfect gentleman from then on. Um... Until the day of the pool party."

"There was something besides him elbowing you in the face?"

It was hard to breathe. I wanted to tell it, but I was so tired of living in it.

"You have to tell me, Mary. We might need more help."

"No, it's not quite that. I don't know what it is, but I know it's not good and I know I have to break up with Gavin."

"Talk, Mary."

"I know, I know." I sat up again. "So, Gavin's mom was letting him practice driving and I couldn't be in the car for that, so we decided they'd pick me up at that neighborhood park near Scout's. We all met there, and his mom was going to drive us on down the street. But Gavin said let's walk because Scout's was close by. He held my hand, and instead of staying on the bike path and going straight to Scout's, Gavin tugged me off into a secluded spot behind the tennis courts. And it was so hot and there were swarms of mosquitoes and he was all *I just want a minute alone with you*, and backed me against a tree and started kissing me."

"I don't like where this is going."

Once I started the story, I couldn't keep it from tumbling out. "And all I had on was my suit and cover-up. My towel, shorts and a t-shirt were in my bag because, duh, pool party, but the bugs were so bad and I felt so naked out there in the woods…"

"And?"

"And Gavin kept me pinned against that tree. I said we needed to go and that I didn't want any kids or tennis players seeing us there, but he pushed his body against mine and uh…" I pointed south again.

"Yeah, I get it." Ivy sprang off the bed and beat an angry path back and forth in front of my bed. "We all understand the basics of natural bodily functions, but the part that's epically unacceptable is that a *possible rapist had you pinned against a tree in a public park!*"

"I know, all right? Don't yell. My mom will fly up here in two seconds."

"Sorry! Gavin's intentions were obvious. He wanted you alone where he could try something, and hoped you'd go along."

"Well, I didn't. I made it clear I had no intention of doing anything with him."

"How'd you get out of it?"

"He put his hand—"

"Ewww…" Ivy rushed to my side. "Sorry. Go on."

"It happened so fast. Before I knew it, he had his hand under my wrap and was headed right for what was on his mind."

"What did you do?"

"I pushed him backward so hard he busted his butt on a log." Ivy snarled. "Good for you."

"I stomped out of there and headed for the safety of Scout's house."

"I knew something was wrong when you got there. How were you so calm? He was holding your hand when you came in."

"He was *squeezing* my hand," I said. "Begging forgiveness. I wasn't going to cause a scene at Scout's party. I thought I'd make a short appearance and then call my ride." I pointed at my nose. "But then, this. I should have never gotten in that pool. I stayed too long."

Ivy stood. "Don't you dare make apologies for being you and having fun." She headed for the bird of paradise. "Ya know? This thing is kinda ugly."

"It is, isn't it? And it's freakin' out my cat."

"What's say we pretend it's Gavin and toss it out the window?"

"Just make sure you open it first."

CHAPTER 9

Ivy

Nothing was more satisfying than the sight and sound of that wooden container busting into pieces on Mary's lawn from two stories up.

But it didn't solve anything.

I turned to my friend with the purple-blue circles around her eyes and wanted to cry and throw things at the same time.

The thought of that creep, Gavin Bagliano, pinning Mary against a tree made me so angry.

I never trusted him.

I closed the window and dusted my hands on my shorts. "Now what?"

"I'll text Gavin and ask him to come by after practice. I should hear him out and break up with him so it's all out of the way before school tomorrow."

I sat at Mary's desk and accidentally bumped Paisley's

feather cat toy. The bell caused her to run straight for me and wait. She jumped for it as it dangled in the air.

I wasn't a bit sorry about the breakup, but I didn't like the look on Mary's face. "Are you all right?"

"Yes. No. I don't know. We've been together almost a year."

I held the cat toy higher. "Listen to me, Mary. Nothing Gavin did was OK. It's run its course. You have the injuries to prove it."

Mary curled onto her side and pulled up the throw. Paisley dragged the whole feather cat toy away and joined her on the bed.

She wiped away a tear. "He's going to be so upset. It's my fault."

"Excuse me? I'm going to assume the swelling is cutting off oxygen to your brain. Because the tough Mary Hunter I know doesn't take crap from anyone, and we both know those things Gavin did to you are not your fault. Guys don't get to fondle us when they want to. You made yourself clear about your boundaries."

"No, I know that. What I mean is, there were lots of times I enjoyed kissing him. I let him hug me and touch my face. He rested his hand on my knee when we watched movies, and I didn't think anything of it. And we kissed a lot."

"I know. Everyone knows. The whole town knows."

"Exactly! So why wouldn't he think he could go further?"

"Hello? Is this the eighteen-hundreds? Do women not have a voice? Did we lose all the rights the women before us fought for?" I yanked my drink off the nightstand. "This is just your broken heart talking. You're trying to let him off the hook. The truth is, he crossed the line. You told him no. You had to knock him to the ground to get away from that tree and he returned the favor by breaking your nose. His actions are inexcusable."

"Maybe mine are too."

"What's that supposed to mean?"

"It means that maybe there were a couple of seconds against that tree when I thought it would feel good to say yes."

I plopped on the end of the bed. "Aw, Mary, are you going to make me Google something sciency?" I capped my empty Dr Pepper bottle and tossed it into the trash. "Listen. Biology 101. You love the guy. Primal instincts affect us too. It's natural to want to feel good. And the things guys' bodies do is natural—however gross it is. They can't help it most of the time, but they sure as heck can help how they act in the situation. Gavin went too far."

"I know. But that doesn't make it any easier to give him up. Most of it was good."

"Yeah? Well, none of it should have been violent."

She nodded.

"I gotta go." I grabbed all my things. "I'll send your mom up. Keep her distracted while I clean up the front yard before your dad gets home."

"Thanks."

"Call me if you need me."

"I will."

"I'm serious, Mary. You're a Warrior. Warriors don't let guys like Gavin push us around. We're in charge of us."

She managed a slight smile. "I know what I have to do."

"Good. Call me when it's over. And Mary?"

"Yes?"

"Intercourse, intercourse, intercourse."

CHAPTER 10

Mary

I'd told Ivy I knew what I had to do.

That didn't make it any easier to do it.

Polite, contrite, and lookin' just right. That's how Gavin came up the walk to my front door.

I met him outside.

He stopped and put his hand over his mouth when he saw me. He had tears in his eyes when he sagged into my mom's favorite wicker porch chair. He knew better than to reach for me.

And I just stood there on the walk. Truth was, I didn't have much to say. All his apologies would make me cry, and all my hurt and doubt kept me from forming real words anyway.

Part of me enjoyed seeing him squirm. I loved the guy but hated his actions. I wanted the life-long friendship without the drama that had broken it forever. I wanted to go back to all the good feels and leave the sharp edges behind.

I knew none of that was possible.

Did it make me a bad person that I wanted him to look at the wounds he left on my face in a moment of uncontrolled anger? I wanted him to study them, think about them, and remember what he shattered. I wanted him to be sorry—truly sorry—for everything.

I also wanted to kiss him and hug him and play with that dark curl of hair that looped around his ear. I liked his embrace and the sound of his heart when we cuddled on the couch. I liked that scent he bought at the mall because I'd smelled it in a magazine. I liked...

I loved him.

I took the other chair.

"Thanks for letting me come by," he said.

"Thanks for all the flowers. It wasn't necessary."

He sat forward in the chair with his forearms resting on his thighs. He twisted his fingers together and picked at his nails as he tried to form words. "It was the only thing I could think to do. You wouldn't talk to me."

"My parents kept me quiet and to themselves a couple of days."

"But you didn't answer my texts."

"Honestly, Gavin, I didn't know what to say. I'm hurt. Like actually hurt, inside and out. I can't believe what happened. You were so angry. And after what happened at the park—"

"I get it, OK."

The twitch of his jaw signaled agitation. I'd been so used to it I almost missed it. But there it was. That twinge of irritation I'd seen grow to full-blown rage.

My heart flopped around in my chest, even as my resolve started to crack.

"I'm sorry about everything," he said. "I know I was wrong. I know I should have never pushed you about anything. What can

I say? I'm stupid. I love you and I lost my mind a couple of times."

"I love you too, Gavin. That's why it's been so hard."

"But you're still breaking up with me. I know you are."

"It's going to be a while for me to heal and get past this, so yeah, I think it's best we take a break and spend some time apart."

Then Gavin Bagliano cried on my porch. Big, splotchy tears splashed on the bricks below, and all I wanted to do was comfort him.

I couldn't. That horrible last day wouldn't let me, but it didn't stop the throbbing of my own face as I fought back my own urge to cry.

"C'mon, Gavin, we'll get past this. We've been friends forever. We can be friends ag—"

"No." He stood and swiped his shirt across his face. "No. It doesn't work that way." He stepped off the porch. "Tell your parents I'll talk to them another day. Your dad's pretty mad right now, but I want to at least apologize."

I nodded. "Sure."

He turned to look at me one last time before he headed down the walk. "Can you just do one thing for me?"

"I can try. What is it?"

"Don't fall for someone else before I have a chance to win you back."

CHAPTER 11

Mary

My mom stepped onto the porch with a cold pack and two large glasses of iced tea. "Here. Relax and put this on your face." She set the tea on the glass-topped wicker table between us. "You want to talk about it?"

"No."

"That's fine. We'll sit here and drink tea."

It only took her forty-five seconds to talk again. "You remember that little black dog your grandma had? Inky? Or Stinky or Pinky or something?"

I slid the pack away to look at her with one eye. "You mean Blinky?"

"Yes. That's the one."

"Is this story going somewhere? 'Cause I promise you this couldn't be a worse time."

"Yes. She rescued that dog, but she really didn't know where it came from, or what it was like."

I gave her the one-eyed stare again.

"Anyway, they got along great. She loved that little dog and had it for a few years."

"I remember."

"And then one day, she was sitting on the couch giving Blinky treats and she dropped one. When she bent to pick it up, she was close to his head, and Blinky snapped right in her face and got a hold of her bottom lip. He bit clear through and could have ripped it off."

I let the cold pack slip off my face and into my lap. "Why would you tell me something like that at a time like this? And also, I don't remember that."

"She didn't want to frighten you. But she had to see a plastic surgeon to sew it up."

"You're comparing Gavin to a dog?"

"My point is, she never figured out what spooked Blinky. She had no idea he had a hidden food aggression. Or maybe he didn't. Maybe he got scared when she suddenly leaned down. Maybe he saw a cat out the window or something from somewhere else or thought she was leaning in to hurt him. But something in Blinky's nature made him snap and hurt the person he loved most."

"Right. Gavin and Blinky. Same exact situation."

"You know what I'm saying, Mary. Scout's grandparents don't miss a thing, and they told me what was on that security footage. And I need you to know a couple of things. One is, it's completely natural you can't look at Gavin the same way. Grandma never got past that thing with Blinky. She always wondered if she might set him off again, and she really was concerned he might snap at you or someone else. When she had the chance to let him go, she did. He went with an older single guy who had a farm down the road and lots of other animals to run with. The man knew about it, and it was the best place for him.

Grandma also didn't have to sleep with one eye open anymore."

I slapped the cold pack on my forehead and took a long drink of tea to keep from crying. "Well, you don't have to worry. I let Gavin go."

"Not gonna lie, honey. I'm relieved to hear that."

"Glad someone feels better."

"No one feels better about any of this, Mary."

Right. I had to remember my parents had safety concerns and could pull the plug on my freedom at any time. "Sorry."

"I know you're going through a lot." She waved a low-flying bee away. "The second thing I wanted to remind you is this: It's generally a fact that a person will show you exactly who they are. You should believe them."

Ouch. Her version of Maya Angelou's famous quote stung a little. Did my parents—who'd also known Gavin his whole life and let me date him for nearly a year—really think Gavin could be a bad guy? I, for one, still held out hope.

But I got it. "I understand. Umm... Gavin wants to apologize to you guys. Do you think Dad will let him live through that?"

My mom smiled. "It'll be entertaining, and I'm sure your dad will make him sweat it out, but it'll be OK." She stood. "But make no mistake. Your dad is very protective of you, and this pool thing is a big deal. He's keeping a copy of that footage, and I'm not saying there's a problem—"

"What kind of problem would there be?"

"It doesn't matter. I'm only saying he's doin' the dad thing. Dads are protectors. That's what they do."

Protectors...

Sebastian had used that word. Could my dad be one of *the* Protectors? Or just a regular dad protector. He did seem to have that superhero vibe about him—if superheroes wore ugly shorts and used criminally bad puns in public. Still, my dad didn't take anything off anyone and he always watched out for the underdog.

Mind. Blown.

My mother stood there looking at me. "You OK? Need an ibuprofen?"

"No, thanks."

"C'mon in the kitchen a minute. Scout's grandma came back by with something else for you."

"Really? Again?"

I couldn't smell much, but the distinct scent of frankincense hit my nose when I walked in the kitchen. That and my mother's meatloaf.

The frankincense brought immediate peace to my mind. The meatloaf, not so much, but I honed in on the frankincense, and Sebastian had been right. It made me feel better, especially about my decision on Gavin. Somewhere, somehow, my supernatural being was close and looking out for me.

My mom put three small bottles in my hand. "Scout's grandma said these essential oils will help you heal. She put rollers on them so you can use them when you need to. This one's for the inflammation, bruising, and pain, and this one is to help you breathe. She said you can rub them on your wrist or your neck or directly where it hurts. It's all natural and won't hurt you." She pointed at the frankincense. "This one is apparently good for everything."

"So I've been told. Did you try it? Because I already smell it."

"No. It's been here on the counter."

And yet, the scent lingered in the air.

"Thanks, Mom. I'm going back up to try and pull myself together for school tomorrow."

"Sure. I'll call you when dinner's on."

Wonderful. The family loaf of meat I didn't care much for.

I stretched out on my bed with Paisley and took a long, slow whiff of frankincense.

Calm settled around me, though my emotions were anything but.

I texted Ivy. *It's done. It was awful.*

Sorry. Want me to come back?

No. It's OK. Details later. The dots on the screen bounced as I thought. *We all need to talk. Do you think we could meet at Scout's this weekend and regroup?*

I'll ask him, but he said his pool was my pool.

How romantic.

Are you sure you want to return to the scene of the crime?

I can't swim, but yes. No reason to waste a hot Saturday afternoon.

OK, I'll try to make a plan. Are you sure you're OK?

Yes. I'm sniffing frankincense. And guess what else?

?

I think maybe my dad's one of those Protector people Sebastian talked about.

CHAPTER 12

Ivy

I couldn't believe it was her.

That night at the pool party, I couldn't believe I'd seen Corey around the side of the house when everything went bad—and talking to Gavin, no less.

She hadn't told me anything about coming to the party, and she hadn't been in touch for days.

I had started to think she was avoiding me, until she sauntered straight toward me in the hall before choir that next week. At near shoulder length, her hair bounced as she walked and exposed pretty highlights when she turned to smile at others.

She didn't exactly smile at me, and though she looked better, more confident, and happier than I'd seen her in months, something was off. She had on more makeup than she'd ever worn. Deep purple eyeliner colored her lash line with the precision of a trained makeup artist, and *some*one had been busy with a contouring kit.

I stepped toward her and, stupid me, thought I'd greet my friend with a hug.

That turned out to be the most awkward welcome-back moment in history.

Corey didn't even open her arms. In fact, she stepped back and looked at me like I was a stranger.

"Corey? Is everything all right? I've been trying to reach you. I saw you at the pool party. Why didn't you come in earlier and say something?"

"Hello, Ivy."

"I wish I'd known you'd be back today. I would've brought you cupcakes or a balloon or something to celebrate."

Corey's cool gaze surprised me. "Then I'm glad you didn't know. But thank you for wanting to draw attention to the fact I'm back from spending time in a mental institution."

"Oh. Sorry. I didn't mean to—"

"It doesn't matter." She stepped around me. "I have to go."

Something was wrong. The Corey I knew never badmouthed a cupcake or a balloon. "Wait a minute, Corey, what's the matter? You've stopped talking to me. Why? I thought we were friends."

"We can't be friends anymore, Ivy." She shrugged. "It's unfortunate, but what can I say?"

"Uh... You can say why we're no longer friends. That's a start." Then I saw the small purple arrows in the cartilage of her ear and the arrow charm peeking out of her shirt. "Wait a minute. Does this have anything to do with the Arrows?"

"I have to go."

"Stop right there, Corey. Why are you acting like an Arrow?"

"Because I *am* an Arrow."

"But Mr. Parrington exposed the Arrows and disbanded them as an unauthorized school group."

"So what? He doesn't control things outside of school. We

never claimed to be a school group. Come to think of it, not one Arrow activity was held on school grounds."

"Yet, the Arrows managed to wreak havoc everywhere on campus."

"Did they?"

"C'mon, you of all people know what a cancer that group was. Paige is gone. Who's even on board with this?"

"We still exist, Ivy, and we still have meetings and plan things together."

"*Why?* Nothing but misery came out of that group." She tried to walk away, but I kept up. "Who's in charge?"

Corey stopped and turned. "I am." Her smile was as wide as it'd ever been.

"*What?* Why?"

"Because I can."

"But why would you want to? Paige was horrible to you, and all her little minions did was torture you under orders from her."

"But like you said, Paige is gone, and I've taken charge of the group."

"And are you going to be running it like Paige? Are you going to be a bully and make other girls feel bad about themselves?"

"Awww, Ivy. Who sounds catty now?"

I couldn't believe my ears. "This is ridiculous. You survived. You overcame your issues and you got better. You're not like Paige. You can't knowingly hurt people or cause pain. You're not that kind of person."

"I'm my own person, Ivy. I choose. I'm in charge of my own life."

Normally, that would have made me feel better. Why did it make me feel nothing but dread? Exactly what did Corey think she was taking control of by picking up where Paige left off, and by leading a band of mean, self-absorbed people through the halls of Stonehaven Academy?

The suicide attempt had been a loud, clear, and desperate call for help. I thought she'd come out stronger as her doctors and counselors worked with her.

How did she come out of that looking like the villain? Did her family and doctors know?

"Fine," I said. "When's your next gathering? I'm technically still an Arrow. I had not heard you were the new leader. Now that I know, I'm eager to see where you're taking us."

"That's not possible, Ivy."

"Why not?"

"Your membership has been revoked."

CHAPTER 13

Mary

I headed into school with a brown handle bag full of my mom's homemade chocolate chip cookies. She'd tied a football-themed ribbon at the top and added a school decal to the side.

I had several things on my mind. How soon would I see Gavin, and how fast would someone ask me about our breakup?

How was I going to get through the day while looking like a walking hematoma—fancy word for bruise I picked up at the hospital?

And how was I going to get that thank-you-gift bag of cookies to Jacob without it being so...*awkward*?

My mom had no concept of what a day from hell I was about to have, but as with everything else, I charged ahead.

Thankfully, Ivy was the first person to get close. Other students gave me a lot of room as if they understood, but more likely, they were waiting for the fallout of the most talked about Labor Day weekend in recent memory.

She approached with caution. "How ya doin'?"

"So far, so good. I've only been here about five minutes, so I'm still optimistic."

"Can I be honest?" Ivy stepped closer and observed my face from too-close a distance.

"Yes."

"It doesn't look as bad as I thought it would."

"Uh... Thanks?"

"No, I only mean it was pretty bad just yesterday, and today it's already looking better."

"Thanks for your honesty. I was able to downsize the tape and lose the gauze."

"Try not to worry about today." She gave me a side hug. "Everyone will get a good look and then move on. It'll be old news tomorrow. What's in the bag?"

"Cookies for Jacob."

"Seriously?"

"I do have to see him eventually, I guess, and thank him for his help. I mean, he carried me to my car. My mom insisted I give these to him today and tell him how much she and my dad appreciate his efforts at the party."

"Ho-boy. She sure knows how to make a strange day even stranger. Couldn't she have taken by his house or something?"

"Why do that when I could show up at school and give him a gift in front of prying eyes on the day after my breakup—a breakup people will think is because of him to begin with?"

Ivy pursed her lips. "Well, first of all, you and I know different about the breakup, and it's no one's business. Secondly, I think your mom is smart. I think she knows you can handle it, and that when it's all out in the open, no one will have anything to gossip about." She glanced at the time. "I'll walk you to your first class."

I wished I was as sure of myself as everyone else seemed to think I was.

Deep down, it all hurt. My heart was broken and I didn't think I could bear to see Gavin. It was homecoming time again. Excitement buzzed in the halls, and I remembered the year before. My wrist corsage was still pinned on my memory board at home. I didn't know how to maneuver through the sadness and distraction of the loss of my first love—especially since it came with the added baggage of his aggression. His pain was clear on the porch the day before, but I couldn't imagine ever being that close to him again.

I tried to stuff the cookies in my backpack. "Thanks for walking with me. I'll see you at lunch."

"No problem," Ivy said. "And we really need to all meet and talk about Corey."

She turned to leave, then made a complete circle. "Don't look now, but Jacob's in this hall."

I didn't even know him well enough to have his number in my phone to text about the cookie situation, but I knew he wasn't exactly on his way to class.

Ivy nudged my arm. "Go ahead. Get it over with. Do you want me to stay?"

"No. Go, or you'll be late. I can talk to him later."

"Why? Take the tardy and get rid of those cookies."

I glanced at my teacher. She had yet to close the door as the second bell threatened to ring at any second.

I ducked behind a column to see if Jacob walked by.

Lucky me.

I held my finger at my lips so he wouldn't speak until the hammering bell stopped its clanging, and Dr. Gianetti closed the door.

He looked over each shoulder and made a slow approach. The hint of a healing busted lip showed up like a fading scarlet line below his nose. "Mary... Glad to see you're back."

"What are you doing in this hall?"

He held up a pass. "I got this note to report to my counselor first thing this morning."

"Oh." Words drifted out of my head like my brain had a slow leak. Now, face-to-face with him, I realized I didn't know what I wanted to say. And worse, the sight of him brought a wave of trauma back from the incident. My mom and dad had been hugging me to death the last few days, but it was Jacob's strong arms that had protected me. He seemed bigger that morning... stronger. I wanted to lean into his embrace again and feel that same bubble of protection and his *I'll take care of you* vibe of safety and comfort.

"Mary?"

"Yes! Sorry. I hope everything is OK. I mean with the counselor."

"It's fine. It's about my transfer credits. Might have to tweak my schedule." He took another step forward. "Are you OK?"

"Yeah." I pointed at his face. "What happened to you?"

"It's nothing. Football practice. I think your boyfriend's still peeved at me." He stopped suddenly and covered his eyes with one hand and dropped his gaze to the floor. "Sorry. I shouldn't have said that." His cheeks reached a shade of red I'd never seen on anyone but a circus clown.

"It doesn't matter. Me and Gavin—"

"It's none of my business, Mary. I shouldn't have said anything."

"Fine." I knew when I'd been dismissed. It kinda ticked me off. Not because he didn't care, but because I'd brought it up. I wrestled the cookies out of my bag. "My mom sent these for you. She and my dad say thanks for your help."

"Thank you, but it wasn't necessary."

"Well, my mom thinks it was, and you should know those are the best homemade cookies in the country."

"No, wait. I didn't mean I don't appreciate it, I only meant I wasn't expecting anything. I was glad to help."

The whole conversation had become stuck and uncomfortable. We were like two birds trying to get the same tiny seed from between two large rocks. We just banged our heads together.

I stood straight. "I have to go, but I wanted to say thank you too. It was an awful night, and I appreciate the first aid and all the other help. Enjoy the cookies."

"Don't go."

It was the tone of his voice that stopped me—not the command. "Why?"

"Because this is weird, that's why. We never finish a conversation like normal people. We've been together three times and haven't ended with a simple *catch ya later* yet. You always leave mad. Or hurt."

"I'm not mad, Jacob. I guess I'm cautious."

"What about me makes you feel like that?"

Good question, considering I wanted him to put his arms around me not that long ago. "I like honesty. It's kinda my motto. *Always the truth so you don't have to keep up with any lies.*"

"You don't even know me, but you think I'm lying to you?"

Did I? Or had I spent too much time under Gavin's possessive thumb, not to mention in the company of newly-discovered supernatural beings… Geez. It was no wonder I was confused.

"Let's reboot." I stepped back behind the safety of the column. "You never answered my question back on the day of the fire."

"You mean the small electrical incident?"

"Cut the crap, Jacob. It was a fire in the wall behind the AC. Everyone knows that."

He grinned. "I'm messing with you. And I didn't answer your question because I didn't understand it. You asked me what I was."

"Fair enough. Why did you pick me for your team?"

"Why did you agree?"

"I agreed because that's what you do. A captain starts picking, and people graciously accept. I'm a good sport, and you didn't answer my question."

"I picked you because I didn't know many people there. I figured if you played soccer, you likely played volleyball too. Some of those girls wouldn't risk breaking a nail to set me up for that winning point."

"There were other female athletes there."

"Agreed. But I didn't know who they were at the time, now did I?"

"And you swear you weren't trying to make trouble with Gavin? Because I don't appreciate being used like that."

"Look, that guy is a jerk in practice, but at that time I didn't know how tight you two are—"

"Were. How tight we were."

"OK, were, and no. I'm a football player with a lot more on my mind than messin' with Gavin. I plan to get a scholarship to play ball, and I've been moved from a large school with lots of opportunities to here because my parents... Never mind. All I'm sayin' is that I picked a competitive athlete who I thought might want to win."

"All right. Thank you for your honesty." I hooked my thumb through the loop on my backpack. "See? We did it. We had a conversation and now I'm going to say *catch ya later* and go get my tardy slip."

"Not so fast. This honesty thing goes both ways."

"What do you mean?"

"I value the truth too, Mary, and I have a question for you."

I had no idea where the conversation was going. "OK."

"What was all that weird stuff that happened when I carried you to your car that night?"

"What weird stuff?" My mind raced to the pool party. I'd

grown used to all the weird stuff, but was convinced nothing supernatural had happened. "You're kidding, right?"

"No. I know you were busted up, but you have to remember that walk to the car."

"I didn't walk to the car. You carried me."

"Yes, I know, and that's when it happened."

"What happened, Jacob?"

He scraped his hand across his short hair. "You really don't remember."

"No. Tell me. It might jog my memory."

"So, I picked you up and Scout put fresh ice and a clean towel near your face."

"Right. I remember that."

"And you rested your head against me." He tapped near his collar bone. "Like way up here because I was holding you high. And you wrapped your arms around me and that ice and that towel were kinda wedged all in there…" He stepped closer.

I let my bag drop and backed as far against the column as I could and slid a couple of inches away from him. "I'm sorry, Jacob, I didn't mean to make you uncomfortable. I was kinda out of it by that point."

"No. Stop. It's not that."

"Then what?"

"Your mom rushed ahead to open the door and get in so she could help you from the other side and take off. I rounded the corner with you, and Gavin was there with that girl."

"What girl?"

"I don't know, but I don't think she was at the party."

"What did she look like?"

Irritation swept across his face. "C'mon, really? She's a girl. Not too tall…" He put his hand by his neck. "Hair about here. I don't know. A girl."

My mind clicked through the girls at the party. Ivy said Corey had showed up at the end and we needed to talk about it, but hadn't gotten around to it yet. "Did you hear a name? Corey, maybe?"

"Didn't hear a thing. But listen. Gavin was talking to her on one side of the walk, and when we rounded the corner, he pushed her toward the other side."

"That doesn't make sense."

"OK, whatever, but that's when it happened. Maybe he didn't want you to see him talking to another girl."

I really wanted to massage my temples, but that was impossible given the whole broken nose situation. I leaned my head against the brick and closed my eyes. "What is happening right now? All I wanted to do was give you cookies and take my tardy, and now I'm trapped in a bizarre conversation loop."

I opened my eyes to Jacob's frosty glare.

He sighed. "Are you finished?"

"Yes."

"So, it happened when I stepped between them. First, there was this really bad feeling. I couldn't get a breath, and I thought I might stumble or drop you... I looked around because it was so strange."

"Uh-huh."

"Then I felt this pressure from outside, but it was a good pressure and it pushed the bad stuff away and I felt bigger and stronger."

"You *are* bigger and stronger. You never would have stumbled or dropped me."

"I know, but it was like stepping through a portal or something in a movie. Are you saying you didn't feel that?"

"Um. What else?"

"It was you. It was as if you were all wrapped around me like some invisible force. You were so close and your body was so warm, I couldn't feel the ice on my chest... It was like we were in a cocoon together or something and we stepped through the bad stuff and you were nuzzled all tight against me—"

"OK, stop." Heat blazed from my toes to my cheeks in a super-hot second. "I don't know what to say, Jacob. Uh... I'm sorry I made you feel weird with my body?"

"C'mon, Mary, it's not about that. It was different, and I can't believe you don't remember. And that smell. I know you couldn't have smelled a dang thing because of your nose, but whatever those plants were on the side of Scout's house were giving off some odor. Like I said, it was like walking through some smelly-space-blackhole-dream portal from a bad movie."

I massaged my temples anyway and let the pull of my cheekbones and nose hurt as they wanted. No, I didn't remember it. Yes, it was possible. Maybe I understood it, and maybe I didn't, but I sure as heck couldn't explain it all to Jacob. My best guess was that Sebastian was near in my time of need. Gavin had been the one to hurt me, so maybe his continued presence only made my supernatural help more alert to my situation. Corey's appearance—if it was even Corey—made no sense in the matter.

But I was apparently some clingy octopus-like all arms and legs warm creature who wrapped myself and my spiritual and earthly realms around Jacob and disoriented him.

Good for me. I sure knew how to confuse a guy, and obviously, I had no control over my movements when things were muddled by injury, pain, confusion—or when someone like Gavin had kept me pinned down and away from the rest of my world... *Wow.*

The discovery was staggering. I'd missed a lot of cues because of Gavin.

Jacob cleared his throat. "What's the matter?"

"Nothing. Just realizing some things."

"And you still don't remember?"

"I'm sorry, I don't." I rummaged in my bag for one of the tiny bottles. "But sniff this." I waved the frankincense under his nose. "Is this what you smelled?"

"Yeah. That's it. Why?"

"No reason. Just clears up one of my questions." At least I knew it was Sebastian who'd been there. How Jacob got into the inner circle of that realm was still a mystery.

"Really?" He challenged me. "You just happen to have that same scent in your bag? C'mon. You have more information."

"I'm telling the truth when I say I don't understand it. If I did, I would tell you."

"Look, you wanted honesty, and I'm being honest. From the day we first met in the café to today, things have been different for me. I don't know what it is, but now I walk along and wonder when I'm going to get sucked into some wormhole. And," he added with a pained expression. "I've done a whole lot of thinking about you. There. I said it. I'm not trying to be all stupid and romantic or anything. I'm saying there's a connection."

I swallowed hard. "I agree. And I'm sorry, Jacob, I wish I had more answers for you, but I don't. I promise to explain if I ever figure it out."

"You mean *when* you figure it out, because you're clearly a step ahead of me in whatever this is."

"All right. *When* I figure it out."

He turned to read the signs in the hall. "OK, I have to go that way."

I'd forgotten how new he was. "Yeah. That hall and to the right."

He turned to me with his go-to considerate and protective glance. "Are you going to be all right? I can walk you where you're going first."

My heart fell into my shoes. He was still trying to take care of me. "No. Thanks. In fact, I'm thinking maybe it was too soon to be here. I might text my mom and head to the nurse's office to see how I feel."

"OK. Here. Put your number in my phone." I did as he asked and he smiled. "I'll uh…catch ya later."

"Hey, Jacob, something like that has really never happened to you before? There's been no other odd activity or feelings like that?"

"No."

"And you've never had a group of friends talk about that sort of thing happening to them?"

"Never."

"Are you a Warrior, Jacob?"

"I don't even know what that question means, Mary."

CHAPTER 14

Scout

I popped the top on a soda can and let the cooler lid drop.

We'd had no fall in Texas. Our seasons that year had been hot, hotter, hottest, and face of the sun. It hadn't even cooled down when we hit October and neared homecoming. And since all our plans to meet the previous couple of weeks had ended in nothing, we decided to spend the night of the homecoming dance together in my pool.

Except me. I didn't get in the pool.

But Deacon the Dolphin flopped, floated, and flailed to his heart's content as the afternoon sun went down behind the house and left the slate around the pool still too hot to sit on.

I did anyway.

Deacon back-stroked his way toward me. "Should we check on Mary and Ivy? They've got the food."

"Nah, they'll be here."

"Dude, it feels great in here. Want to try?"

"No, it's much better out here on the bridge to Hades as I work up a wicked case of butt-sweats."

Deacon snorted. "Trust me. A good dip in your own pool will cure your butt-sweats. Also, don't talk about butt-sweats in front of the ladies." He stopped swimming and hugged the side. "Can you explain something to me?"

"I'm sure I can. Eventually."

He smacked a splash of water my way. "That's for your butt-sweats."

"What's the question?"

"I get how you're afraid of the water. You earned that one fair and square, but don't you take showers? And drink water? And you're sitting right here." He flicked water my way again.

"Stop it."

"Fine, but I'm curious, that's all."

"It's not the water. It's what the water can do. I have control of the shower, but I don't have control of the ocean. It's too big."

I wasn't going to tell him I didn't even have control of the pool. I thought of being alone and getting a cramp and not being able to swim and slipping under the water. And that led to thinking of others who'd become submerged and couldn't get out.

It was an anxiety thing. It was PTSD. I wasn't going to let it play out by way of a panic attack in front of my friends.

"I'm working on it," I said. "It's the rush of water over my head and that muffled sound. You know, that wave of water in your face when you can't take a breath."

Deacon pushed away and floated back. "Brother, you know we've got your back. When you're ready to try to get in here, you'll be fine. Between the four of us, what could happen to you in your own pool?"

And what could happen to a family trying to escape rising water? My dad thought he could see the road. I knew the hard way a car could be washed away in just three inches of water.

"Dude. Sorry." Deacon nudged my foot. "Didn't mean to say it like that."

"Nah, you're good. I'm going to text Ivy." I tapped out the message and changed the subject. "Where are we on the ski trip?"

"Yeah." Deacon shook like a puppy and sprayed water my way again. "We need to talk about that."

"Then get out of the pool, will you?" I tossed him a towel and started to move chairs closer to the table. "Ivy says they'll be here soon."

"All right. The latest is that all our parents say it's fine to go, but we have to earn some money."

"Duh."

"The first payment is due after the informational meeting at the school in two weeks. Then we have the whole month of November and part of December to earn."

I swiped dust off the table. "How much money do you have so far?"

"Not much. I've been selling things with a local app—old games, systems, tech, sports equipment, stuff I don't use or wear anymore. My parents said they'd match what I make, but it's going slow. I'm trying to get some jobs in the neighborhood. I washed out and sanitized trash cans all last weekend. What about you?"

I shrugged. I wasn't about to tell him I'd saved every penny I made over the summer and could pay for both mine and Ivy's trips. She was the only reason I wanted to go, but I could never make that offer. "I'm doing OK. I think Mary's parents offered the matching thing too. Ivy asked her Aunt Connie if she'd forget her birthday and Christmas and give her cash for the trip, and she's selling all the clothes Aunt Connie gave her that she won't wear. She's also a dog-walker for all the people in her complex who work late. She makes good money, especially now that the word's out and they text her when it's an emergency. Like when they have to work late or there's a traffic issue."

"Houston's a big city. There's always a traffic issue getting home at night."

"Yep. That's what she's counting on, but we also need pocket money. We have a ways to go."

Deacon paused as he held a chair and slipped into his flip-flops. "Any ideas what to do about that?"

Grandpa walked by with a handful of tools on his way to the shed. "Pressure washer."

"Hey, Grandpa."

"Hi, Mr. White."

"You need money? I got a pressure washer."

That got my attention. "You'd let me sell your pressure washer? What else is in that shed we can get rid of?"

"Take it easy, son, you're not selling any of my tools."

"Then what about the pressure washer?"

"I'll let you use it to make money."

"How?"

"It's not that difficult, son. You boys go door-to-door and see who needs their driveways and walkways done."

"Oohhhh. Good idea. You think people would want that?"

"Well, we don't have much winter and the holidays are comin'. People want their decks cleaned for company. Maybe even their gutters or the green stuff on their siding."

"Nice," Deacon said. "And if a pressure washer is what I think it is, it's like using a super-powerful squirt gun to knock dirt off stuff."

Grandpa scoffed. "It's a little more complicated than that, but if you're willing to work, I'm willing to teach you how to use the thing and not take out any windows or hurt yourself."

"How much can we charge?"

"I'm already letting you use my pressure washer. Don't you

think the two of you could use those phones you always have your noses in to do some research?"

"Yes, sir," Deacon said. "Absolutely. We're on it."

"Yeah, thanks Grandpa. We'll talk to you later. Looking forward to it."

Ivy came around the house with Mary. "Whatcha' all looking forward to?"

"Finally," Deacon grumped. "What'd you bring to eat?"

"Sandwiches."

"There better be a full-sized, multi-level-meat-stacked Italian in there."

Mary pulled off her sunglasses. "Or what? You're going to sit and watch while the rest of us eat because that was rude?"

"Ouch," I said. "Let me get you some cream for that burn."

"Don't ever attempt to use that joke or one like it again, buddy." Deacon held a chair out for Mary. "Sorry. May I please have the full-sized, multi-level-meat-stacked Italian I hope is in that bag?" He bowed and held out his hand. "Or anything else you would like to give me because I'm not picky and appreciate the effort."

She reached inside. "That's better."

Ivy laughed. "Here's the chips."

I grabbed a Dr Pepper from the cooler and opened it for Ivy. "Here you go."

She glanced up at me from under extra-long lashes. Those were new. With a hint of midnight blue. And a bit of sparkly something-or-other on her eyelids. And why did I know all that?

She patted the chair next to her. "C'mon. I got that Philly cheesesteak sandwich you like."

She always said those things as if she hadn't noticed my whole ribcage had collapsed inside my chest and crushed my vital organs. "Thanks," I said on what I figured was my last breath.

Ivy unwrapped her sandwich. "You didn't answer my question. What are you guys looking forward to?"

Deacon dumped a pile of chips on a napkin. "We have a new way to make money for the ski trip. We're going to pressure wash stuff."

Mary shrugged. "Sure. Why not? You two with a high-powered machine—either powered by gas or electric, doesn't matter—what could possibly go wrong?"

"Hey now," Deacon said. "We got this under control. But you might need to help us spread the word. We'll make a flyer your parents can share online or text their friends. I'm thinking one subdivision at a time."

"That'll work," I said.

Deacon dipped his head and glanced my way. "Psst."

I rubbed my mouth. "What? Something on my face?"

"No. Something you said earlier. Are you going to be OK with this pressure-washing gig?"

"Why wouldn't I be?"

"It's a lot of water and lot of power—and maybe not a lot of control. Depends on how well your grandpa can explain to us what to do."

"Thanks for asking, but I think I can handle a pressure washer. It's not like we're going to blast each other in the face with water."

Deacon laughed. "OK, yeah I hear it now. Just checking."

"We'll be fine," I said a little too loud. "I won't point my nozzle in your face as long as you don't point your nozzle in mine."

And then you could have heard a pin drop.

Mary and Ivy blinked in cartoon-like unison.

"Guys," Mary said. "Is there something you want to share with us?"

CHAPTER 15

Mary

I slipped into the pool and found a comfortable spot to lounge on the steps while Deacon tossed the last of our trash in the barrel beside the house. The near ninety-degree heat, even as the sun went down, made the pool the most comfortable place to be.

Scout found a seat on the edge. "You gonna swim, Mary?"

"I don't think so. I'm pretty much healed, but I don't feel like letting water rush up my nose yet. It's hot, but I'll probably sit here and watch you guys."

The last of the fading green and yellow bruises of my once black-and-blue face had disappeared in the last week.

"You look great," Scout said. "You can't tell anything happened."

"Thanks. I feel like it took forever to clear up."

"It has been a while," Ivy said. "But I'm glad you're better and that we finally managed to make this time to talk—just the four of us."

Deacon joined us in the pool. "So, where do we start?"

I knew they were looking at me. "Let's start with Gavin. I know we've been texting, but let's get it all out there."

"No one's here to judge you or cause you pain, Mary," Ivy said. "We don't have to talk about Gavin."

"Yes, we do," I insisted. "He's not who I thought he was and it's weird. Between the pool party and what Jacob said, I don't know what to think anymore."

Deacon stopped swirling water with his hands. "Is he still trying to get back with you?"

"Yeah. He leaves me little gifts. He taped a rose to my locker. He came to talk to my parents. I wasn't there, but he talked to them like we were still a thing. So strange."

"You mean so much like a stalker," Deacon said. "Did you ever find out if he was the one who was creepin' behind you late that night after you had to work concessions at the football game?"

"I don't know what that was about. All I know is that someone was following me to my ride."

Ivy's eyes widened. "And you weren't scared? How do you do that? I would have run back to the stadium or fell in with the first group of people I saw."

"I wasn't worried, that's all. There were people around."

"About Corey," Ivy said. "We all agree she was the girl who Jacob saw with Gavin at the pool party, but we don't know why, right?"

"Right," Scout said. "But I think that was a coincidence. She came by late and Gavin was trying to stay close—"

"But not close enough to actually help," Deacon said.

"In his defense," I said. "I didn't want him close."

"I know," Scout continued. "What I'm trying to say is I think they just ran into each other around the side of the house.

"Right. I see how the timing lines up, but I don't understand what Jacob said happened on the walk. What he said was like full-blown Warrior stuff that even we don't understand. I told you about my nighttime stuff and my drowning story. What Jacob described is like those fights I have. What triggered that response from Sebastian and our supernatural help?"

Everyone stayed quiet.

No one wanted to admit what we all thought.

"Can I ask a logical question?" Scout asked.

Deacon smirked his way. "Have we ever been able to stop you?"

"Let him talk," I said.

"All right, listen. We now know Gavin's got some issues. And we thought Corey was getting well, but all she's done is become what tormented her. Sebastian warned us about enemies. Could Corey and Gavin be on the same side?"

"If they are," I said. "It's not ours."

Even after what I'd been through with him, it was so hard to look at Gavin as not really being on my side. I thought all our assignments and battles would be with *real* bad guys, not the people I'd known my whole life. Not the people I loved.

"I think the supernatural thing with Jacob might have been a fluke," Deacon said. "An accident. You can't help what you are, Mary. Jacob just happened to be the one helping you at the time. We don't know much about the realm we're spinning in and out of. It may have been something that will never happen again."

"Maybe," I said. "But there is something about him."

"Like what?"

"Like he's familiar. Like Sebastian was the first time I saw him in the garden. Jacob and I had a connection the first time we met. I can't explain it."

Ivy pushed off the stairs and took a cooling loop in front of us. Water rippled across my body as she came to rest again nearby. "Maybe it can't be explained. We've all been over-thinking everything since we met Sebastian, and there's been very little action. I think we'll know an issue when we see it."

"But how do you do that? I spent almost a year with a guy who clearly has problems. He hid his aggression very well for a long time."

"No, he really didn't," Ivy whispered as she leaned in. "You knew something was wrong."

"And I chose to ignore it," I whispered back. "And now I see that control he had over me kept me from seeing and doing other things and meeting new people."

"Well, it's over now."

Scout tilted his head our way. "Anything you need to share? This is supposed to be a meeting of our great minds to catch up on Warrior business."

"No, nothing that will help," I said. "My mind isn't so great right now. I'm still confused and angry about Gavin, but I have to forgive him and move on. That door is closed."

"What about Jacob?" Deacon asked. "Even if he's a coincidence in all this, I'm with Mary. There's something there. He keeps turning up."

"Then what do we do about him?" I asked.

"We watch him," Deacon replied. "Or more like *you* watch him. You're the one he's connected to."

"Great. I get to keep an eye on two guys who are a part of one of the worse nights of my life."

Ivy bumped my shoulder. "At least you know which one isn't going to hurt you."

"Do I know that? Just because Gavin's the one who hit me and Jacob's the one who helped me? Jacob might be a fake, and Gavin might be truly sorry and worthy of a second chance."

The look of horror on Ivy's face was almost funny.

"No wait, I don't mean I'm taking him back. I'm only saying… I don't know what I'm saying. Again." I pointed at my head. "My mind isn't so great right now."

"No worries," Deacon said. "Give yourself time."

"Forget those two," Scout said. "On to Corey. Do we know anything about the new Arrows?"

Ivy's expression changed to visibly agitated. "Can you believe that? After everything she's been through. It's like she went to the psych hospital and they took out the real Corey and replaced it with a vengeful and angry Corey. I get that she has to take her life back and find a safe place to cope, but really, the Arrows?"

Scout changed positions and used a towel to make a pillow to rest his elbow on the concrete. "Maybe she wants to make it different. Maybe it's her way of making things right in that group."

"Um... No. Not a chance," Ivy said. "It was like talking to Paige herself that day in the hall, and I was clearly dissed in her little declaration about me not being an Arrow, and therefore, not being her friend."

"Sorry that happened to you," I said. "You had so much invested in her and the friendship."

"Totally. I thought we were friends, but let's remember something we talked about before. Corey was my assignment. I completed my part. Something's gone wrong there, but I don't feel any obligation to step in, you know? I'm sad, and I feel like I must have done something wrong, but—"

"You did nothing wrong," Scout said. "She's alive. You did everything right."

"Yes, I know she's alive and got help, but do you really think the Creator's plan was to use us to help, and then for Corey to end up an Arrow? What are we missing here? I feel like my assignment ended, and I miss my friend, but if this was the ultimate ending, I don't think Corey's OK."

Deacon did a somersault and ended up floating on his back. "What I'm hearing is we have more questions than answers."

"Yep," Ivy said. "And nothing's happening. We waited weeks to get together and talk and we have nothing new to add."

"Maybe that's a good thing."

"Or maybe," Scout said. "It's the calm before the storm."

Ivy shivered. "Don't say that. We're not looking for a storm. Let's maybe hit the hot tub and talk about something else."

Deacon flopped out of the pool close enough to Scout to irritate him.

"Really? You've got this whole area to do your Deacon the Dolphin thing and you have to do it at the same spot I'm in?"

"Ooops."

Ivy laughed at them. "I guess we all missed a heck of a homecoming game last night."

Everything about homecoming reminded me of the year before. It was all just sad.

Deacon held out his hand as I stepped into the warm water. "Yeah, Mary, your boy Jacob is every bit the beast I said he was. We wouldn't be winning anything if not for him."

"Yeah. I'm glad he's doing well. He's working for a college scholarship. Not that we talk much, but he did tell me that."

Ivy grabbed a bag of popcorn from Scout. "Not to remind you of anything, Mary, but are you sorry you aren't at the dance? I know a couple of guys besides Gavin asked you."

"No, I am totally fine not being at homecoming. But Deacon, how are you holding up?"

"What? Why?"

"Oh, I don't know. Maybe because you lost Claire Cannon to another guy two years in a row? How does that keep happening?"

"Yeah," Ivy said. "How do you expect to pull off your great ski trip romance if you can't even get her to a homecoming dance?"

"I have it all under control. I'm leaving myself room to work."

Scout settled into a chaise. "Sounds more like you're holding the door open for someone else to cuddle with Claire in front of the fire in the Colorado mountains."

"Like I'm going to take advice from the guy who's had the same two years to take a certain someone..." He pointed his head toward Ivy. "And yet, here we are."

Uh-oh.

I glanced at Ivy and didn't know how to help. According to her, they'd had an awkward talk where it appeared Scout asked her to the dance, followed by a one-minute conversation where he'd talked her out of accepting because he knew she didn't really want to go.

Or something like that.

"I wouldn't worry about us," Ivy said. "We're saving every penny so we can be on that ski trip and watch you *not* sip hot chocolate with Claire Cannon—only at a higher altitude."

"Funny."

"Oh, hey guys, check this out."

Scout left the chaise and planted himself with his phone at the edge of the hot tub, so close he nearly dangled his feet. He was right there...

"Oh, never mind."

"No! You can't do that. What is it?"

"Well... I was checking for stuff from the dance, but it's not important." He clicked the screen black.

"It's fine," I said. "I know Gavin is there and everyone's having a great time. Whatever."

"But did you know who he was going with?"

"His mom told my mom he didn't have an actual date and was going along with a group of friends or something."

Scout turned the screen.

Deac got closer. "What the what?"

Ivy gasped. "There are so many things wrong with this."

The four of them stood there—all smiles. Jacob towered over

the others with his arm securely around Cassidy's waist. And Cassidy had her arm looped around Gavin, who had his arm wound around…

Gavin had a date after all.

"I guess that's part of the group," Scout said. "Makes sense. They are football players, and jocks stick together."

"But Jacob and Gavin hate each other," I said.

Ivy snorted in disgust. "Look at that. Gavin's tie matches her dress. The flowers in their corsage and boutonniere are the same. This has been planned a while."

I returned to my spot. "Pass me a soda, would you Scout?"

"Sure."

I popped the top. "Corey and Gavin." I took a drink. "Gavin and Corey. Didn't see that one comin'. Did you guys?"

CHAPTER 16

Shanar

Pathetic. Insignificant. Human.

I waited in my supernatural form at the late, earthly hour, and snatched the boy by his collar.

I slammed him into a tree. As he slid down the trunk, the sleeve of his suit jacket caught on a protruding stub of a branch. Fabric ripped from his arm—along with a couple of layers of skin. Blood seeped through what was left of the cloth that dangled from his shredded shirt.

He dropped to his knees and shrieked into the quiet night as he pulled sticky fingers from the wound on his bicep.

"Get up," I commanded.

He staggered as he stood. "What was that for?"

"We need to talk. You've accomplished nothing."

"It takes time."

"It doesn't when you're not wasting it."

"Mary is hurt, and angry, and suspicious. I'm doing what I can."

"Do more. She must be kept under control and distracted."

The boy pulled off his jacket and used what was left of his shirt to cover the oozing series of gashes on his arm. "How am I supposed to explain this? Huh? My parents are tired of hearing how I'm getting hurt on the field." He growled as he pulled fibers from his jacket out of one of the deeper scrapes. "And what do you want with Mary anyway? She's just a girl."

Humans. The stupidest of all beings.

"She is not just a girl. She possesses something she is not supposed to have. I must take it to maintain balance in our realms."

"That's it? If she has something you want, just take it, so everyone's life can get back to normal. Why am I in the middle of this?"

My anger cracked the sidewalk beneath his feet. "Ignorant fool! Do not presume to guess what I am or am not willing to do."

I felt his arrogance grow, even in the face of my anger. He was a brave one—for a nanosecond at least. I'd give him that.

"What are you going to do? Open the ground and swallow me?"

"That can be arranged," I warned. "But for now, your only job is to remain close enough to Mary for me to get what I want."

"I'm out," he said. "I talked to my parents as you suggested and got those details. I don't work for you. I don't owe you anything. I'm old enough to make my own decisions. So, if all you want is to take something from her, you can manage that without me."

And then the putrid little puke turned his back on me.

It was my pleasure to do as he asked.

The large tree I'd blasted him in to groaned as the concrete cracked further and disturbed its roots. Nature usually rebelled when I altered its surroundings. My darkness choked the Creator's perfect, life-giving balance, and my negative energy often simply...killed things.

The oak shook and leaves fell like rain as the earth split far enough and fast enough to trap the preposterously naïve boy's left leg.

"Now that I've regained your attention..."

"Let me out of here!"

"I wouldn't move too much if I were you. I assume you need that leg in one piece to play football."

He struggled against the pinch of shifting ground around his upper leg. Roots and rebar twisted and creaked as he clung to a scarce solid piece of concrete path. New spots of blood appeared on his pant leg and bloomed until it dripped.

The begging was about to start.

"What do you want from me?"

"The same thing I've always wanted from you. Mary."

"I'm doing what I can. Get me out of here."

"Not so fast." I hovered closer to him, but I doubted he could see a thing. "You feel that blood draining from your leg? Never mind. Doesn't matter. Your blood intrigues me. It is, after all, the reason your parents and I met."

"Yes, I know. They told me. I made them tell me about those additional details you said I was missing. That's how I know I don't have to work for you."

"Oh stop. Let me tell it. It's one of my favorite stories. Now. There you were, your blood positively polluted with cells designed to steal your life—and you'd done nothing to deserve it. But see, your father and his father and his father had a long and twisted history with the Destroyer. And that made it possible to wreak havoc and take over your life. Because one time sooooo long ago, someone decided to accept help from the Destroyer. Just one journey into darkness, one walk into the gloom, any act of separation from the Creator can open doors far into the future for the Destroyer to walk through."

"But my mother said—"

"Shhhh, shhh, wait. I like this part. So, anyway, when you were a baby and got sick with a blood cancer, it was almost too easy to convince your dad I could save you. It's not hard to blind someone whose eyes are already dimmed by years of living in the cellar. Your mother took more time to persuade, but one high fever and a bout of pneumonia sealed the deal. *I'll do anything*, she'd said, without giving any thought to the magnitude of her choice. In her defense, I didn't play fair, and they were so weak. But then... A catch."

"Yes, I know about the catch."

"Your mother was so desperate. *Use me... Use us*, your mother said, and willingly gave herself and your dad to me. She convinced me they were more good to me than a little boy. *Use us*, she'd said. *And then when he's old enough to make his own decisions, take your hands off. Let him alone and leave him free to make his own choices.*"

"Exactly," the boy said from his hole in the sidewalk. "And I've made my own choice. I don't want to work for you."

"Anyway," I continued as if I hadn't heard. "I always loved a good mystery. I was excited to see how that one would play out. Their plan, no doubt, was to raise a good boy in the midst of their own despicable lives in hopes you would free yourself." I disrupted the ground a little more, and the kid wailed. "But you didn't."

"I did!" he screamed. "Now let me out of here."

"No. Don't you get it? You've already taken favors from me. As soon as you were old enough to make some moral choices on your own, you chose your father's path. You wanted to win the geography trivia contest, but you didn't want to study. When I offered an opportunity to cheat, you took it. How many times have we done that? You wanted to win a Pinewood Derby race in the Cub Scouts. I gave you the fastest pretend car. You wanted to excel on the football field. I gave you strength. You wanted Mary. I put you in her path and boom—two birds, one stone."

"I was a child when I made some of those stupid requests."

"Yes, but you already knew right from wrong and you chose wrong and never looked back. I've put good and satisfying things in your life. Do you really want to give them all back right now? No continued good health? No football, popularity, or success? No Mary?"

Did I mention I didn't play fair?

All anyone in his family ever had to do was ask the Creator for help.

Somehow, no one ever did.

And why would they? Why take pleasure, strength, or power from the Creator's world when the Destroyer's gifts were so much more fun?

Soooooo much more fun.

The Creator tried to reach him, but brightness barely lit the cage of evil his consumed parents built around him. It's hard to see life when the curtains of death are pulled tight across the window.

Still… Everyone always had a choice, and everyone always had a chance. The Creator's offers of redemption were infinite, but one solid rejection was all the Destroyer needed to take control.

So, the boy continued in the way of his parents and, when the girl defeated death, it was him I chose to make an Agent and take back what Sebastian took from me—the girl's life.

The kid never fully understood how I'd planned to use him, or what his part was in the destruction.

It didn't matter. He was willing—or at least he would be by the time I got done with him.

"What's it going to be?"

"Get me out of this hole."

"So, you've made your choice to continue to cooperate with me?"

"No, but I'm no good to you if I've punctured something vital and bleed out in this hole."

He had a point, but I remembered even a blind squirrel stumbled upon a nut once in a while.

"Fine. That does look like a lot of blood." It took no effort to shift the ground again.

The boy pulled himself out with considerable effort and turned for home. He looked like he'd been hit by a truck.

"Mary belongs to me," I called after him.

He turned back. "No. She belongs to me."

CHAPTER 17

Mary

My chest burned as I looped the track one more time. The cool November air bit my cheeks, a welcome change from the too-hot Texas October we'd had. The regular walkers hugged the inside lane as I jogged past on the outside.

"Lookin' good, Mary!"

I waved to the older couple who lived on my street and came out to exercise three times a week. "Thanks."

By the time I made it back around, they'd headed for the gate. I paused to grab my water from the bench. "You done already?"

Mr. Carmichael pointed toward the poles. "Lights didn't come on. It'll be black as a raven's wing out here soon. You best get home too."

I hadn't noticed. "Oh yeah. The time change last weekend. They haven't adjusted the timers. I'll remind someone tomorrow."

Mrs. Carmichael pushed a fluff of silver-black hair away from her forehead. "Thanks. C'mon. We'll give you a ride home."

"No, thanks. I have another two miles to run."

Her husband pulled off his Houston Astros cap and scratched his head. "I don't feel right about that. There's no one else around tonight."

"I'm fine," I said and managed what I hoped was a convincing smile. "You know it's not going to take me long to make eight laps. And I promise I'm going to run straight off the track, out the gate, and down the well-lit bike path as soon as I'm done."

"Well, that is true, but if I don't see you zip down the street in a reasonable amount of time, I'm going to come back. Or worse. I'm going to call your mom."

Then he laughed.

Mr. Carmichael thought he had jokes.

Truth was, I'd probably be finished before the Carmichaels made it to their car, stood and discussed their post-workout smoothies, and debated whether or not they needed to get almond milk and blueberries for breakfast on the way home.

But I smiled and thanked them because I did appreciate the concern and small-town intimacies of the suburbs. It'd been a rough fall with the breakup and the injury and all the truths I'd discovered about myself and my relationship with Gavin. His weird new association-friendship-alliance with Corey stuck in my gut like broken glass. No one could figure that one out, especially since he still relentlessly pursued me. *Wanna go to Starbucks? I just want to talk. Can I walk you out? Do you want to work on that project together?*

No. I didn't want to do anything with Gavin, and even though I believed he was sincere and thought *some*day we could get back to that innocent place where we'd grown up together, no amount of lemon-filled cupcakes or pink roses placed strategically in my path was going to change my mind. His actions had morphed from sincere and desperate to stalker-like and pathetic. I'd spotted him behind me and Ivy in a movie theater when the lights came up. Had no idea he'd been back there, and he'd disappeared by the time I stumbled up two rows to confront him. Once, he appeared in a booth across a restaurant where a group of us had met to discuss the ski trip. All alone, staring my way, vanishing when I looked again—but he'd paid the bill for my chicken alfredo. Still, the whole time he was being consistently spotted with other jocks and their band of groupie Arrows—especially Corey.

I jogged toward the gate and used the filtered light from surrounding streetlights and distant businesses to leave the athletic complex area of campus and make my way to the main road. It's not like I didn't know the place as well as my own backyard, and despite the number of leaves that still clung to the trees, there was enough light from the gas station at the closest intersection to see the path.

I texted my mom. *Leaving school.* She didn't need to know the timed field lights had failed to come on and that the school's security lights hadn't worked since the week before when either lightning took out the power box—or, as Scout said, Mr. Silva had tried to adjust something. That'd made us all rethink the small-electrical-incident-slash-fire.

I laughed out loud as I thought about his comments, but that and the rustle of my windbreaker didn't cover the distinct sound of cracking sticks in the brush nearby.

I kept walking.

Squirrel? Racoon? Armadillo?

The brush kept crackling.

My patience with Gavin had grown too thin. I stomped faster toward the main road as obvious footsteps among fallen leaves picked up behind me.

I turned on him. "Gavin, I swear I've had enough of this. You really need to back off."

A large figure tumbled onto the sidewalk as the bright light of a cell phone flashed in my eyes.

I felt in my pocket for my own phone and turned to run.

I wasn't afraid.

I also wasn't an idiot. That body was too big to be Gavin. I just figured I'd accelerate my jog home.

"Mary, wait."

I turned back. "Jacob? What the heck?"

"I'm sorry I scared you."

"You didn't scare me."

"Stupid phone." He turned the light toward the parking lot. "That flashlight icon shows up ten times a day when I don't need it. The one time I try to swipe and find it, it's nowhere."

"What are you doing here? Football practice is long over. No one's here."

"I know. I came back to run."

"Why would you do that? You guys are playoff bound. Haven't you worked out enough for one day? I know the coach is killing you."

"It helps me think. Clears my head. And we don't get many nights this cool."

"But you live a ways from here. I thought you ran on the track at the Y or in your own neighborhood or something."

He pointed the light in my face. "Is there a reason for this interrogation? It's an open track. I go to school here."

"Sorry, but it's… It's nothing and none of my business. Run where you want, but I wouldn't do it here. Between the time change and the electrical problems, the timer isn't right."

"Obviously." He killed the light and stepped toward me as his keys dangled at his side. "Otherwise, I wouldn't have come here to stumble around in the dark. Do you have cat-vision or something? It's pitch black out here."

"I'm just real familiar with the grounds." He was dressed for a run and couldn't have known I was there. His appearance had nothing to do with me, and once again, I'd let Gavin's disturbing habits get in my head. "See you tomorrow."

"Wait. I'll drive you home."

"I can't do that. Not that I don't trust you, but I just got my license, and I'm about two weeks away from getting my grandma's car. My dad didn't sell it when she died. So, it's mine. If I don't get in any trouble. And I told my mom I was headed home. On my own. On foot."

He stood tall and crossed his arms, towering above me. "Not that I don't enjoy your rambling, but a basic *no thanks* would have sufficed. Now I'm wondering why you had to include the part about *not that I don't trust you*. I thought we were past weird conversations. Why would you have to tell me it's not that you don't trust me? I mean, we've been through some stuff."

"Again. Sorry. I meant that about driving. I promised my parents I wouldn't get in a car with other teenage drivers, and yeah. Lame. I'm going home."

"I'll walk with you."

"That's not necessary."

"Oh, it kinda is."

"But you have your car. You should go find a place to run where you won't possibly step on a skunk or something equally smelly or gross in the dark. Also, it could be dangerous."

"Rambling again."

Why was I doing that?

He clicked his alarm. The blink of the lights illuminated a rear paper license plate and the shiny finish of what had to be a brand-new car. Interior lights stayed lit and faded to a soothing shade of blue before dimming completely.

"Is that yours?"

"Yes. Now do you want a ride?"

"It's amazing, and yes, I truly do want a ride, but no, I can't."

He laughed. "You're something, you know that?"

"Why? Because I don't want to mess up my chances of inheriting a car that has beige cloth upholstery, no place to charge my phone, and smells like an old lady's lilac perfume? Did I mention the radio is stuck on an all-talk station?"

He laughed again and headed for the bike path. "Never mind, but believe me, I'd trade my new car for your old one any day?"

I rushed to match his stride toward my house. "Why?"

"Because your old beater comes from the right place. That pricey piece of machinery back there doesn't."

"Where does it come from?"

"From one of two successful people who think if they give me a car like that it'll make everything OK." He slowed. "It won't."

"I'm sorry, Jacob. I know your parents' problems have been hard on you."

"Yeah, well, I won't be in the middle much longer. Once I head for college, I'm never coming back."

I nodded, but I couldn't imagine it. I had even less of an idea of how to help. "It's almost Christmas break, and after that you'll just have three semesters to go. Next year you'll be a senior and you'll be really busy. You'll be fielding all your offers to play college ball. You'll be on to the next phase of your life before you know it."

Something about that made me sad.

He picked up the pace again. "What is Gavin doing to you?"

"Nothing. Why would you ask that?"

"You don't even know what you said back there, do you?"

"When?"

"When I found you at the track."

"You mean when you fell out of the woods?"

"Don't do that."

"What?"

His jawline tightened as he walked even faster. "Try to

change the subject. When someone asks a question, the other person should answer. What do you want for dinner? A steak. Did you pay the electric bill? No. Are you having an affair? Yes, aren't you? Yes." He stopped and bent to rest his hands at his knees and breathe. He stood with a blast of emotion on his face. "Lying is a waste of time and it hurts people. You said this yourself, Mary. You value honesty."

His truth melded with mine and clicked like a lock and key. "And you hate a lie."

"And that's the same thing. My parents lie to me because they think they're protecting me. My coaches lie to me because they want a better performance and to make themselves look good. Friends lie to me to get something, and girls lie to me to be popular. So, when I ask you what Gavin is doing to you, I want an answer, because no one who claims to care about me ever just *tells me the freakin' truth!*" His fists trembled at his sides as he came down from the loud and painful declaration. "I'm sorry."

I grabbed his hands. "Don't be sorry. You're right. We talked about this that day and you're right."

"I overreacted."

"Yeah, but you have a lot on your mind. I can see why a good run on a cold night like this would make it better. I get it."

"I shouldn't have said any of that to you."

"We're friends. You can say anything you want to me."

"I'm sorry."

"Don't be sorry. Just stand here a second."

I grabbed my phone and texted my mom again. *I'm fine. Jacob is walking me home.*

I took his hands again. "Now. Look at me. You asked me a question. The truth is, I don't know what Gavin is doing. We were together almost a year. He was aggressive and it's over, but he's still trying to make up for everything and it's getting weird. He shows up where I am, and he inserts himself in my life at the same time he's dating Corey, I think. It's so strange. When I heard someone behind me tonight, I assumed it was Gavin because he's always just...*there*. I'm not afraid of him, but I don't know what he's capable of. And that's the truth. I don't know what to do about him. I don't know what he's doing."

Jacob swiped his hand across his mouth. "OK. I see. Thanks for telling me."

"Listen, Ivy is the only one who knows all this. You can't repeat it, and you can't mess with Gavin. I know you two have had your problems on the football field, but—"

"He's not worth my scholarship, Mary, that's for dang sure."

I smiled. "Good answer."

"Don't get me wrong, though, you're worth everything—"

"What?"

"Uh… Nothing. I was trying to say I can't let something go if I see it."

"Whoa, whoa, whoa. I can take care of myself. I'll do what I have to do if it gets any worse. This isn't your problem. Do you hear me?"

"Yeah. I hear you."

"Good. Now let's run."

"What do you mean?"

"We're gonna run. Of course, you'll have to hold back or I'll end up two miles behind you, but let's just run. There's a loop around the park in my neighborhood and it's all lit, so let's just run."

I turned to take off, but he swooped me into his arms. It was the first time a guy had pulled me so close in what I thought was a romantic way since Gavin had been so pushy. My instinct was to jerk away and bolt—or even take a swing. I quickly reset my brain before the moment was lost. It was Jacob, not Gavin. Still, while I remembered the comfort and safety when Jacob helped me at the pool, I also remembered pain and a lot of blood.

I shook off the bad memory.

He was so tall, his embrace had lifted me off the ground. He loosened his grip and I slid down his body like a super-sleepy, boneless kitten. I lifted my gaze to his.

"Glass," he said.

"What?" My breathless rom-com response surprised and annoyed me.

"There are two broken beer bottles right in front of you on the path. I didn't want you to step on them."

Ser-i-ous-ly?

"What?" Crap. I'd done it again.

He took two steps back and set me on the ground. "Don't step on the glass."

"Thanks." I curled my arms around him and rested my head on his massive chest. "Thank you for watching out for me. Again."

He returned my hug and swept his strong hands across my back. I felt nothing but heat, and for the second time, the distinct connection of a lock and key.

Click.

And then we ran.

CHAPTER 18

I^{vy}

It was the grossest thing I'd ever seen.

Well, maybe only one of the grossest things I'd ever seen. My mother had recently gotten a raise at work and used it to reward me with a couple of streaming subscriptions to watch what everyone else had already seen. I'd been seeing some medical and science things that were beyond disturbing.

Then I saw what I saw by the locker room.

Corey and Gavin groped and grinded against each other like a couple of barnyard animals—but with more slobbering—and considerably more grunting.

I turned to get away as Corey slid down the wall. I considered where her mouth was headed and knew I was gonna have to have my eyeballs scrubbed out of my head.

I ducked around the corner and made a sound when I brushed a trash can.

All their noise stopped, so I did too, and flattened my back against the wall.

"Someone's there," Corey said.

"No one's there," Gavin answered.

I decided if I heard footsteps, I was going to keep walking. What could they do? Give me crap for interrupting that? Ha! I didn't even know the consequences of what they were doing if a teacher came along.

The rustle of clothes—ewww—told me they weren't going to check. I was on my way out until someone spoke.

"Wait," Corey said to Gavin. "Not until we talk about the pep rally."

"What about it? All you and the Arrows have to do is make sure Jacob is late to the gym. He needs to walk in after it's started, and this is very important, he needs to walk in on the end that exits to the parking lot, not the end from the campus hallway. Oh, and like it's real obvious he came in after the rest of the team."

"He's the star player. If anything, Coach will want him leading the guys through the blow-up arch. Something tells me they'll know he's missing."

"Then your people will have to get real creative, won't they? If you need help from my guys, let me know."

"So, we delay Jacob and send him in a certain door. Why?"

"That part of the plan is really none of your business."

I'd held my breath so long my heart took over and started to beat out of control. Shallow breaths didn't help, but at least I wasn't dizzy. I had to hear the plan. Knowing Gavin's mean streak and Corey's gullible nature... Wow. The combination of a diabolical mean guy and a do-anything-for-him minion could be dangerous.

"I'm serious, Gavin," Corey said. "If the Arrows could get in trouble, we should know."

"You won't get in trouble. If all goes well, the Arrows won't be on the hook for anything."

"What are you going to do?"

"The less you know the better. Just delay Jacob and send him in the area we talked about, and make sure you're close to an exit."

Close to an exit...

The words reverberated in my head as Gavin's muffled voice disappeared in what was probably him doing his best to pick up with Corey where they'd left off.

I covered my ears and headed for the door.

Move child...

Once outside, I crouched against a brick column and closed my eyes. Not one person roamed that end of the campus. All the words and images tumbled in my head and I couldn't make sense of them. And where was Mary? I knew I was supposed to meet her by the locker room after her soccer meeting, but no one else was around. Why wasn't anyone else around?

Move child...

"Yes, I heard you," I whispered into my own chest. "I understand, but what am I supposed to do?"

While completely unbelievable and strange, the voice had become so familiar to me, it was no longer accompanied by the sense of a cool hand grazing my cheek. Was it weird that I was growing so in tune with my Warrior abilities that all I needed to hear was the voice?

The smell of smoke hit my nose. Not cigarette smoke, not barb-que smoke, not campfire smoke, but the hot-plastic scent of an electrical-type fire—a lot like the smell of the small electrical incident and/or the not-quite-a-fire from the ice cream social.

I opened my eyes and moved farther between the column and the shrubs to avoid being seen. A little cloud of black smoke appeared and hovered before my eyes.

I squeezed them shut again. "Please tell me I am not actually seeing a ball of smoke..." I looked again and the mass had grown. It pulsed in front of my face like an active storm cloud. Dark, but still fluffy, the swirling puff released more of the burning smell.

I raised my hand and drew a finger through it. "I see you. What are you trying to tell me?" I'd gotten pretty brave about the whole hallucination thing since I'd last had one. Even my heart rate had slowed.

Tendrils curled around my hand and dissipated into the air.

There was going to be a fire and...something else? It wasn't clear. The fire wouldn't be like the one in the Saints Café. It would be bigger and scarier, and Gavin had something to do with it.

Peace surrounded me as I stood to tap out a text to Mary.

Soccer meeting? Where are you?

She responded fast. *What meeting?*

We were supposed to meet today.

No. Tomorrow.

I sent a poo emoji. *My bad. I'm a day off. Where are you?*

Post weight-lifting smoothie with Jacob. Sorry we got our wires crossed. Wanna come?

Can't. We need a Warrior meeting 911.

Are you OK?

Yes, but we need to talk. Corey came out the door without Gavin. *Gotta run. I'll call ASAP. All fine right now.*

I fell into step with Corey as she headed from the athletic building to the front of the school. Her cold look didn't stop me from trying.

She glanced back at the door and then to me. "What are you doing here?"

"I had a mix-up with Mary about a meeting spot. What about you?"

She didn't answer, but it was clear she wondered if I'd heard or seen anything. "I have to go. My ride's probably already here."

"I miss you, Corey."

She stopped and turned my way. "What?"

"I miss my friend. You see, my friend had a rough time and went away to get help. When she came back, she was different and didn't want to be my friend anymore. I miss her."

She took off walking again. "Stop talking about me in third person—or whatever that is you're doing."

"Then stop acting like we don't know each other. What happened to you in that hospital, Corey? I visited you all the time and you seemed better."

"I had lots of visitors, and I learned a lot about myself. I'll never not be in control again. No one is ever going to bully me, and I'm going to be the one in charge of *me*."

I grabbed her arm to slow her down. "Are you sure about that?"

She jerked her arm away and spun. "What do you mean?"

"We've talked about this before, Corey. Don't trade one kind of manipulator for another. Who got to you in that hospital? Did someone threaten you?"

"No," she spat out. "Someone empowered me."

That took the air from my lungs. Nothing about her behavior seemed safe, smart, happy, or logical. Sebastian promised the Destroyer had allies. People like Gavin and Paige made sense. Could they have convinced Corey to take a darker path? Someone had twisted her brain around backward while everyone else had been working to straighten it out.

And I had no idea what to do about it.

I stepped back. "I'm here if you need me, Corey."

"I don't need you."

"At least be careful. Especially with Gavin."

"No, Ivy. *You* be careful."

CHAPTER 19

Mary

Jacob held two smoothies. "You said surprise you. I have a veggie apple kale thing and a veggie carrot spinach thing. No extra powder because it's late. Just pure wellness blends."

I tried not to make a seriously disappointed face. "The apple one, I guess?"

"I'm kidding." He set a plastic cup and straw in front of me and pulled out a chair. "I got you chocolate banana something. It's vegan, but still sounds promising."

"Oh, thank God. I'm not sure I can do kale."

"No one can really do kale, Mary."

I pulled my notebook out of my bag. "What'd you get?"

"I still have to do the spinach thing. No more sugar today."

I considered his size, athletic ability, and discipline. "You must have to consume an enormous amount of calories and protein a day."

"Yeah. I'm sure our housekeeper is really sick of cooking

chicken. She does a whole bunch of food stuff for me on Sundays and stocks the fridge."

I slid a stack of papers across the table. "That's nice. Weekdays are busy. Especially for you right now."

He thumbed through the pages. "What's this?"

"I sent some docs to your laptop, but thought you could use these notes for your term paper. Your junior English teacher was also my creative writing and journalism teacher. She likes things a certain way. My notes and her feedback will give you an idea of how to make your term paper stronger."

He dropped the top page and took a long drink. "You dug this stuff out for me?"

"Yes, Jacob, that's for you. I thought it might help. Now, did you bring your history notes so I can quiz you?"

"You were serious about that?"

"Why wouldn't I be serious? My mom said you could drive me two miles to my house as long as we were working out and studying. I'm close to getting my car, and she's probably spying on me right now, so yes, I was serious."

"For real? You suburb people are weird."

"Hey! There's nothing wrong with us small-community people. It's good to know your neighbors. And this is Texas. Yes, it's true half the people you meet are armed and drink too much sweet tea, but that doesn't mean it's not a great place to live."

"I'm teasing you, Mary. I don't mind it. I'm just used to living in the city like I did in Dallas. Not outside it. And I know Texans very well." He took another slurping pull on his straw.

"You can't possibly be enjoying that."

"It's not too bad." He stood. "I'll get my tablet out of my trunk." He paused and touched my shoulder as he passed. "I appreciate the study help. I was only surprised because no one who's ever suggested I study with them actually meant there'd be studying."

I felt my right eyebrow creep up at his comment. We had the

most bizarre relationship going. Most days he was either too serious and reserved, or too loose with personal information and humor. I didn't always get when he was trying to be funny, but I recognized his clever but brutal sarcasm, though it was never directed at me. It was as if he didn't have a lot of experience with casual friends.

But that was the problem, wasn't it?

Jacob didn't have any friends.

He was at a new school where everyone saw only a possible state football championship for the first time in school history. They'd probably push him into baseball right after that.

He wasn't close to his parents, and he'd gravitated toward my unusual friend group from the beginning. His camaraderie with his team was only because he was so good, and homecoming with Cassidy had, by his own admission, been a fluke of two people who didn't have a date.

Jacob was lonely.

He'd latched on to me and the Warriors that first day at the ice cream social and we'd been linked ever since. Still, I didn't know where he fit there, if at all, but it made me feel a whole lot better he seemed to be on our side rather than the alternative.

Our personal connection was different. The comfort and familiarity between us couldn't be explained. We had no history, no ties, not even a whole lot in common. But we worked like that lock-and-key certainty that came when we were together. We just…*worked*. It wasn't overtly romantic or strictly a friendship. He held my hand when we crossed a street and always watched out for me. I was doing the same for him.

We needed each other and we belonged together—and it defied explanation.

I pulled the zippered pouch my grandma had given me out of my bag. The soft, worn leather was comforting under my fingers as I dug for a hair band and a pen.

Lost in thought, I mindlessly doodled on the back of my

notebook. Warriors. Sebastian. Jacob… My phone jarred me from my artwork with a series of texts from Ivy.

Jacob dropped his tablet and a wadded-up review sheet on the table. "Everything OK?"

"Yeah… Ivy's got something going on. She said she'd call when she could. Sounds important."

"Do you need to go?"

"No, she'd say if I did."

"What's the A for?"

"What A?"

"On your bag there."

I'd forgotten the monogram on the pouch. "Oh. My initials."

"Is your middle name Angel?"

A chill rippled at the back of my neck. "Why would you use that name?"

"Angel? It's not such a stretch."

I couldn't imagine what he possibly meant.

He pulled my notebook across the table and held it up for me. By my own hand, I'd drawn no less than a dozen angel wings in various shapes and sizes.

"Oh. That."

Thank God. If we'd had one more supernatural, telepathic, or otherwise psychic-like circumstance to navigate that day…

"Mary Angel. I like it."

"That's not my name."

"I think it probably is."

"It's not." I opened the review sheet. "Let's see here. You'll have to answer a couple of essay questions on test day, but otherwise, I can quiz you on some multiple choice. I hope all your answers on this review sheet are correct, though."

He turned his tablet my way. "You can double-check me, but I'm ready. Hit me, Mary Angel."

"Stop." I finally had to laugh. His delivery couldn't have been funnier. "That's not my name."

"Hey, Mary Angel?"

I looked up.

"Gotcha'. You answered to Mary Angel."

"No, I didn't."

"You did."

"My name is Mary Antonia Hunter, and you need to study."

"I like Mary Angel better so I'm going with that, and you didn't answer my question."

"You didn't ask a question. You're just tormenting me and stalling for time."

"Oh, sorry." He leaned in. "Mary Angel, can I kiss you when I take you home?"

CHAPTER 20

Scout

I closed the door to Mr. Silva's office with a soft click and turned to my anxious friends. "What's the emergency? We have about ten minutes before Mr. Silva comes back. He's pretending to be occupied somewhere else so we can talk."

Deacon snorted. "Who knew Scout's bromance with our school custodian would turn out to be such a perk?"

"Shut it, Deacon. We don't have much time."

"All right," Ivy said. "Here's the deal. There's a big pep rally Friday morning to send the guys off to the playoffs. Gavin and his band of…whatever demon-like people he knows, are going to try to pull something. They're setting up Jacob. The Arrows—led by Gavin's new evil sidekick, Corey—are helping him." She glanced at Mary. "Sorry."

Mary dropped her gaze. "No need. It's become clear around here the Arrows and the jocks have become a thing."

Deacon gave her a side hug. "One of my brothers said they're having those weird campfires out in the woods behind the country club where he works. Like way out past the lake after hours."

"I know," Mary said. "And apparently it's pretty gross. Certain things are now required of the Arrows to be able to spend time with certain football players."

That piqued my interest. "What things?"

"You know," Mary said. "*Things.*"

I still didn't get it.

"A sex thing," Deacon said. "We're talking about a specific sex thing, Scout. Perhaps you've heard of it?"

"Leave it alone," Ivy said. "We only have ten minutes, and I've already had to sanitize my eyeballs once this week because I accidentally walked up on something, so can we move on?"

I didn't like that Ivy was uncomfortable. "What did you walk up on?"

"Never mind." She glanced Mary's way again, and it was clear they'd already talked.

"Oh. Got it. Gavin. Corey. Sex thing. Sorry, Mary."

"Will y'all stop it?" Mary snapped. "I honestly don't care anymore about that, but what I do think is hilariously ironic is that some of those girls are in the Purity Club."

"I can explain that," Deacon said.

Mary's shocked and wide-eyed expression was almost as funny as Deacon's statement. "You can explain the Purity Club connection? Are you a member?"

"No, of course not. But I talked to my mom about this."

Then it was Ivy's turn to look a mile past awestruck. "You talk to your mom about sex?"

"Well, it's more like she talks to *us* about sex, but if you'll let me explain—"

"I can't wait for this," I said.

Deacon gave us a deadpan stare. "You don't deserve to hear my vast knowledge on the subject."

Mary laughed. "C'mon, Deac. Whaddayaknow?"

"There are five kids in my house," he said. "Five boys. *Boys.* All we talk about is girls, sports, food, and video games. And my mom eavesdrops. So, when she hears something, she gets right on in there and tells us how it is."

"What does this have to do with the Purity Club and the sex in the woods?"

"That's my point. They aren't having sex in the woods. Or at least they don't think they are."

"What?" I grimaced until my eyes closed. Then one eye popped open. "What do they think they're having?"

"Don't even try to make me say all the words because I know I'll pay for it later, but according to my mom, there are some girls and guys who think certain sex acts aren't really sex. They don't feel like they're breaking any rules because they aren't really…you know…"

"Alrighty then." I glanced at my phone. "And now we only have two minutes to discuss how we're going to make like Warriors and stop a disaster. Ivy?"

"It's a fire," she said. "I think Gavin's guys are going to start a fire during the pep rally and make it look like Jacob did it. They're using the Arrows to distract him and make it look like he could have done something. I think they want him off the team and kicked out of school."

Deacon crossed his arms. "Seriously? They'd blow the game just to get to Jacob?"

"I think Gavin hates him that much. And there's more. I don't know why, but I believe there's something else. It isn't clear. Gavin seemed adamant Jacob be in a certain place at a certain time. I couldn't hear everything, but there's more to this than just a fire."

"We should warn Jacob," I said.

"No!" Mary dropped onto the folding chair by the door.

"Why not? I thought you trusted Jacob."

"No," she repeated. "I mean, I do trust Jacob, but no, don't warn him."

"Why?"

"Because I don't know what he is. I say we make a plan in case there's an actual fire. We can watch out for Jacob. If he's one of the good guys, he'll come out all right. And if he's one of the bad guys..."

"He'll be exposed," I said. "I like it. Clever, Mary."

"Thank you. Now, what do we do? We're talking a fire. Do we warn Mr. Parrington?"

Ivy pulled on a strand of hair and wrapped it around her finger as she thought. "And tell him what? That I saw a vision of a smoke cloud and smelled the stench of an electrical fire?"

"Good point," I said. "Especially after we've had so much trouble here with all that. We could look guilty of something. Mr. Silva's been working with an electrician, but he's beside himself. The electrical problems make no sense."

"Or," Deacon said. "They just haven't found them all yet."

"Right. If the Destroyer is using Gavin and the others to cause problems, who knows what they're doing or who could be hurt?"

Deacon leaned against the wall. "Anyone else think it's weird that some kids would be messing with electrical stuff? I don't even have my phone charger plugged in by the sink where I brush my teeth. You know... Electrical stuff and water."

"Right...," I said. "I'll help you with that later, but right now, you also have a point. If all this electrical misfiring is connected —the fire behind the AC, the problems with the security lights and cameras—some teenager is taking some really scary risks to mess with that."

"Unless it's an adult," Ivy said. "Sebastian said the Destroyer would use all kinds of people to try and hurt us and others."

"Maybe it's the electrician," Mary said. "Or any adult who

could get in here unnoticed during that pep rally and cause problems. Parents will be here for that."

Ivy shrugged. "What do we do? I got the impression it was about framing Jacob and not necessarily burning down a school full of students."

"Yeah," Deacon said. "But you know how fast that can get out of control. We have to be prepared either way. We're either stopping a fire or rescuing students when it goes three-alarm."

"Or," Mary said. "Exposing Jacob."

Ivy stepped to Mary's side. "Or uncovering an adult enemy."

"Maybe instead of possibly exposing Jacob, we're saving him," I added.

Deacon sighed. "Well, we just have a big ol' mess, don't we? We can't be everywhere."

"No," I said. "But I can start here. In this office. This is Wednesday. The pep rally is Friday. I'll try to get through Mr. Silva's records and get his log-in to get into the system and see what the security cameras are doing—when they're working."

"You can do that?" Deacon seemed surprised.

"I can do a lot of things. I have a feeling the cameras being down are part of the plan. Or at least a small part of it. With everyone running loose that day and all the visitors, Gavin or whoever is helping him has to count on one camera to know where Jacob is."

"Yeah," Mary said. "But doesn't that mean it'll also catch us and the Arrows out and about? Mr. Parrington's not going to know who to believe if he sees us all running the halls looking for trouble."

"There has to be adult help," Deacon said. "You don't think—"

"No, I don't," Scout said. "If anything, Mr. Silva is somehow one of us."

"You know that for sure?"

"I know that for sure."

Ivy twined her fingers in mine and planted a tiny kiss on my cheek. "Thanks for being a genius, Scout."

I may have seen stars and a wall of black for a sec.

Mary grabbed the doorknob. "What next?"

"Keep your eyes and ears open," I said. "Video chat late tomorrow night." I swiped a folder off Mr. Silva's desk that I intended to return by lunch, and pulled my girl toward the door. "Don't worry. No one's burning up in this school."

CHAPTER 21

D^{eacon}

It was mass chaos.

And that was before everything happened.

The Stonehaven Saints had never been to the playoffs before, or so close to a state title in anything. Everyone wanted to cheer the team on and see them off. I don't think the principals expected to see so many extra people show up for a pep rally. Parents and grandparents and locals came out of the woodwork. The community newspaper came for pictures and interviews, and Wayne had to call in extra security at the last minute.

Like I said. Chaos.

Scout and I filed into the gym with our class to our assigned grade-level section. While everyone else chattered and prepared to cheer loud enough to earn the coveted spirit stick, Scout went over blueprints and diagrams with me on his phone.

"It doesn't make sense," he said. "The random fire and the

electrical problems don't add up. I scoured Mr. Silva's records. Like I said last night, I don't think the electrician knows what he's doing, but right now, all the cameras are working properly. If I can get enough signal in here, I might even be able to get back in and see for myself."

"What are all these Xs?"

"Those mark spots where there have been previous repairs or updates. They're not old, but they're not new either. The other marks are where it appears things need to be upgraded. And look at this." Scout scrolled through several more pictures. "Here's where Mr. Silva's notes line up with what's been happening recently. See that? Mr. Silva is noting where he feels there are issues, but it doesn't look like anything is being done."

I scanned the crowd, but there was no way to pinpoint anyone. "Where are Mary and Ivy?"

"They already peeled away from the crowd and are in a hallway on either end of the gym as planned."

"Which means we need to get to the ends of these bleachers and near the doors to watch for Jacob to get in. He'll either be right on time and with the football team on that end, or he'll be late and come in this end—if Mary and Ivy don't bust up whatever the Arrows are doing to misdirect him."

"And," Scout said. "If he gets in on time, he's probably safe, but there's still the matter of a fire. If Ivy said she saw fire, that girl knows there will be a fire."

"Let's go, then."

"Wait." Scout grabbed my arm. "Look at this view."

I glanced at the picture and didn't know what I was looking at. "What is it?"

"It's the gym. See it?"

"Look, Scout, there's no way I'm going to see what you're looking at and we're out of time, so spill it."

"They did a two-year fundraising campaign a while back to update the gym. They maybe got as far as updating the lights to

LED and revamping some disgusting locker rooms, but I think I read the project tanked. Bad management, no money, whatever. But look at all these spots Mr. Silva has marked around the gym. He's got big red circles around our joke of a press box, the scoreboards—"

"Can I have your attention, please?"

"Crap. We have to go before everyone gets quiet and we can't move."

Scout bolted.

The band started the fight song as the cheerleaders lined up at the opening of the inflatable arch in the corner.

I stumbled toward the end to try and sit near the doors Jacob was supposed to come through late. If we hadn't been herded like cattle into the gym in the first place, I might not have had to step on not one, but both of Claire Cannon's feet. I couldn't even eek out a decent apology as the acrid fumes from the fog machine hit my nose.

Really? The fog machine inside the gym on *that* day? Between that and the cheerleaders, I couldn't even tell if Jacob was with the team as they barreled through.

A teacher stopped me near the end. "Sit down, Mr. Sanders."

It wasn't a bad place to stop. I texted to our group. *No eyes on Jacob from here.*

Scout texted back. *He's not with the team.*

Dang. That meant he'd been derailed. I only hoped Ivy and Mary hadn't been also.

I continued to search the perfectly normal pep rally as Mr. Parrington introduced the coach. Drum claps and whistling rang in my ears as I counted the exits on each end. There were plenty of doors, but far too many people to get out fast. Any mass movement would be no less than a stampede. Even the older bleachers could collapse under the constant and sudden movement of terrified students.

"You better be around, Sebastian," I mumbled to myself. "Scout's right. If Ivy said fire, she meant fire."

I glanced at each scoreboard. My hands pulsed warmth.

I texted. *Scout. Scoreboard?*

Yeah?

Look. Why are they on? The one down here isn't fully lit. Flickering.

Diagram says issues.

I just knew.

But Mary and Ivy didn't.

IT'S THE SCOREBOARD ON MY END! Mary, Ivy, what's happening?

Nothing, Ivy texted back. *Some guy in a navy jumpsuit stopped to ask me about a bathroom.*

Me too, Mary wrote.

Jacob? I asked.

All answered no.

It's too crowded, I texted. *He could be anywhere. And who wears jumpsuits?*

Electricians, Scout texted back.

Then I spotted the navy jumpsuit come through the door as the coach rambled on and the crowd cheered. He talked of introducing the team, but Jacob's chair in the front row was noticeably empty. Was anyone going to address that the star of the team wasn't there to be introduced?

I have eyes on navy jumpsuit. He's taking a vid w/his phone, I texted and then snapped a photo of him. *Something's not right with this guy. And where is Jacob?*

Here! Mary texted. *Walking in now.*

I glanced at the scoreboard and then at navy jumpsuit.

The rest was a blur of noise and confusion.

Over the next several seconds, four loud pops—like gunshots—rang in the air. It was enough to stun everyone into silence, and then into screeching panic as many clearly thought it was an active shooter.

Drops of white, liquid fire fell from the scoreboard like a fireworks display as it exploded and sent bits of hot debris into the air.

I was stuck in slow motion as my gaze landed on Jacob who paused to look up.

I ran for him—but so had Mary.

She slammed into him as what was left of the swaying board burned and plummeted to the gym floor. Unidentifiable pieces skittered for yards as students dodged, tripped, and wrestled through the mess.

I opened my mouth to scream for Sebastian, but nothing came out.

I heard a voice in my head. *I'm here.*

I glanced up. The explosion had left everything near the scoreboard on fire.

As alarm bells raged above us, I struggled to get to Mary.

"You guys OK?"

"Yeah. Let's get out of here."

But even though the Warriors had been seconds ahead of everyone on what was going to happen, we were not prepared for what happened next.

Everyone had run away from the falling scoreboard and toward the opposite exits. That would have been great except for one thing.

I met Mary's gaze with sheer terror. "The doors are closed, Mary. We can't get out."

CHAPTER 22

Mary

I understood what would happen the moment Deacon said *scoreboard*.

I knew Jacob had been delayed somewhere out of my reach. I knew the navy jumpsuit guy was not a coincidence. I knew we were in for a fight.

When Jacob rounded the corner in a hurry because he knew he was late, I tried to stop him. He slipped in the first door he passed, and right toward the middle of the end wall of the gym to then race to his seat.

And I was on him like stink.

I didn't look up. I only looked ahead and tackled him in hopes I'd push his massive body far enough away to be safe. We tumbled to the floor amidst blistering drops of melting plastic, hot glass, and clanging metal.

I heard nothing as I pulled my arm from under Jacob's

weight. Pain flooded my elbow with the movement, but I kept using it.

"Keep going!" I pushed him.

He grabbed for me. "Not without you."

"I'm here. Head for the door." I slipped on what I hoped was vomit and not blood. In my confusion, I'd blocked out the noise, but I caught sight of students in full panic as they moved like watercolor blurs in various states of shock and zombie-like movement.

That could have been anything on the floor.

Deacon stepped toward us in much the same way. "The doors are closed, Mary. We can't get out."

"What?"

"Look. They're crashing against the doors. They won't open."

Mr. Parrington's voice became a blob of unintelligible thunder over the crowd. I think he was trying to say what they heard were not gunshots and that everyone needed to calm down and exit.

But there was no way to exit and terror grew.

"Deacon! Don't lose it now!"

"Yes! I'm good. What is this?"

I felt the suffocating hands of Shanar around my neck. I couldn't think any faster. I tried to close my mind to the outside. I fought in my supernatural realm and tore his hands from my throat. The problem was, I was still very much in the real world in the midst of a disaster.

Focus... Sebastian, we need you.

I'm here.

What's happening? What do we do?

It is as I explained. The Destroyer would see you dead, but you do not have to die.

And neither does anyone else...

Where does your help come from, Mary?

The Creator. And you on his behalf.

So, what is to be done?

"Mary!" Deacon yelled. "We're running out of time. Fire is coming down this wall."

"Think logically, Deac. There's no reason those doors are locked. Scout showed us last night. There's no emergency lockdown on them, and even if there were, it wouldn't stop escape, only entrance. This isn't a natural force. It's a supernatural one."

"Are you saying the Destroyer is holding the doors closed?"

"Why not? This is just all-out war. Use your powers."

"What powers? My hands heat up and maybe that warmth heals things. The last thing we need in here is more heat."

"Turn it on the doors."

"And do what? Melt them closed even tighter?"

"Go!" I pushed him toward the farthest door, a good ways from where the scoreboard used to hang. "Push it open. I'll help, but so far, you're the only one with actual visible and physical powers. Together, we are all the force we need to defeat the Destroyer. Sebastian is here to help."

"I know. I heard him."

"Then grab the bar and push."

I pulled Jacob along and noticed blood. It trickled down the side of his face. I had no idea where the wound was, but it was on his head. He slumped against the wall.

I joined Deacon at the door. "Jacob can't help. He might be hurt, and I think it has to be us."

"We need to hurry. The smell is getting bad."

A blast of air passed through the gym. "That's not good," I said. "It will only feed the fire."

"Where is that coming from?" Deacon asked.

I glanced behind us. No doors had been opened to create a path for wind to pass through. "I don't know."

My heart dropped as I caught sight of the navy jumpsuit guy. He seemed to be making half-hearted attempts to help at the other end. Then there were others who didn't seem to be nearly as concerned. Some of Gavin's football friends, some of the Arrows, a few others who were stone-faced and seemingly unconcerned.

I caught the scent of ugly truth as sure as the burning electrical stench in my nose.

They thought the Destroyer would take care of them.

We were surrounded by enemies. The lines had been drawn in the sand. The war of good and evil was a real one, and we were up to our necks in it.

I turned to Deacon. "We've totally got this."

Footsteps thundered up behind us. Ivy and Scout grabbed the door.

"Go back," I commanded. "It's safer down there and they need help."

"Not on your life," Scout said. "Sebastian sent us."

"And there's no safety for anyone if the doors don't open," Ivy added.

"Everyone focus," I said. "Focus on the Creator. Imagine the Destroyer disintegrating away from the door. He can't win. He's not able or allowed to win."

We closed our eyes.

"Push!"

CHAPTER 23

Deacon

Everything was black.

I closed my eyes like Mary said. I tried to focus. I imagined crashing through the doors and the Destroyer's forces to free everyone.

But nothing.

I thought I had died. My body split from itself somehow and I was detached from the action. I couldn't feel anything, and there was so much...*black*.

A swirling mass encircled me as my vision came back. "Your talents are wasted here, Deacon. Look at you and your friends pushing on that door. Hopeless. The firefighters are literally minutes away, but you and your friends are still going to die. What's above you is going to come down in blazes at any time."

My own common sense rattled me into some form of thought. "I'm still alive. You said *going to die*. I'm not dead yet. I just need to focus."

"Ah. Smart boy. I'll make this quicker. You don't have to die. All you have to do is swear allegiance to me and become my Agent like so many of your other friends here have done. I'll get you out of here safely, and tend to all your needs and desires, blah, blah, blah, do we have a deal?"

"No, we do not have a deal. Why would I make any deal with someone I don't know?"

"Oh, smart boy, I think you know who I am. I know Mary. She told you about me. And I believe I know your mother. Your real mother."

My body lost its footing on the ground below my detached being. The door wouldn't budge, and I slipped.

I'd faltered, and the dark force knew it.

Focus...

"Let's see. I know your real mother from way back. She tried so hard to resist me, but times were rough. Now, let me think. I believe she's still alive. I could probably arrange a meeting, but that depends on you. And you two can talk and talk, and she can explain to you how much easier things are when you work for me."

How many times had I wondered about my parents? How badly did I want to know? I considered all I'd learned and seen in the past year, and nothing about my current ominous out-of-body and near-death experience was positive or helpful in any way. There was nothing peaceful about me dangling around my own body while people screamed in fear and my life was threatened. I pictured my great-grandfather's face. He never would have fallen for that.

"I know who you are," I said. "You're Shanar, and I don't work for you. I work for the Creator."

"Suit yourself, smart boy. For now."

A pinprick of light permeated the black. Green and purple hues trickled through the darkness until bright white light chased it completely away.

I was with my body again.

Deacon, listen to me.

Sebastian?

Yes. You did a good thing. Now, remember what Mary said and open the doors.

I don't know how.

Yes, you do. You are the power.

My eyes flew open wide. "I've got it! Don't push with me. Push *on* me. Channel all your Warrior energy *through* me. Help me. I got this."

I placed my hands on each bar of the double doors. "No way, Shanar. Not today, Destroyer."

Scout, Mary, and Ivy pushed my body until my face smashed against the heavy steel door. Things cracked in my torso as they pushed again. I placed my palms flat on the surface as hot warmth traveled through every vein, and pure strength burst from my fingertips.

The door flung open.

"Next door!" Mary screamed.

I reached for Jacob and lifted him from the wall and over my shoulder. "This door's open," I yelled as loud as I could to the others as I carried him out and propped him in a corner near the front. I held his head in my hands. "You'll be OK."

The crowd rushed toward me as I came back in to work on a second door.

"Let's get to the other end," I said. "The other exit is too close to the fire in the wall and ceiling. It's clearing out on that end."

We shoved our way through the pulsing crowd and hit the first door we found. The swarm noticed and more people ran out.

We fell into a rhythm. I flattened my palms and pushed, and the others backed me up with one quick shove and a burst of powerful energy.

People poured out as we worked. When we got to the fifth door, it flapped open on its own.

The Destroyer had released his grip.

CHAPTER 24

Mary

The football game was moved to the following Friday.

The school was closed for three more days after the weekend.

The gym was closed indefinitely.

One lady and one student twisted their knees—both left knees—in the crowd, and one dad was taken to the hospital as a precaution because he couldn't breathe. Someone said it might have been a heart attack, but later decided his long-untreated asthma couldn't handle the smoke in the room.

Seems Deacon and I had gotten the worst of it, and Jacob's head injury…

Well…

No one died.

Scout's grandma arrived at the top of the stairs with a tray that held popcorn, a bowl of chocolate-covered peanuts, a bag of pretzels, and fruit.

Scout knocked pillows off the ottoman and patted it. "Here. Thanks, Grandma."

"No problem. How you guys holding up?"

I grabbed the cloth on my sling and used it to pull my arm off my lap and change position. All my parents had done for days was field phone calls from those concerned, interested, or snooping around. My dad hadn't even gone to work Monday or Tuesday, and the whole community was up in arms about the safety of the school and the trauma of those who'd been there trapped in the gym. "I'm fine, thanks, but I'm tired of all the attention."

Scout's grandma laughed. "I'm not sure how you're going to avoid the attention since all the stories are about how you four saved the day. All the news stations have come around."

Ivy plopped on the couch and pulled a fluffy throw across her lap. "It's true, Mary. You saved Jacob's life."

"Where is Jacob?" Deacon asked.

"He's at his third different neurologist trying to figure out what happened with his concussion and if he can play ball. He may come by in a bit."

Scout's grandma put her hands on her hips. "Well, let me know if you need anything." She stepped to the mini bar and poured water in the small machine she called a diffuser.

"Whatcha' puttin' in there, Grandma?"

"Couple drops of vetiver, cedarwood, lavender… It'll make it smell great up here and help you guys rest and focus and get ready for tomorrow." She clicked it on and a scented cloud puffed out the top. "If you need anything, I'll be downstairs."

Deacon winced and held his side as he bent to wave the fragrant air in his face. "Smells good. Your grandma is cool."

"She's a hippie," Scout said.

"Did everyone's parents get the text from Mr. Parrington?" Deacon asked.

"Mine did," I answered. "They said he wanted to see all of us in the morning. What do you think he wants?"

"No tellin'," Scout said. "Probably the usual *why is it always you four* routine."

"Have you been able to get back into the program for the security footage?"

"Nope. Either Mr. Silva's access has been revoked, or the whole system is fried and there's nothing to see."

I laughed. "If you want to see something, just check the hashtag *StonehavenGymFire* and look at all the cell phone video people managed to capture during the chaos."

"I don't want to see it," Ivy said.

Scout picked up the bag of pretzels and then dropped them again. "I can't eat. I'd rather get an injury report. Mary?"

"Bruised bone." My elbow ached with every word. "Maybe a hairline crack. Sling and ice for now. Deac?"

He took a seat. "Two cracked ribs and a bruised stir...strinium..."

"Sternum," Scout said. He pointed at his own chest. "You mean right here? Your breastbone?"

"Yeah, yeah, that thing. And the worst part is, there's nothing they can do. It hurts to laugh, cough, and sleep. It's getting better, but man. I can't even breathe deep. The doctor says if I'm not movin' around more tomorrow when he listens to my chest, I might have to blow on a machine several times a day. I don't know what that's about."

"It's about keeping your lungs clear," Scout said. "Never mind. You'll feel better tomorrow. Ivy?"

"Nothing here. I feel like I've been hit by a truck, but no real injuries."

"Same," Scout said.

I glanced at my friends. "Where do we start?"

Ivy leaned forward. "I'll start. I want to talk about the navy jumpsuit guy. Probably not an electrician."

"Thank you!" Scout smacked his hand on a stack of crinkly pages by the couch. "No, he probably is not. And after running it down with Mr. Silva, he has proof the guy was a new sub-contractor for the company that came out about the problems. It's a whole thing. A work order was cancelled and re-submitted—school budget crap and all—and that guy showed up, and things got worse. I only hope Mr. Silva doesn't lose his job over it." He rustled through blueprints of the gym he'd originally borrowed from the library.

Ivy nudged his shoulder. "Tell them the other thing."

"Yeah. You know how we couldn't believe the timing of the whole electrical fire in the scoreboard? And how could anyone possibly arrange it so perfectly as to when Jacob came in the door? I think it was more than that. I think it was a small explosive device designed to go off and trigger the fire. And." He held up his phone. "I think the navy jumpsuit guy used his cell phone to detonate it."

I could barely get the word out. "Bomb. You think there was a bomb in the scoreboard."

"Yes. A device small enough to bring down the scoreboard and start a fire without taking out the whole building. Everything was designed to look like a simple electrical malfunction—like everything else."

Deacon turned his phone in his hands and then dropped it on the couch. "You mean I can blow up something with my phone?"

"No. But if you wanted to, it's possible. Terrorists have been using cell phones with explosives for a while now."

Deacon poked his phone as if he were newly afraid of it. "Does that make what happened a terrorist attack?"

Scout shrugged. "All I know is that the investigation got a whole lot more complex once the fire marshal took a look around. I believe they called in additional investigators. Federal. But don't tell anyone that. It came from Mr. Silva."

"We were right about there being an adult involved." I considered what that meant as it related to Gavin. "But what was the end game? Gavin obviously has it in for Jacob, but why not try to kick the crap out of him after school or something like normal people do?"

Deacon reached for the popcorn. "Gavin's jealous of Jacob and obsessed with you, but how did he get from that to a terrorist-like attack?"

I rubbed my forehead. "He may have made some stops along the way."

"What do you mean?"

"There were some incidents before the gym fire. Jacob's car was keyed—"

"No way. His new ride?" Deacon asked.

"Yes. He also had a tire slashed. And someone messed with his equipment, bashed in the family garage door, and trenched their yard."

Scout's face reddened. "How did we not know about this? It plays right in to what happened in the gym. Jacob was a target. He could have died. Shouldn't we be telling some cop about this?"

"Look, I already feel bad enough about it. I literally found out the morning of the pep rally. Jacob didn't guess for sure it was Gavin like we would have. He said he thought it was random and his dad was on it but it was hard to prove. And the whole time, I'd been getting secret gifts and rose petals in front of my locker and little stuffed animals on my doorstep. I'd told him to stop and my dad even talked to him, but I do wish I'd known about Jacob's vandalism. Those are crimes." I sagged into the couch. "I don't know what to do. That's not the Gavin I grew up with. What's happened to him? What kind of kid gets with an adult and sets up something like what happened at school?"

Ivy picked up a piece of chocolate, but didn't put it in her mouth. "Speaking of the navy jumpsuit guy, there's more."

"What?"

"There's something about that guy. He's familiar. Maybe I've seen him before? I don't remember when or where, but he's familiar. I don't know if it's a warning in my head, or if I saw him around campus, but keep your eyes open. I don't think he's going away."

"But what do we do with that information?" Deacon asked. "This isn't a graphic novel or a fantasy. That guy's out there. In the real world. He needs to be in jail."

"Yes," Ivy said. "And I believe he's dangerous and did every bit of what Scout thinks he did. But everybody in the room had their cell phones out recording something. What reason or proof do we actually have to tell anybody to go after that guy? *Anyone* could have triggered that explosion."

Deacon leaned forward but stopped when it hurt. "But your gut feelings are your gift, Ivy. If you say navy jumpsuit guy is bad news, then he's bad news. You were the first to say Gavin couldn't be trusted."

Scout held up his hands. "Let's back up and think. Our assignment was to help with the fire, right?"

"Right."

"And, in doing that, we uncovered problems at the school with the electrical. And, from what Ivy overheard, it looked like Gavin was trying to set Jacob up to take the blame for the fire. Like he caused it."

"But it didn't turn out that way," I said. "It doesn't look like Jacob did anything. It looks like Jacob was a victim."

"Or maybe he wasn't," Scout said. "Ivy's vision clearly indicated fire. We focused on fire. Jacob only came in as collateral damage because Gavin hates him and Ivy heard about it. Gavin's not smart enough to have planned everything. Maybe he just did what navy jumpsuit guy told him to do. He was trying to prank Jacob and get him in trouble, but whoever was really pulling the strings made it so much worse."

I used my good arm to rub the tired muscles in my neck. "I'm so confused. That makes Gavin a victim too."

"Maybe," Deacon said. "But that would still mean he went along with something he knew might hurt someone."

"And where does that leave Jacob? He could have died."

Scout shrugged. "Could he? You were there to save him, Mary. If the Destroyer's master plan for that day was to kill one person or a hundred, it still all depended on what we did about the initial assignment—and that was the fire."

"I'm beginning to think this whole thing was a trick," Deacon said.

"Or a test," Scout added.

"How could it be a test?"

"Bad people are going to do bad things whether we know about them or not. We can only help if we listen and use our abilities. We did. We showed up."

"And Sebastian came to help like he said he would. We're still learning, but the Creator gave us an assignment that was over our heads."

"And now we know that can happen," Ivy said. "But we still don't know who the real good guys and bad guys are. Maybe it's time we bring Jacob in and find out which side of the fence he falls on. He didn't exactly appear to cause any problems on fire day, but then again, we didn't have eyes on him."

"Hate to admit it," Scout said. "But he didn't help, either."

That didn't sit right with me. "You're really going to go there? His injury took him out of the fight."

"Just making a point. Jacob came out neutral."

I leaned my head back against the cushion and repositioned my arm. "I don't think we should reveal anything to Jacob yet. I trust him. I really do. I think he's on our side, but I also trusted Gavin, so what do I know?"

"For what it's worth," Scout said. "I'm undecided about Jacob."

Deacon nodded his agreement.

"This is only an opinion," Ivy said. "But I feel like Jacob's a good guy. Don't attribute that to my gut just yet. My intuition is much better about definitely saying who *not* to trust and Gavin and navy jumpsuit guy are in that category. My gut-jury is still out on Jacob."

My elbow throbbed, and my shoulders ached from the fight and from readjusting my body movements to accommodate a sling. Jacob had become so much to me, and I questioned everything all over again. I couldn't make another mistake like Gavin.

Deacon remained quiet. Too quiet.

"What is it, Deac?"

"I uh… have something important to tell you all."

"Now's the time," Scout said.

He glanced at the others, but his gaze landed squarely on mine. "I've met Shanar, Mary. I've been where you've been. We had a conversation. He calls the people who work for him Agents. He asked me to be one. I think you know what I said."

Disbelief slammed into me so hard it took a while to form words. "You found the other realm," I whispered.

"More like it found me, but yes."

"When?"

"In the gym."

"During the pep rally?"

"Yes."

"What are you saying, Deac?"

"I'm saying either Gavin or Jacob works directly for Shanar. One of them is a full-blown Agent of the Destroyer."

CHAPTER 25

Deacon

The school was not the same when we arrived.

Mary and I showed up together to find the parking lot in chaos. The gym was blocked off with a temporary fence and flapping yellow caution tape. No cars could go that way, so everything took longer. Large thuds banged every minute or so as debris was dropped into big roll-off dumpsters.

I couldn't shake the feeling of dread as I passed the site. I knew everyone was safe and we'd done our job, but the Destroyer himself had been right there in our midst. I'd experienced something dark, and though I came out all right, I couldn't stop seeing the swirling mass of Shanar I'd met face-to-evil-face. I didn't want to see or feel that ever again, but somehow I knew I would. I wasn't looking forward to it, and I didn't like the new cloud of doom that seemed to hover over our school.

How had Mary done it all those years? How did she keep up

the fight and stay so completely cool-headed about it? Her *normal* was everyone else's worst nightmare.

"What a mess," I said.

Mary paused and took a long look at the growing debris. "Could have been a lot worse. Just thinking about it kinda knocks the wind out of me and I feel it right here." She pointed to her heart.

"I know."

She protected her elbow and headed inside. I trudged along behind her, helping her hold one side of her heavy bag since we both had to get to Mr. Parrington's office. Neither one of us were sure how we were going to get through the rest of the day after that. I couldn't carry my backpack like normal with my jacked-up ribs and sore chest.

"Wait up!" Jacob skidded to a stop beside us. "I got that, Deacon," he said and offered to take Mary's bag.

"That's OK," Mary said. "We're going to the same place for a meeting."

"I'll see you after first period then, and help you out today."

"That'd be great," she said.

Mary's eyes lit all up like a flashing video game. I knew she and Ivy had been discussing every angle of Jacob's sudden appearance in our lives. I wanted to believe he was one of the good guys, but I'd seen too much and was still rattled by my visit with Shanar. I couldn't get close to someone who might be an Agent, and that made everything awkward. Things were off when all the Warriors didn't agree, so Jacob was in that weird gray area between trust and no trust, and we were all conflicted about it.

"I have stuff for you and Ivy in my car," Jacob said to her. "My mom sent all the ski clothes you can borrow for the trip."

"Great news. At this point we need all the help we can get. I can't exactly baby sit little kids with my arm like this."

"Humph." I rolled my eyes. "You think you have problems?

Do you know what a beating me and Scout take with that pressure washer? We just had a five-day weekend and could have added a wad of cash to our pocket money, but we could only do so much with my ribs."

Jacob looked disappointed. "I could have helped."

"We thought you had a concussion. I'm pretty sure the only thing more dangerous than jarring ribs is jarring a brain." I thumped the side of my head. "But you're good for the game Friday?"

"Yeah. Three different doctors said I'm good to play ball."

Mary blinked up at him with a sappy smile. "I was so relieved when you told me that last night. And you're sure? You can't take any chances with a head injury."

"So, it was a mild concussion?" I asked.

Jacob shook his head. "It wasn't a concussion at all, and I actually wanted to talk to you about that."

I glanced at each of them. Why did I feel like I was being ambushed? "Me? Why?"

"Look, Deacon, I did have a concussion. Believe me, I've had a concussion before, and I know I got clipped hard by something that fell. I was dizzy, disoriented…I had a brief loss of memory about the incident…" He paused to take a deep breath. "I'd be dead if not for Mary."

"You don't know that," she whispered. "Don't even say that."

"It's true and I know it. We all do. We all were there." He turned to me and lowered his voice. "Now, look. I know this isn't the best time, but I'd really like to ask you some questions. There's been so much weirdness since we all met, but I'm tired of being confused about everything. We all know what happened that day. You picked me up and got me out of there, Deacon, and no offense, dude, but I'm at least twice your size and I don't think you've ever been inside a gym."

He had a point, but I didn't like his tone. I didn't remember everything clearly myself. "No offense taken. I have no idea what happened, and I'm sure I couldn't do it again."

He turned to Mary. "That thing that happened on the night of the pool party. You asked me if anything like that had ever happened to me before and it hadn't. And I've never had a group of friends like you all. I was honest about all that. But I have had questions, and after all this, I know there are bigger things at work here. That day was insane. The things I've heard you guys say…"

"Let me stop you right there," I said. "Yeah. It was a weird day. I wish I knew more." I turned to leave. "I'm glad you're OK, but we have to get to a meeting."

"What did you do to my head?"

His question speared me to the core. I turned back too fast and felt the pull in my chest. Truth be told, I still didn't remember everything. "What do you mean? Are you asking if I tried to hurt you?"

"No, of course not. The opposite. You helped me. I felt it, but I'd kinda like to know what happened to my concussion. I know I had one, but the last I remember of it is when you carried me to the corner and put your hands on my head. You told me I'd be all right, and I *know* I was injured. I'm tellin' you I've had a concussion before and I know there was a hit and some blood. By the time I got to the hospital, I was fine. I felt something in your hands when you—"

"Let's not get carried away." I stepped forward. "If I was that dang talented, don't you think I'd fix my own ribs or touch Mary's cracked elbow?"

"I don't know what happened in there, but I know something did. It'd be nice if someone would trust me enough to share it with me."

"Yes," I said. "That would be nice."

CHAPTER 26

Mary

Deacon finally slowed down outside Mr. Parrington's office.

We leaned against the wall and dropped our things. "You were too hard on him, don't you think?" I asked.

"How so?"

"He only wants answers, Deac. He's as confused as we get sometimes. He doesn't understand this place we've found ourselves in."

"I don't understand it either, and I sure as heck don't want to discuss it with someone I'm not sure I can trust."

"Fair enough." I offered him a bottle of juice from my bag.

He opened mine and then worked on his own. "It's not that I'm not happy you've moved on and have something going with Jacob, but—"

"You don't have to explain yourself. I've been thinking a lot about what you said and I want you to know I understand. That whole thing with Shanar…" I shivered.

"I'm not getting much sleep. I close my eyes and see myself looking down at us trying to crack those doors. How is that possible? How is *any* of this possible?"

"I don't know. I wish I did. I can only trust the Creator and believe Sebastian has our backs."

"Well, all I know is I'm mad. What supernatural being has the right to invade my mind and my thoughts? That can't be right."

"It shouldn't be," I agreed. "But yet, here we are." I bumped my bottle of juice with his. "Here's to us. A couple of oddballs who have to keep that angry edge and direct it toward those who would cause harm." We took a drink. "I'm serious, Deac. One of the only ways I stay sane is knowing I'm on the right side of the battle. Don't let fear and anger pull you down."

"Easy for you to say. You've been at this a while. I only recently got manhandled by an evil force in the school gym."

"Maybe, but you've had those hands your whole life and you sure figured out how to use them when you needed to. Everyone has a choice, Deacon. We both chose to live."

"None of this seems real anymore."

"What do you think happened with Jacob? Your hands were firing at maximum capacity at that pep rally. If you touched his head during all that, you likely fixed whatever was wrong in there."

"How can he be so sure he had a head injury? He's not a doctor. There was probably nothing wrong with him."

Scout and Ivy arrived from another hallway.

"What's it look like on that end?" Deacon asked.

"It stinks and made my eyes water," Ivy said. "But it's not too bad." She nodded toward Mr. Parrington's office. "What do we do in there?"

"The usual," I said. "Always the truth."

Scout leaned one shoulder on the wall and shoved his hands in his pockets. "Within reason, I hope."

Ivy laughed. "Can you imagine?"

Deacon remained stoic. "How can you laugh at a time like this?"

Ivy dipped her head. "Sorry. Just trying to stay positive."

Scout stood straight. "You OK, Deacon? How's the ribs?"

"They hurt."

"Sorry, dude. Can I carry your stuff today? We go pretty much the same way all day."

"No. I'm good."

Deacon's doubt and rage continued to grow on his face like a building storm. Who could blame him? He'd been put in a place he didn't ask to be, and it scared him. He wanted out. Who wouldn't? But after all he'd seen, I didn't think he could be anything other than a Warrior. And being in the school didn't help. He was right. The air had a sinister feel to it.

I didn't like it. Not one bit.

"Listen, Deac. You have to concentrate on the good part. Shanar can't hurt you. This life is weird and we'd all rather not know what we know, but we do, and we have a responsibility."

He closed his eyes and fought for a deep breath. I knew he was in pain.

Scout touched his arm and plucked his bag off the floor. "C'mon, buddy. None of us asked for this, but we have to stick together in there."

Mr. Parrington rounded the corner and motioned for us to follow him inside. He was not his usual happy self. There was no skip in his step, no goofball comment as he stepped into his office and closed the door behind us.

Ivy shot me a concerned look. Leave it to her to catch a whiff of despair and want to help.

Scout too. His analytical but compassionate heart found the wounded animal every time.

It seemed Deac and I were the ones perpetually locked and

loaded for physical battle—and we had the injuries to prove our call.

I sat and was amazed at our team, but also stunned again at the magnitude of it all.

What else were we supposed to do?

The clearer it became, the muddier it was.

Scout finally spoke after one of the signature long pauses Mr. Parrington used to see if we'd volunteer information. "How is everything, Mr. Parrington?"

"It's not good, Scout. Not good at all."

"How is Mr. Silva? He's been very upset about everything... It's not his fault, you know."

"I know." He turned his laptop toward us. We stared at the school logo floating on the screen until he spoke again. "I have something to show you, but I thought we'd talk first."

I moved in my seat to reposition my arm.

He caught that and nodded my way. "Are you all right?"

"Yes. I can lose the sling tomorrow and see how it feels."

"How exactly did that happen?"

"I think when I tackled Jacob all his weight came down and kinda smashed my elbow into the floor. I remember feeling that. It wasn't bad. I think it was the angle."

"Right. What about you, Deacon? How are you?"

"Healing, sir. What about the others who were injured?"

"Everyone appears to be fine." He twisted a paper clip between two fingers until it pulled apart. "And everyone gives you four the credit for that."

We did what we always did. We looked away and at the ceiling and mumbled things like *we were in the right place at the right time, there were other people helping out, we did what anyone would do, we didn't do anything special...* And my personal favorite: *...it was nothing, we were glad to help.*

"I'm going to ask you to stop repeating all that and be straight with me. For a change."

Scout seemed to take offense to that. "Excuse me, sir? We always answer your questions as best we can."

"That's not going to work this time. I need to know everything that was going through your minds that day. Why you were positioned where you were. How you came to be reacting before there was anything to react to."

"Are we in trouble?" Deacon asked.

"Not that I know of," he replied. "I've talked to all your parents and I told them we'd be having this conversation and that I was going to show you a video."

I considered the possibilities. There had to be a hundred different clips of the chaos circling social media. Whatever he had couldn't have shown anything detrimental to us.

He waited another long moment before he started the clip.

We scooted closer to see the grainy split screen.

"I thought the cameras were down," I said.

"Mr. Silva must have gotten things going after we looked at the issues," Scout replied.

Deacon scrolled through his texts. "Look at the time. These views are exactly when we were texting, but I can't tell what I'm looking at."

"There," Ivy said. "That's me outside the doors watching for... There's the creepy electrician guy. He's asking me the way to a bathroom. I don't see any Arrows."

"Now here," I said. "Same guy on my side. That was fast."

"He knows his way around the building," Scout said. "And look at the time. The tape skipped a bit."

The picture changed to an overall view of the gym.

"I can't make anything out," Deacon said. "There's people everywhere and not everyone is sitting down."

Scout tried to maneuver the touch screen and nothing worked. The picture only got worse. "Time, Deacon?"

"Same time as the text where I mentioned I saw the scoreboard flicker and wondered why."

"Where are Gavin and Corey?" I asked.

Scout shook his head. "No way to tell. OK, look. This blurry figure is the electrician coming in. This one is Jacob coming through that door and Mary through that one. Deacon, that's you going to help." The screen filled with a bright, white light. "Kaboom."

Air stuck in my throat as I watched myself tackle Jacob. What looked like a fiery piece of something *did* fall and knock his head as we escaped. The blob on the floor represented the exact time my elbow crashed and bruised. "Look. There's Deacon and then we turn to escape."

"Where's the electrician?" Ivy asked.

Scout paused the video. "Can't see him. Looks like he headed for the opposite end as soon as…"

Mr. Parrington leaned in. "As soon as what?"

"Um… Just a sec. OK, look. This is where Mary and Deacon head for the door, but Jacob appears woozy."

"Look at him," I said. "He's grabbing for me and Deacon and he's trying to get to the door, but he's wobbly. I don't remember that part. I know he stayed with me, but I don't remember him trying to drag us both. It's not like we weren't trying to get to the door."

"This happened so much faster than I remember," Deacon said. "And now everyone is realizing the doors won't open so they go to the opposite end away from the scoreboard fire."

"And look at that," I said. "Looks like you pointed and told us both to head the other way. I don't remember that."

"I don't either, but I see it. We were in shock, I guess. Jacob is trying to get to the door with me until he couldn't stand up anymore and you helped him against the wall."

"And," Mr. Parrington said. "You can't see them, but Scout and Ivy are coming to the dangerous end. Why?"

Scout shrugged. "Because Seb—"

"Because we had to help Mary and Deacon," Ivy said.

"Why didn't you all go to the other end if you knew you could get the doors open?"

"No time to waste," Deacon said. "The crowd was too intense at the other end. I knew if we could get one door open, it was a start. We went to the other end as soon as we could."

"But first," I said. "Look at that. Jacob was right. You picked him up and took him out like a firefighter."

Deacon's expression was one of shock. "I don't know. I don't remember it all."

We sat in silence as that first door flew open. My heart jumped with joy at the success, even though I knew how it ended. I wanted to be proud, but all I could consider was what could have happened if we hadn't done what we were called to do.

Would the Creator have sent someone else?

The camera flickered and the picture pixeled and blurred as things got worse and then better.

We didn't say a word, but I knew all we thought about was timing. What happened only took seconds, but in our time, it seemed like long, prickly minutes.

And everyone had to be wondering when Deacon had his out-of-body experience.

It'd happened in another realm, and we realized then that time was different in parallel places.

We knew more from seeing the tape. We knew less. We knew nothing.

Mr. Parrington closed his laptop.

"Can I get a copy of that?" Scout asked.

"Not for a while," Mr. Parrington said. "There's an open investigation, and I wasn't supposed to show it to anyone. That scoreboard didn't catch fire because of an electrical issue. I think everyone knows that. The problem is, we're a mid-sized private school in a sleepy suburb of Houston. Why would we be a target? More importantly..." He slid the laptop to the side. "Why would you know about it in advance?"

"Wait a minute," Deacon said. "You said we weren't in trouble, but now you're saying we knew about a crime before it happened—as in maybe we were a part of it. I'm pretty sure that means we'd be in trouble."

"He's not saying that," Scout said.

"Then what is he saying?"

Scout let out a heavy sigh. "He's saying he knows we had advance notice and he wants to know how and why."

CHAPTER 27

Deacon

"Scout!" I snapped, fearful of what he was about to reveal.

"What? We did have advance notice, so what difference does it make? Ivy needs to say what she overheard."

"So, you do know something about this." Mr. P leaned back in his chair.

I glanced at Mary. She was as cool as she ever was while our world was crumbling around us. I knew it made her feel better to have Jacob's possible head injury explained and to see he was the only other student who didn't run away when it got ugly. I saw it too. I still wasn't convinced, but I saw it. The guy barreled toward the door to save Mary—and probably me—even though he could barely stand up.

Mr. P left his desk and pulled his chair around to circle up with us. A sharp sting of pain hit my side as I moved to make room. "What are we doing now? Playing support group?"

Ivy got antsy in her seat and chewed on her thumbnail. I

hadn't seen her do that for months. She, more than anyone, was going to feel it deep down if anything was off.

So far, everything had been off since we came back into Stonehaven Academy.

The principal leaned forward and rested his arms on his knees. "I'm sorry I showed you that video. I realize now it was too soon. It was a traumatic day and I shouldn't have made you look at that. You probably know I told your parents I'd make sure you saw a counselor today."

"A counselor?" Ivy asked. "How about the school lawyer? My mom had to outrun a reporter this morning to get me here on time. She doesn't need that kind of pressure. She got a call at work yesterday from someone wanting to interview all four of us on national TV. Who's protecting us from all that?"

"You're safe here at school."

"Really? Because we had to pass extra security to get here, and this feels like an interrogation." She slapped her hand across her mouth. "Sorry, Mr. Parrington, I'm not trying to be rude, but this isn't getting us anywhere."

Scout reached out to squeeze her hand. "Everyone needs to stop."

Mary used her good arm to pull her chair forward. "What is it, Scout?"

"It's this meeting. No offense, Mr. Parrington, but you've been trying to *handle* us since we came in that door. You know us well enough by now to know that doesn't work. Waiting in silence for us to crack, showing us that video and watching for clues, coming around the desk for this little pow-wow like you're one of us... We deserve better. We've always told you exactly what we know. Why do I feel like we're not on the same side anymore?"

"That was not my intent, Scout. We are definitely on the same side. I only want to know what happened."

"Then maybe you should do some talking too. Honesty goes both ways."

I couldn't help but hold my breath, though it hurt like crazy. Scout was turning tables like a pro. I was gonna buy him lunch —if we ever had another normal day in the Saints Café.

CHAPTER 28

Mary

Mr. Parrington took his chair and went back behind his desk.

"All right. Full disclosure. It's probably not my best move to share these things with you, but I don't see much reason not to since I may not be here much longer. Besides that, I'm really curious."

Scout scrubbed his fingers across a new patch of peach fuzz on the side of his face. "What do you mean you may not be here much longer?"

"Well, the organization that handles our accreditation and governs our school, along with this school's board of directors, aren't super happy with me right now. We've had problem after problem around here. Student achievement is down and discipline issues are up. We've had one fire, numerous electrical problems with the security system, a possible issue with a district-contracted employee, and a near mass casualty explosion event—also known as a pep rally. You can see why they're concerned for student safety."

"None of that is your fault," Ivy said.

"Oh, but it is. I'm responsible for what goes on here and who comes in and out. I'm waiting for the other shoe to drop. Someone's bound to use this as an opportunity to sue me for something and I don't know how much backing I'll get from the board—except for when they ask for my resignation to appease the angry mob of parents—and I oblige."

He paused to reach for his cup of coffee. "We had some bright new families move in this year, but many parents have pulled their students from our program. That loss of income doesn't help our reputation or the budget."

Something he said rattled me. I glanced at Scout who looked me straight in the eye. We were thinking the same thing. *New families*. What was different, who was new, where had they come from, and how many were there? If the Destroyer was coming for Stonehaven Academy at full force, wouldn't it make sense he'd send his troops to attack from all sides?

We were so focused in our own world and what assignment was put in front of us, that we were missing what else was going on. Our own flimsy, underdeveloped plates were already full.

We were outnumbered.

Scout cracked his knuckles one at a time. "Was the number of new students this year particularly high?"

"Not necessarily in light of the growth of the community and our expansion projects. Plus, we had a lot of kids come over from the other side. Siblings of current students aged up."

I'd forgotten Paige had a sister. That right there could have caused a ruckus in the universe if she were anything like her older sibling.

"We've had some nice surprises with new students," Ivy said. "If not for Jacob, I don't think we'd be in the playoffs."

Her well-intentioned comment landed like a thud.

Deacon didn't miss the opportunity for one more jab. "Yeah. Imagine. If Jacob weren't here, we probably wouldn't have had that pep rally at all."

The last thing we needed was for Mr. Parrington to sense the fracture in our team. "Uh… What else can we do for you, Mr. Parrington? We've all seen the same video. You know what we did, and I have a feeling student enrollment is not why we're here."

"That is true, Mary." He picked up the paper clip he'd mangled earlier. "Truth is, you're here because I love my job and I don't want to lose it. I love this school, and I love this community. I do a good job here, but I am clearly missing something. I think you all know what that something is."

We just sat there.

"You know," he continued. "Everything you say here is confidential. I would only share information if it means we get to the bottom of the fire. And we have to get to the bottom of that fire. You understand that, right? If it wasn't electrical or just some student prank gone really wrong, it means someone intentionally tried to burn down the gym."

All we could add without going full Warrior on him was what Ivy had overheard.

So much for *snitches get stitches* and all that.

I raised an eyebrow toward her. "Do you want to tell him what you heard, Ivy?"

"Tell him about the Arrows while you're at it," Scout said.

So, she did.

She told him about Corey and the rebirth of the Arrows and the disgusting scene outside the locker room.

Scout tried to help. "And I only knew about the electrical problems because Mr. Silva helps me with my Portuguese and I knew he was concerned that nothing added up. It didn't take an engineer to see this place is an electrical nightmare."

"And speaking of electricians…" Deacon held up his phone.

"This guy is suspicious, but I suspect you know that. We're pretty sure he had something to do with this."

"He's right," Ivy added. "I swear I've seen that guy somewhere, but I don't know where. I don't know who he is, but I agree. I think he had something to do with it."

"I see." Mr. Parrington slid his empty coffee cup to the very edge of his desk. "I knew about the Arrows, but to my knowledge, they are doing absolutely nothing on campus."

"They're not," Deacon said. "My brother said they meet in the woods far out behind the country club. He works there."

"Thank you. I can get the county sheriff on that." He looked disappointed, as if we would have shared more. "As for the electrician, yes, we're aware."

He stood and took a walk around his office.

And once again, we waited.

Scout finally cracked. "Can we... go now?"

Mr. Parrington spun on his heels and clapped his hands together. "You know what? No, you cannot. Because, you see, while this has all been very entertaining, I still don't know any more than I did. This little chess game, as usual, has been fun. Scout, you were at the top of your clever game with the whole *handling* move, but you said it yourself. The whole country wants to talk to the heroes of the *Stonehaven Gym Fire*, and you really thought after that monumental feat you were going to be able to come in here and tell me you know nothing?"

"Well—"

"Not a word, Mary. You four once again saved your classmates and a bunch of other people from certain catastrophe. I keep looking at that video and wondering how you did it and *why* you did it when you could have run to the other end like everyone else. You didn't panic. You didn't flinch. You took fire —*literal fire*—and ran into the fight. Not only that, you ran in there with a plan. Which means you had enough foresight to *make* a plan! You were in position. You had jobs. You worked like an elite team in the armed forces. Do the Navy SEALs know about you? Because they could learn a few things."

"Thank you, sir?"

"Don't be smart, Deacon. I know those doors were locked tight and not meant to open. I was on the other end with a group of grown men grabbing every tool we could find to free everyone. So, just tell me… Where does that come from? *Please!* I'm begging you… Tell me how it is that you four ordinary teenagers keep doing this?"

I glanced at my fellow Warriors.

I got two shrugs and a nod.

Deacon stood. "Let me."

"Sure."

"We're not ordinary teenagers, sir. We're Warriors, commissioned by the Creator to carry out assignments. Everything we told you is what we know to be true. For whatever reason, the Destroyer has sent Agents to wreak havoc on this school."

"Is that so?"

"Yes, and from the feel of things, he's settled in like a cloud of doom over this place. The real question is not how I got through those doors, but why and how were they sealed shut to begin with? And who, Mr. P? Who wanted a gym full of people to die?"

CHAPTER 29

Ivy

We all rushed into the hall and away from the office as fast as possible.

"Remember that time I said we'd just had the weirdest principal visit ever? I was wrong. *That* was the weirdest principal visit ever."

"No lie," Scout said. "Did you see his face when Deacon dropped the truth on him? *Boom!*"

"Sorry," Deacon said. "But I'm tired of all the secrecy. We are what we are, and things are getting more dangerous. I guess Mr. P could repeat what I said or call my parents and tell them I've lost it. I don't care."

"He won't do that," Mary said. She chewed on her bottom lip as she thought. "That clip and him seeing it may turn out to be the best thing that's ever happened to us."

"It's true," Scout said. "Up until now we've only been able to talk about things that happen after the fact. With the video right in our faces, we were able to actually see ourselves in action."

"And no one can dispute it," Deacon said.

"Or explain it," I added. "Maybe we should have warned Mr. Parrington after all."

"I wouldn't go that far," Mary said. "And don't go putting *Warrior* under extracurriculars on your college apps just yet. We still don't know who we can trust."

Deacon made a turn and came back. "See, that's the other thing I don't get. Why is it so darn hard to figure out who the good guys are?"

Scout sneered. "Uh… Because the bad guys aren't going to announce their presence and tell you they're bad guys? Because they're deceitful and evil and out to hurt and confuse us?"

"No, I know that. What I mean is, why is it so hard to trust that someone really is a good guy? Shouldn't it be more evident?"

"It's not hard for me," I said. "I feel it. Usually right away."

Deacon jabbed his finger in the air toward me. "Right. You're an emotional Warrior. You trust your gut and feel things."

"And you're a physical Warrior. You problem-solve with actual power. That's a much different gift than mine. I knew through discernment and instinct and supernatural vision the fire was coming."

Mary stepped closer. "And Deacon was there to take care of the doors."

"Which is hilarious," Deacon said. "Because I'm the least muscly guy there is. Jacob called it. I've never seen the inside of a gym."

"But that's not what this is about, though, is it?" I asked. "It's a completely supernatural manifestation when we need it. When it's our assignment."

"Right," Mary agreed. "It's for a time and a place."

"C'mon, Deacon," Scout said. "Don't you know? Your gifts

aren't for the ordinary times. They're for the extraordinary ones."

He considered that for a moment. "But there's another thing. We can't be the only ones."

"I never thought we were, did you?"

"I didn't," Scout said. "I think there's a group of Warriors everywhere there's a group of people. Sebastian said there were many kinds of people who work for the Creator. Guardians, Protectors... And Sebastian called himself an Enforcer. But I don't think people get to see many of those. That's like realm-level existence there. I think the rest of us keep our feet on the earthly ground most of the time."

"But that also means there's a group of Agents from the Destroyer," Deacon said. "Everywhere."

"Yes," Mary said. "But we need to take a break here. We've been over this a hundred times and I know we'll go over it a hundred more. Deacon, I think you're still reeling from your visit with Shanar. It changed everything for you. It made it all no-turning-back real. You believed it before, but now you *reeaally* believe it, and it's caused you to take a deep dive in the meaning of it all. Believe me, I've been there, but you have to give your mind a break and figure out how you're going to handle all the information without your head exploding."

Scout nudged my arm. "Speaking of things exploding..."

Gavin and Corey came our way. She hung off the side of his body like a bad sweater.

They stopped when they should have kept walking.

"Here they are," Gavin said. "The heroes of the Stonehaven Gym Fire."

Deacon bristled. "You know what they say. If there weren't any villains, you wouldn't need any heroes."

Gavin held up his phone as if he were going to take a picture.

Mary stepped in front of us. "Put that down. No one is supposed to be recording anything in the school right now, and we certainly didn't give you permission to take a pic of us."

"C'mon, you all are famous. You have your own hashtag and everything."

"Move along," Deacon said. "We have to get to class. Good luck in the playoffs."

I admired Deacon's restraint. He was pretty calm for someone who'd been in pain, on edge, and questioning everything since the fire.

What I didn't like was Corey's sullen and fractured appearance. She looked as much a bully victim as she ever had with Paige, but she clung to Gavin as if he were her savior. It made me sick to think she'd fallen into another pit and could feel hopeless enough to attempt to take her own life again.

"Corey, can you talk a minute?" I glanced at the others.

"Yeah." Scout got the hint. "Hang out a minute? Talk about the ski trip?"

Corey didn't speak, but Gavin did—all the while looking only at Mary. "We're on our way to our mandatory support group to talk about the fire. Waste of time."

"I don't think so," Mary said. "A lot of people are shaken up. Some students have left the school."

"Good riddance."

"What's your problem, Gavin? Are you afraid people might talk and figure out what really happened?"

"Are you?" he shot back.

"What's that supposed to mean?"

"I don't know. Maybe that it's a bit strange you're always right where the trouble is?"

A muscle in Deacon's jaw twitched. "Where were you? On the other end? As far away from actually doing anything as possible?"

"Whoa!" I refocused to Corey. "You're coming on the ski trip, right? Maybe we can have some time to talk and catch up."

I barely got a blink of recognition out of her.

"What is this?" Mr. Parrington's louder-than-usual voice echoed behind us. "Where are you all supposed to be?"

"Sorry, Mr. Parrington." Gavin's cold, hollow gaze had morphed to his warm and charming one. "We were talking about the ski trip."

"Talk about it some other time," he said. "Get to class."

Gavin and Corey moved on. We tried, but Mr. Parrington stopped us.

We had no idea what was coming next.

"Is the ski trip going to be a problem?" the principal asked.

"No," Mary said. "Why would it be?"

"No particular reason. I got the final list today to check for discipline issues. Despite the time you spend in my office, none of you have any actual code of conduct violations."

He laughed. I guess he thought that was funny. We didn't.

"What about your injuries? The trip is right around the corner."

"I see the doctor tomorrow," Mary said. "I don't think it'll be a problem."

Deacon let out a little bark of laughter. "I can't ski anyway, so if all I have to do is watch I'm OK with that, but my mom's making me see my doctor too before I go."

Mr. Parrington stood there and stuffed his hands in his pockets. It was as if he had something he wanted to say but didn't know how to say it.

"Is there something else?" I finally asked.

"You know, there are a lot of people signed up for that trip. Are you sure you're not going to have any problems with anybody?"

Deacon was annoyed again. "We don't look for trouble, Mr. P."

"Yeah, yeah, I know. Trouble finds you."

"I'm glad you understand. Now, can we go?"

"I also wanted to let you know there is some scholarship money available for the trip. A couple of students had to drop out and their parents forfeited their payments for anyone who needs help."

I wanted to say something. I'd walked the legs off a hundred dogs, but I was still short for the last payment. I also needed spending money. Mary and I had borrowed all the clothing we needed from Jacob's family who skied all the time, but I lacked snack and coffee money and needed to buy some decent underwear.

"We've got it covered," Scout said.

"Actually, I don't have it all covered…"

"No," Deacon added. "It's covered." He pointed at Scout. "Mr. Moneybags here didn't tell me when we started our pressure washing business that he already had more money saved than the Microsoft guy. We put a lot of what we earned in a jar for the four of us. We got you."

"That's your money, you guys. I'll fill out the forms and walk more dogs—"

"This isn't a discussion," Scout said. "It's already done. Forget about it."

I lowered my voice and tilted away from Mr. Parrington. "Can we talk about this later? I'm embarrassed enough already."

Mary wrapped her arm around me. "We need to get to class. Can somebody wedge my bag on my good shoulder, please?"

"I'll carry it," Scout said.

"I've got Deacon's," I said.

Mr. Parrington looked us over one more time. "You four really stick together, don't you?"

We didn't answer, and truthfully, were getting tired of the bizarre conversation. The man had tortured us enough for one day.

"Just one more thing."

We turned back.

"Y'all have a safe Thanksgiving next week and I'll see you back here ready for finals after that."

"Thanks," we all mumbled.

"You too, sir," Deacon said.

"And hey! Guess what?"

Now it was just getting stupid.

"What?" Scout asked.

"I think I'll be on that ski trip with you."

Deacon audibly moaned his unhappiness. I think Mary would have elbowed him in the ribs—if she had a working elbow and he had working ribs.

"You see, an administrator has to be on every school trip."

"I thought this was a parent-and-student-organization-sponsored trip," I said.

"It is mostly, but still. A school official has to be there."

"Thanks for telling us," Scout said.

"No problem. Thought I'd let you know. Just in case."

"In case of what?"

"You're our school Warriors, remember? Never know when you might need backup."

CHAPTER 30

Mary

I hugged Jacob when he stepped off the team bus.

"Hey, Mary Angel."

My face warmed. "Stop that."

Gavin wasn't too far behind him. I swear he crashed into us on purpose on his way to meet Corey and his parents. I avoided the bump to my still-tender elbow because Jacob held me so protectively in his arms.

"I'm sorry about the game," I said.

"Yeah, it's disappointing."

"You played well, though. Anybody interested in you for college could see that."

"I guess."

"And there's always next season. So, you got knocked out in the first round this time. Next year you'll go all the way."

I backed off while other players, coaches, and fans congratulated him. Our whole community had come out on the cold

November night to support the team despite the loss, and everyone needed something to feel normal about after the fire. If the end of football season helped that happen, then it was OK it was over. They'd gone as far as they could, and I don't think anyone was really worried about Jacob's career. He was a massive, talented fish in a little, tiny pond at Stonehaven. Recruiters had been hovering since they were allowed to hover, and Jacob's parents weren't going to miss an opportunity.

Mr. Parrington stood with everyone and clapped until the last player had exited the bus. If he had anything else to say to any of us, it hadn't happened. His stalling and shake-my-head comments in the hall left us wondering what he really thought.

The general consensus was that he was messing with us.

Jacob hung his arm across my shoulders and brushed his lips at my temple as we headed for his car. Small gestures like that were as far as we'd gotten. After he'd asked to kiss me over smoothies and I'd been too shy and tongue-tied to say yes, he'd backed off and settled for those moments that seemed completely natural but didn't cross any lines. Everyone assumed we were an official couple and we likely were, but we'd never had a conversation about it. The lock-and-key thing just kept happening.

He hoisted his bag onto his shoulder. "I'm hungry. Can you go eat?"

"I would love to, but here's the thing. It's only been a week since the fire and my parents are being strict about where I go. Strangers are still trying to talk to me, and there's been no answer on the elusive electrician everyone wants to find so..."

"But they said I could take you home, right?"

"Yes."

"Let's get some food and take it back to your house. Can we watch a movie or something?"

It sounded perfect to me, but why would the star of the football team choose that over a house party where he'd totally be the guest of honor?

"Of course," I said. "Are you sure your parents aren't waiting on you to do something special?"

"Nah. I think they left the game toward the end when they were sure we weren't going to pull it out. They're off doing whatever it is they do to torture each other and aren't concerned about me."

"I know your parents love you, Jacob."

"I'm sure they do. In their own way."

It was the saddest thing I'd heard all day.

I took his hand and held on tight.

Hours later…

After we ate too much fast food and shared two kinds of milkshakes.

After my dad followed Jacob around our kitchen and talked football.

After we watched the most ridiculous horror movie ever and I got scared anyway.

It was then we were wound up together under a soft Sherpa throw on my parents' couch. We were warm and half asleep with messy hair and our shoes off but our socks on. We were close—but not too close—as my parents fell asleep down the hall.

Jacob stared at me in the flicker of the light from the screen, and I willingly crept to where he hadn't asked me to be, but I knew I belonged. He wrapped his arm around me, and I nestled against his chest.

And I remember everything.

The lightest scratch of his fresh Saints t-shirt on my cheek, the earthy scent of him, the sound of his heart…

He rubbed his hand across my back. "I don't think I ever said thank you."

"For what?"

"Uh... For saving my life? You brought me cookies for helping with a nose bleed, and I forgot to thank you for tackling me to avoid certain death. What do you mean *for what?*"

"You were still hurt. I wasn't fast enough."

A low chuckle vibrated in his chest. "Really? How do you not see how big a deal that was? No one else raced in to help me. You could have been hurt too."

"You were hurt," I argued.

"That bang on my head and a skull-crushing death from that falling scoreboard don't even compare. And don't change the subject. You were there for me. Like my guardian Mary Angel."

Every time he called me that, something stirred. Whether it was the growing affection between us or the actual particles of angel being Sebastian said I carried with me, I didn't know.

I snuggled closer. "And you were there for me with the broken nose, so we're even."

"Not even close."

"It's not a competition. We helped each other." I then added the sentence I'd used a lot, and never intended to use it on him to explain Warrior business. "I was at the right place at the right time."

"You know what that also means, Mary?"

"That means something else?"

"Yes. It means I was at the *wrong* place at the *wrong* time. One can't exist without the other. If it is necessary for someone to be in the right place, it's likely because someone else is in the wrong place and needs something else or someone else to be in the right place. It's about balance."

Mind. Blown.

I pulled away and studied his face.

He looked uncomfortable. "What did I say?"

"You sound like Scout," I said. "We have these deep philosophical discussions all the time. Then I have to go home and Google a bunch of stuff."

"Just you and Scout?"

I smiled because he sounded jealous. "Not only Scout. Scout and Ivy and Deacon and me."

He smiled because he knew he'd given himself away. "OK. Just checking." He curled a piece of my hair around his finger. "What's Deacon's problem with me?"

I didn't hesitate. "He doesn't trust you. Yet."

"I'll have to work on that."

"But back to your original point about timing and balance… Why were you late to the gym? Coach must have been furious you weren't there to come in the pep rally with the team."

"It was the dumbest thing. First a couple of girls tried to stop me because they wanted to write about the football game for the online school newspaper or something. Then, I knew I was late, so I headed straight for the doors the team came in, but some maintenance guy stopped me and told me I had to go around. He said he was working in that hall. I couldn't believe that was happening during a pep rally, but I took off to get to the other side."

"Navy jumpsuit?"

"Yeah."

"That's the electrician who may or may not be a real electrician."

And it was a couple of Arrows who'd stopped him in the hall, but I wasn't going there yet.

"And that proves my point," he said. "My wrong place was your right place and it saved my life. Now, the only question is —and remember all the crazy stuff we've been through since we met—why is your right or wrong place always my right or wrong place?"

"Because we're each other's balance," I whispered.

Lock. And. Key.

Balance… I remembered the word from our conversation in the garden with Sebastian. It seemed like a thousand years ago, but I recalled the moment he looked at Scout and Ivy and spoke of balance. Scout was Ivy's, and she was his.

And Jacob was mine.

What did it mean?

I caught Jacob's startled, but slightly amused gaze. "I'm sorry," I sputtered. "That sounded too uh…forward, I guess? I'm sorry. I didn't mean anything serious by that. We hardly know each other."

He shrugged. "But I agree."

"What?"

"I agree."

"What exactly are you agreeing to?"

"It's us. It's you, Mary Angel. It's a thing. I don't know what it is, but it's a thing."

"A thing?"

"Yeah, I'm just gonna roll with it. No hurry. No pressure."

"You're making fun of me."

"Not a chance. It's a thing."

I truly didn't know what to say.

"Really, Mary, it's fine. We're fine. Don't overthink it." He pulled me close again. "Let's watch the rest of this stupid movie and I'll leave before your parents wake up and realize I'm still here."

He thought we were a thing? What kind of thing? We barely knew each other. We hadn't kissed. We cuddled and talked and watched out for each other, but nothing more. And he thought we were a thing. I didn't know where all he'd grown up or what the dysfunctional situation was with his parents, but he seemed as sure as one person could be about another. And it wasn't in the same pushy, disturbing way Gavin had tried to overwhelm me. Jacob was calm and laid back and didn't get all agitated ten times a day over things that didn't matter. His whole personality was in sharp contrast to his size and his aggressive presence on the field. He acted on things when he needed to, and stayed out of it when he should. For months we'd weaved in and out of each other's atmosphere, always aligned in some way. From simple study groups to complex situations like the fire, we were always in some way a team.

Jacob was simply…balance.

He was *my* balance.

His breath tickled my ear as he pressed his cheek against my hair. "What are you doing for Thanksgiving?"

"The usual. My mom and dad are going to serve food downtown in the morning, then we'll eat later."

"You don't go serve?"

"I do, but this year my mom said I probably needed to stay away and rest my elbow. I said I'd be fine, but I'm usually a runner with those big metal pans and it's probably not a good idea. Plus, if I'm home I can put the turkey in earlier." I traced little circles on his arm. "You're invited to come eat with us."

"I was actually going to ask you if you'd like to come to my house. If the timing is right. Don't want to interfere with your family plans."

"I'd love to. We'll work it out. If we plan it right, we'll get to eat dessert twice."

"Yeah, well, don't get too excited. Mine don't actually cook. Or serve. Or really talk to each other. It's usually a stuffy catered thing with people they've invited from work. I don't know them."

I realized again how little I knew about his family. Deacon said he'd been to his house when they first met him and had gone by to give him a ride. He called it a mansion, but hadn't been inside. Deacon often exaggerated, but did admit he and Scout made most of their pressure washing money in Jacob's subdivision.

"Can I ask you something, Jacob?"

"Anything."

"You don't say much about your mom and dad, and when you do, it's negative. I'm not trying to be nosy, but how did you end up here? Why did they move a talented guy like you in the middle of high school? Houston's a big city, but you're out here in the 'burbs. You said when we met you it was a business move and your parents hate each other, but they're still together, right?"

He scratched the side of his head and took a deep breath. He started to talk twice before he actually got something out. "You really want to hear this?"

"Of course."

"It's not a fun story, and I don't share it."

"You can trust me if that's what you're worried about. I won't blab it to anyone."

"I know. It's more about the subject matter. I don't want it to change anything between us."

My heart fluttered as I sat back onto the pillow near my end of the couch. It sounded serious. Was there something he could say that would change my opinion of him? Had he done something so bad I wouldn't look at him the same way?

It was very possible. Gavin had.

"See? You're already pulling away."

"No, Jacob, you just sound so serious." I hugged the pillow. "I'm listening."

"I have to tell you now. We had an agreement, remember? You always want the truth."

"And you don't want to hear a lie."

"Right, so I'm up to my neck in it now, aren't I?"

I shook my head. "Say it, Jacob. We'll make it through a true story. If we can't, we've got other problems."

"All right. You know how everything always comes down to money?"

"Honestly? I don't know what the answer to that is. It appears your family has a lot of money, so I'm gonna trust you know what you're talking about."

"Yes. Trust me, because everything comes down to money one way or another."

"Got it."

"So, my mom and her brother—"

"Your uncle."

"Yes. My uncle. And their dad—"

"Your grandfather."

"Yes, my grandfather. Can I finish this story?"

I squeezed my pillow. "Sorry. I'm trying to imagine all the players."

"My grandfather started the business years ago. My mom and her brother helped him build it, and eventually they went public. It's huge now. My dad technically works for them."

I resisted the urge to raise my hand. "What's the company?"

"There are several now, but my grandfather developed a kind of material that goes in everything from sports equipment to shoes for old people. It's gotten stronger, lighter, cheaper to make, and whatever... They sell it to all kinds of manufacturers. It's probably in your soccer cleats."

"Seriously?"

"Yes, seriously. Anyway, this business is a very big deal, and it's still about family. The four of them hold the top positions and collect big paychecks. Everyone's happy."

"But..."

"But everyone isn't happy. Because they're keeping secrets."

I waited. I held my breath. I didn't move.

"When I was about four," he continued. "My uncle started molesting me."

I couldn't hold in my wheezing gasp.

"Hold on," he said. "I'm fine. Let me explain."

I nodded.

"It was classic grooming behavior. I know that now."

"Grooming behavior?"

"Yeah. It's what they call the process of how children are drawn in by sexual offenders. If you look it up, you'll see a list of common things molesters do. My uncle could have written a handbook. He bought me big gifts for no reason, tried to spend alone time with me like a buddy, often photographed me, made comments of a sexual nature I didn't understand, there were some inappropriate touches, and it goes on... But it never got physically severe because my nanny, the woman I spent the most time with, figured it out."

"Thank God. And she told your parents?"

"Yes."

"And what happened?"

"They fired my nanny."

"Why? She watched out for you."

"Yes, but she had knowledge the family didn't want her to have, and she wanted to tell someone about it. That's when everything started to crack."

"How?"

"My mother didn't want to believe her brother was a pedophile. But now I believe not only did she and my grandfather know, but I think they'd seen other things. She may have even been a victim in some way of her older brother's behavior when they were young. And my dad... My dad just wanted to kill him."

"How did you all get through it?"

"We didn't. That's the problem. We went on as if nothing happened because that's what my grandfather commanded. That's where the money comes in. Wealthy people don't want their dirty secrets to get out, and they can pay to keep them quiet. What would it look like if the family child molester was exposed just when we went international? And acting like things didn't happen did nothing but cause tension between everyone—especially when my uncle had children of his own."

"Oh no."

"Yeah, but don't worry. My grandfather has everyone on a tight leash. You wouldn't believe how much money he spends spying on his children to make sure they don't do anything he can't cover up. Everything is a lie."

"I'm sorry, Jacob."

"I hate the holidays. I can remember being ten or so and having to sit at a long table with the whole family. My uncle bounced his kids in his lap and it made me sick. Still does. I wondered if he would do something to his own children. We all lived close to each other and had this big family image to uphold—for the sake of the company—so I kept an eye on my little cousins."

"You were a kid. You couldn't possibly watch everything, and it wasn't your responsibility."

"No, but I got between them every chance I could. We'd hide out together and play games."

"You were their protector."

Protector...

"I tried."

"Where were the adults?"

"Somebody had to keep the business going, didn't they? That's the worst part. Those four hate each other—my mom, dad, grandfather, and uncle. In private, they'd stick knives in each other's backs if they got the chance. But in public, nothing is wrong."

"Where are your cousins?"

"Still in Dallas. They're like in middle school, and I know they stay away from their father. We're close and they tell me things, but I think one of them is already experimenting with drugs."

"How did you end up here?"

"My grandfather's getting older. My parents don't deal with my uncle outside of work. They haven't for years. My parents are only sticking together so they can kick my uncle out of everything when my grandfather dies. That's their plan, anyway. It'll get ugly and they'll ruin him. My parents live separate lives otherwise. So, I'm here because they expanded their presence in Houston. My dad heads up the sports division of everything. He sells the materials to the companies who make your cleats."

"Let me guess. He was a football player."

"Yep. So, it doesn't matter what school I'm in now. He has connections and can get me tryouts wherever he wants. And if I make it all the way to the pros, I'll be expected to represent the company."

"You feel trapped."

"I am trapped."

CHAPTER 31

Shanar

I appeared at the side entrance to the boy's house. "Why so late, boy?"

He punched his code into the family's security system.

"Answer me," I demanded. "The football game was over hours ago."

"Yes, and speaking of that, where were you? You promised some big plays for me. You didn't deliver. We lost."

"Oh, you didn't lose because I didn't deliver. You lost because you're a wretched human with no talent. And you were distracted. And you haven't held up your end of our bargain."

He dropped his bag on the flagstone walkway and kneed open the door. "I do have talent," he ground out between clenched teeth. "I was not distracted, and you haven't done your part."

I swirled into the doorway and stopped his progress. "Says the boy who I've rewarded with much success lately in every material way, and who is smothered with attention by girls who offer every form of affection."

"I only want one girl."

"And I want that girl too."

He attempted to push through me. I allowed him to pass, though I could have easily swallowed his entire flesh-and-blood body. Of course, my power would have disintegrated every bone in his body. Nothing would have been left for his family to find. He would have simply…vanished.

"Let's be serious for a moment, shall we? Mary is mine. You are to bring her to me. She got away from the Destroyer on my watch, and I cannot move any further up in my realm until the loop has been closed on my mistake. I do not intend to lose her again. You will lead her to me and I will defeat her *and* that piece of angel she carries around with her." I wrapped my dark force around him and squeezed. "And then everything will be back to normal."

"What piece of angel? What does that mean?"

"Your girl is a clever one, that's all I can say. A clever and tough one. She really wanted to live. She summoned that being and didn't stop until she'd saved her own life."

He twisted away and pressed his back against the laundry room wall as I hovered closer and closer to his face.

"You stink," he said. "How is it you smell so much like the back end of a skunk? I would think a supernatural being could do something about that."

"Boy, you continue to amaze me. You certainly have a pair of brass ones on you to say the things you say to me. Do you not realize I could end you right now?"

He quieted.

"No smart-aleck answer to that? Do you want to die tonight? Tomorrow maybe? The problem is, you are the best one to lure Mary to me. If you do that, I will continue to hold back the curses your family put on you. I will keep you safe and even productive throughout your earthly life. You will not suffer or want for anything as long as I get what I want."

"I don't want Mary to die."

"So, you want to die?"

"No. I want to live. With Mary."

"That is hilarious."

"Can't you just defeat the angel part? That's the thing that aggravates you the most, right? That you were assigned to take her life and she fought back with the help of her guardian angel? And won?"

"Humph. Guardian angel. You know that's not a real thing, right? It's just something people tell themselves to feel better when they're scared."

"Whatever. I want this to be over."

"Our relationship will never be over. You have made that choice. However...," I spun in my massive, smoky cloud and sent curling, almost artistic wafts of dark matter around the room. Houses, money, cars, boardrooms, bedrooms, exotic locales, and images of his own secret desires appeared and disappeared before his eyes. "... I will take care of you. After I have what I've asked you for, the rough times will be behind you, and you will have your whole life to live on my gifts, and someday, die a happy old man."

"Is this some kind of joke? This is a parking lot carnival magic tric—"

I grabbed him by the throat before the last letter of his word left his tongue. "I am not a joke. I do not play games. You are an Agent of the Destroyer, and you will complete your task."

Red streaks shot through his bulging eyes as I held on. "Lure Mary to me by whatever means necessary. If you do not, I can promise the terror I will rain down on you, your family, your school, your community, and everything the sun and moon touches that you care about will come swiftly, but last a long, excruciating time. Do you understand?"

His body went limp in my grasp. He was trying to die. No such luck.

I dropped him.

"This is the last time you will see me while you're still alive. Consider it my last warning." I pressed on his throat. "Lure Mary to me. I will do the rest."

CHAPTER 32

Mary

I awoke with a start and clawed at my neck as I gasped for air.

Shanar.

I prepared for a battle that didn't come. Was it really only a nightmare?

I glanced at the clock and turned over to scratch Paisley behind her ear. Three-thirty in the morning.

Jacob and I had talked for hours, and I'd only been asleep a short time before the dream startled me awake.

Something wasn't right.

Jacob's secret washed over me again and filled me with anger and sorrow. I wanted to get my hands around his uncle's neck and squeeze. I wanted to hunt down the secret-keepers and make them pay for allowing that beast to roam free and possibly hurt other children. I wanted to hug Jacob and never stop, but still...

I sat straight up.

When it came to fight, flight, or freeze, I seemed to have arrived in the *come out swinging* camp.

But I was a Warrior. Not a vigilante.

I texted Deacon. *Are you up?*

I am now.

I need to talk.

His sleepy voice whispered across the line. "What's up?"

"This world is one messed-up place."

"Duh."

"I spent half the night with Jacob."

"Also, duh, and news that could have waited till morning."

"No, it's not that. Jacob is on our side, Deac. He may not be a Warrior, but he's something. Something special."

"Awwww... So sweet. *Not*. I'm done now."

"No, wait. I need help with something."

He yawned. "All right. I'm awake now. What happened?"

"People are evil. The Destroyer suffocates families and infiltrates lives and kills things. That's why we're here. That's our purpose, to do what we can to help."

"Uh... We know that, Mary. That's what our assignments are about."

"Right, but have you ever considered how big the job is? It's not just about Stonehaven Academy or limited to our own understanding. We interact with people every day, and we have no idea what their personal battles are."

"OK, calm down there, superwoman. I don't think we're supposed to know all that. We couldn't handle it. We can only take care of what's put in front of us."

"But I just woke up with a bad feeling. Something isn't right. I thought Shanar was here, but he's not. But just because he's not here, doesn't mean he's not nearby and tormenting someone I care about."

"Stop." Muffled sounds rattled in my ear as Deacon moved around—and probably dropped his phone a time or two. "Listen to me. You need to get some sleep. You've already made your choice to stay alive and work for the Creator. You can't do anything else. We'll never understand this thing we're caught in, but it's happening. We have to roll with it and do our best."

"That was easier before I knew how big it all is."

"Girl, you're gonna have to pull yourself together now. You've always known how big it is. It's just that you did it for so long alone with Shanar, it seemed small and normal to you. The rest of the world's been either self-destructing or getting stronger as usual, depending on who you ask. We're not the first Warriors to be called. We won't be the last."

"You're sure there are more of us."

"Get. A. Grip. Yes, there are more of us. Many more of us. Not only that, I believe there are twice as many of all the others Sebastian talked about. The Guardians and the Protectors."

"Why do you think that?"

"Because I think the Guardians and the Protectors do a lot of work before we're ever involved. I think they solve a lot of problems before we're aware. I think the kind of battles we have to fight are at the point of no return. Busting out of those gym doors was big-time Warrior stuff. It's what we were built for. It's why we survived. We're for the last resort battles. And the even bigger guns like the Enforcer Sebastian? That's our backup."

My thoughts continued to scatter. I couldn't pull them all back fast enough. Why did it feel so out of control? Being on the front line for a last resort battle seemed like a lost cause situation that could kill me.

"You're right, Deac, I know you're right. It's been a confusing and upsetting night, that's all. Sometimes it all creeps up and startles me all over again."

"No worries. We all have our ups and downs with it. That's why it's so important we stick together. Now tell me about Jacob and then try to sleep, OK?"

"Yeah... You know how when we discovered our abilities and started talking about them, we also discovered we all had interesting backstories?"

"Yeah."

"Well, I know Jacob's backstory now. I understand where he came from, and I can see how he's been gifted to protect people. He's been protecting me—and us—since we met him."

"A lot of people have interesting history. That doesn't make them heroes for the Creator."

"Well, it doesn't make them bad guys for the Destroyer either. In fact, I think there are a lot of good people who have come from bad situations and have turned it around for good. Not only that, I think there are truly good people. And Jacob is one of them."

"Are you lightheaded from kissing on that muscle head half the night?"

"That is definitely not what we were doing. We haven't... uh..."

"So, the jock has no game."

"There are deeper things going on here than making out."

"There's always time to make out."

"Should I ask Claire Cannon about how lightheaded she is from making out with you?"

"This is me hitting *end*."

"I don't want to die, Deac."

"Awww, Mary, who said anything about dying?"

"This whole thing is getting bigger and more out of our control. That fire was next-level evil."

"Yes, things are getting more intense, but Sebastian warned us about that. We're OK as long as we rely on our help. That's why I have so much trouble trusting Jacob or any new person who comes along and looks too good to be true. I have to be sure someone has my back in a fight."

"The Creator has your back, Sebastian has your back, and I have your back."

"And we all have yours. No Warrior is dying on our watch."

"But death snuck up on me once, Deac. It almost had me."

"No worries, Warrior. Death can't sneak up twice on the girl who refused to die."

CHAPTER 33

Ivy

The weeks became a blur.

With Thanksgiving so late in the month, it was already December when we went back to school after the break. Finals took the bulk of our time, and long study sessions with students we didn't know well took away from our Warrior visits. Then, all that was left was as much dog walking, pressure washing, and babysitting time we could all squeeze in before Christmas and our ski trip.

On Christmas Eve morning, I met Scout at his house to finish filling gallon-sized bags of necessities for people on the street and in shelters. I was going to go with him and his grandparents to hand them out that afternoon.

And I had to walk some dogs and tend to some cats for apartment complex people who were out of town...

And spend some quality time with my mom and Aunt Connie...

And pack for the ski trip...

And how was I going to get it all done?

I snuck past Scout as he came down the stairs, and hit the light in the pantry. It was the fastest place I could find to hide his Christmas gift.

It wasn't like it was small either. I had to put it in a giant Santa Claus handle bag. My mom went a little crazy with the tissue paper.

There may have been too much glitter on Santa's beard.

Scout was waiting for me as I stepped back out into the kitchen.

"Whatcha doin' in there?"

"Umm...saltines?"

"No. You don't eat those. Cardboard and sodium, remember? Your words."

"Pretzels?"

"Try again."

"Yeah. I got nothin'. Stay out of the pantry."

"OK." He gathered me in one of his tentative friend-zone-like hugs. "Happy Christmas Eve."

I gave him the usual awkward squeeze-n-pat thing.

Then I tried not to strangle him when he walked away—even though he'd gotten new cologne or soap or fancy-guy, mountain-breeze body spray or something and smelled so, *soooo* good.

But *ser-i-ous-ly*?

What did a girl have to do to get a real kiss from a guy?

I'd had enough. I knew for a fact Scout did not think of me as only a friend. He just didn't. He couldn't. I'd caught him looking at me certain ways. Nothing rude, sometimes goofy—like a dog looked at an empty bowl—but never disrespectful.

And there's no way I was that dumb or oblivious.

All the signs were there. He just *didn't freakin' kiss me*!

"We're all in the dining room," his grandpa said.

I joined Scout and his grandparents and a few other people who were circled around the large table with piles of supplies.

Scout handed me a bag. "Every bag gets a pair of warm socks, packets of antibiotic stuff, bandages, a protein bar, a toothbrush, toothpaste... You get the idea."

I joined the assembly line and glanced around the room.

Scout's grandma paused with a candy cane in the air. "What's the matter, hon?"

"Nothing. I was just wondering if there was anything for the little kids."

"Not yet, but we did get a late donation check and were wondering what to do with it. You and Scout can run in the supercenter on the way out and grab some coloring books and crayons or maybe some puzzles or card games to hand out at the women's shelter. They can use everything."

"Sure. That'd be great."

I remembered a time me and my mom had been a few dollars away from going to a shelter. There were some rough days before she got her meds regulated and Aunt Connie had to step in. Again. I couldn't imagine ever going back. I'd been almost homeless, but wound up in private school with good grades, friends, and basic necessities.

And suddenly, I was a Warrior. Somehow, that gave me a sense of added responsibility.

I wanted to help, and I enjoyed it.

"That's a darling sweater, hon. Did you get it for Christmas?"

I glanced at the basic, but festive, red V-neck. "No, ma'am, I found it in my Aunt Connie's closet."

"Well, it's lovely on you."

Scout's grandpa nearly knocked him off his feet when he *accidentally* bumped into him. "Yeah, Scout. Sweater," he whispered way too loud and pointed at the neckline.

I don't know who turned redder. Me, Scout—or Grandpa.

"Yeah, that's a great sweater," Scout squeaked out. "It's red."

It became painfully obvious I wasn't the only one who thought Scout needed help in the passion department. Did *every*one know how ridiculously lame and innocent our romantic relationship was? No wonder his grandparents never seemed to worry about us being alone upstairs in the rec room. We were as far away from hooking up as we were from the North Pole.

I stood there and tried to let the heat of embarrassment fade from my cheeks.

But I'd already lost my place in the baggie brigade and had to stop and check every one I'd stuffed for toothpaste.

Scout's grandma sent me a wink and a smile.

Some other old guy I didn't even know wiggled his eyebrows at me.

"OK, that's enough." Scout dropped another pile of socks on the table. "Ivy and I have something to discuss." He yanked me by the hand and dragged me toward the door.

I kinda liked take-command Scout.

He paused at the entry and looked around. "We'll be in the pantry. Leave us alone."

They laughed and snickered behind us, and I forgot all about the gift in there.

He pulled me inside and closed the door.

I wrenched my hand away. "Really, Scout? The pantry? This whole big house, and you drag me in the pantry?"

"I choked. They're making me nuts, and I remembered you were just hiding in here yourself a minute ago…"

I looked all around though I'd been in there a hundred times gathering snack food for Scout and the others. "It's fine. It's a nice big pantry. But uh… Why are we here?"

Scout leaned in and cupped the left side of my face in his hand. "Glitter," he said and grazed the pad of this thumb across my cheek. "This piece of glitter has been flashing at me like a

Vegas marquee since you stepped out of here earlier, and I didn't want it to get in your eye."

Breathless, I backed into the shelf. "Oh. Thank you."

A tower of sugar-free gelatin boxes tumbled to the floor.

Stupid gelatin.

Stupid glittery Santa bag.

Stupid Scout for being so close with that new body spray…

He pressed closer, and by the time he had his other hand on my face, his lips had already gloriously collided with mine. Not in a messy, awkward, hesitant way. More like a soft and perfect, confident, just-right way.

It was a Christmas miracle.

In a walk-in pantry.

He rested his forehead against mine—after a while. "Sorry. I didn't want to do this here. I had this whole thing planned and wanted to give you your gift later, but then those twisted old maniacs out there and the sweater… I couldn't wait another minute to kiss you."

I pushed him back as far as the pantry would allow. "Hold on. You couldn't wait another minute to kiss me?" I punched him in the arm.

"*Ouch*! What was that for?"

"Oh, I don't know. I've been waiting for over a year for you to make the first move, and all of a sudden you can't wait another minute and have to drag me into a pantry on Christmas Eve? What changed? I was beginning to think you didn't want to kiss me. Or would ever want to kiss me. One minute I think we're this big thing, and the next you're shoving me in or out the door when we say goodnight. Do you know what your mixed signals have done to my already busy brain? And don't even get me started on those times you kissed me on the cheek or *patted my arm*!"

As usual, he waited for me to stop my rant.

"First of all, we are a big thing. A huge thing. We're the only thing."

That sent me back to breathless and wobbly.

"Secondly, we've had a long, super-weird year. I knew with the way I felt about you, I couldn't just kiss you like it was some casual hook-up. I knew once I started kissing you, I wouldn't be able to stop. And with all the exciting and confusing Warrior stuff, and fires, and ski trips, and your supernatural psychic-like abilities..." He grabbed me by my shoulders. "I didn't want to mess with your thoughts. I wanted to be sure you were sure."

"Scout, you are way too wise and too good for this world."

"And see? That's another thing. My great-grandmother used to call me an old soul. A very old soul—if you understand and believe that stuff. And I don't know anything except that I know this isn't typical teenage stuff. In my head we've already been married for fifty years, and no guy my age is supposed to feel this way or say this stupid stuff."

"It's not stupid."

"It kinda is, Ivy, but I can't explain the way our bond feels to me."

"It's not stupid, Scout, because we're not normal teenagers. I don't know what we are, but we don't interact in the world like others do. I don't know what to do with all the feelings either." I wrapped my arms around him and pressed my lips near his ear. "I just wanted you to kiss me," I whispered.

It wasn't long before he pressed his fingers into my waist and stepped away—and onto a box of bowtie pasta and a bag of egg noodles he knocked down when I punched him.

"Right," he said. "But just so you know, all this kissing and ear-whispering, and hugging... Well, I won't be able to leave the house much."

I literally laughed out loud. Like laughed so hard and fast I lost my breath. "Stop it."

"No. I'm a gentleman. I need to stand over here in the corner a while."

"We'll get through it, Scout."

A sharp knock on the door startled us both.

"You OK in there?" His grandpa asked. "We're going to leave in twenty."

"We'll be out in a minute," Scout barked.

"OK, OK, just letting you know."

I put my hand on the doorknob. "Um… thank you for dragging me into the pantry. It's cleared up a lot of things."

"Don't go."

I raised my eyebrows toward the door. "You know they're all standing out there."

"Yeah, I don't care. I want to go ahead and give you your Christmas present."

"OK." I tapped the giant bag on the floor with the toe of my boot. "I guess I could give you yours too. I wish I could have taken it on the ski trip with us. I imagined us sitting around the fire and watching it snow and you opening it, but it's too big to lug on a trip."

"OK, then. You go first. Have a seat with me."

"We're in a pantry."

"Over here at the end. This spot used to house fifty-pound bags of dog food and a step stool. We'll fit."

We scrunched against the wall and stretched out our legs as I tugged the giant bag toward us. "I hope this is OK."

"Why wouldn't it be OK?"

"It just might not be."

Scout pulled the thick, twelve-by-twelve album from the bag. He moved his fingers across the lettering under the plastic cover. "You made me a scrapbook." He opened it. "Of my family…"

"Yeah, I did. I talked to your grandma about that stack of pictures up there. Seemed more and more of them fell off the shelf every time I came by. She said she always wanted to put them in a photo album for you, and I asked her if she thought it'd be OK if I made a scrapbook."

"She knew about this?"

"She helped me. When I saw a couple photos of you all someplace like Disneyworld, she'd try to pin down the dates, or give me a better picture from her collection. I documented everything the best I could. It's chronological. I think it helped your grandma too."

He flipped to a Christmas page and traced the reindeer and candy cane stickers that decorated the edges. "This was a couple of years ago. We got new phones and video games."

"It's a good memory, Scout."

He turned past Cub Scout camp and his parents' anniversary party. He smoothed pages and touched tiny 3-D charms that dangled on ribboned birthday packages until his eyes welled with tears."

"OK." I tried to close and take the book. "You can do this in small doses. I thought it might help you when you want to remember good times. And we can make more pages and more scrapbooks. Anything that would bring you comfort."

It took him a while to speak.

"I'm sorry," I said. "It was too much. Your grandma said it was time. We were wrong."

"No, Ivy. It's perfect. I can't believe you did this for me."

"I would do anything for you, Scout."

He paused and lifted up to reach behind a box of corn flakes. "This is for you."

"Are you serious? You had my Christmas gift hidden in the pantry? How could you have known we'd end up in here?"

He shrugged. "I didn't. I put it there for later so I didn't have to run back upstairs if the moment struck to take you for a romantic walk in the park or something."

I turned the small, wooden box in my hand. The silver

hinges and tiny clasp were already an interesting gift. I found the snowflake necklace tucked inside on black velvet. "Scout, this is beautiful..." I tugged the chain loose. "But it looks like it was too much. It looks antique or something."

"It is. Some other lady had it a long, long time ago."

"It's like lace. I can't believe the detail." A small red stone twinkled at me from the center. "What is that?"

"It's a garnet."

"A real garnet?"

"Yes, a real garnet."

"This is too much."

"No, it isn't. It's a garnet, not a real emerald or a canary diamond. Garnets are like an affordable cousin or something. And it doesn't matter anyway. Whatever it takes."

He took the chain. "Here. Let's get it on you. Ever since I saw you in that sweater, I wanted to see it on you. That's what all those old clowns out there were attempting to tease me about."

I lifted my hair. "They knew about the necklace?"

"My grandma checks my browsing history. I leave crumbs for her to find so she doesn't get suspicious. She saw I was searching for an antique snowflake necklace and no one can keep a secret around here."

"How did you know I would like an old snowflake necklace? Never mind. It's amazing. I love it. Thank you."

"You're welcome." He pulled the scrapbook back onto his lap. "You even have NASA paper. Who knew they had NASA paper? This is our last trip to the Johnson Space Center."

"Scrapbookers have a piece of paper or an embellishment for everything. It's true. The craft store owns me. I've never seen a real snowfall..." I touched the necklace. "...but I have a snowflake punch in my craft box. I'll be making a page in my journal about the ski trip."

"See what I mean about being in sync? A red sweater—"

"Snowflakes and the pantry. How did we do that?"

"Who knows?"

I held his hand as he looked at a couple more pages. "I'm sorry if the scrapbook is too much for you."

"It's not."

"I would never want to break your heart at Christmas."

"You didn't break my heart at Christmas, Ivy. It was already broken. You helped put it back together."

CHAPTER 34

Deacon

My cracked ribs took a long time to heal.

The doc said I was young and still made of rubber, but cracked ribs were cracked ribs. I was fine most of the time, then I moved the wrong way or laughed too hard and felt a tug and a pain.

Hours in a crowded van didn't help. For the most part. we slept and played games on our phones, but after a while, the snacks ran low and everyone wanted out.

I'd been only dry and miserable for the most part, then we hit a rest area once we'd gotten into Colorado snow. Many of our three vans full of people hadn't ever seen real snow and proceeded to have a snowball fight outside the cold, brick structure that housed metal toilets—also very cold, according to the girls.

OK, I was one of them. Not who complained about the cold toilets, but who played in the snow at a rest stop.

Long story short, where I was once dry and miserable, I was then wet and miserable.

Jacob and Mary sat curled up together in deep discussion most of the time, and since Scout had finally gotten his game on with Ivy, they did nothing but try to suck each other's faces off and cuddle without being separated by Mr. P.

And then there was Claire Cannon, two rows ahead of me and completely oblivious of my interest. The others were right. I was never going to have the nerve to get close to that girl.

Everyone had someone, and Claire Cannon didn't know I wanted her to be my someone.

So, I realized it was going to be a wet, miserable, and boring trip for me.

I didn't have my girl, and I wasn't going to be able to master skiing with my lingering pain. I was gonna try, but fully expected to wind up at the bottom of a hill with a piece of my rib stuck through my lung.

Good times.

"Deacon! Wake up." Ivy pulled my headphone away from my ear and flicked my earlobe. "We're here." She snapped it back on my head.

"Where? The lodge?"

"No. Well, kinda. It's check-in. The place where we get our gear and stuff."

I glanced out the frosted window. "Look at that line. It's out the door."

"No, c'mon. It won't be that bad. Erin's mom has this thing beyond organized. Our stuff and all our passes are already supposed to be set aside for us. We just have to make sure everything fits. Especially the boots. There are people here to help us."

"Do you have any idea what you're talking about, Ivy?"

"No, I do not, but I have my checklist on my phone."

I rolled my eyes. "Then it's all good."

My first step outside the van was into a slushy pile of melting snow.

Ivy danced around me as we got in line. "Look. I can see my breath. That hardly ever happens in Texas."

I held my nose and tried to blow pressure out my ears. "You know what else never happens in Texas? Fluid in my ears and this ringing sound. You hear that?"

"That's the altitude. My ears popped all the way up the mountain." She rummaged in her pocket. "Here. Scout's grandma made me this peppermint oil mixture. Sniff it and rub some on your forehead or on your neck or something. I don't remember. I also have something for ears. I'll find it when we get to our rooms."

"I can't wait."

"Look, Deacon, you worked really hard to be on this trip. Who shoved a stick up your butt between home and here?"

"Sorry. I'm not feelin' it yet."

"Well, snap out of it, will ya? Even this parking lot is beautiful."

From icicles on the log cabin-like building to snow-covered branches, she had a point. Though it was getting dark fast and the temperature continued to drop, I couldn't miss the blanket of glistening snow along the road and the scent of clean, crisp air. Snowcapped peaks loomed in the distance, just above a line of tall, thick pines that were about to be swallowed by night.

Ivy nudged me. "Some view, huh?"

"Yeah, but right now I need out of these wet shoes and into a vat of hot chocolate or something."

Ivy laughed and looped her arm through Scout's. "Totally. Don't worry, we should be in front of a fire soon and relaxing before tomorrow's day on the slopes." She stepped closer and looked at the ground. "Don't be obvious, but look over there. That super-cute girl has been watching you this whole time."

I jerked to look immediately.

"Smooth," Ivy said.

"The one with the blue hat and short hair?"

"No. Red winter headband and box braids."

I took another less obvious glance and nodded. *Wow, I* mouthed to Ivy.

"Yeah, and don't be a dork because she's walking this way."

Ivy smiled wide. "Hi, I'm Ivy and this is Scout."

Scout had been talking to some others and had no idea what was happening. "Hey," he said.

"I'm Deacon."

I'm sure that's what came out of my mouth, but all I heard in my head was *her smile is beautiful, her smile is beautiful, her smile is beautiful because she crinkles her nose...*

She shoved her hands in the pockets of her puffy jacket and leaned forward. "I'm Charlana, but don't call me that 'cause I won't answer. Call me Char."

"Nice to meet you, Char."

"You look cold. Where's your winter gear?"

"Still in my duffle, uh…buried under all the other bags." I scratched the side of my head. "I didn't think that one through."

"But you'll be on the slopes tomorrow?"

"Yeah. And I'll be dressed for it."

"Good. See you up there tomorrow."

"No, wait. Are you from Colorado?"

"No. Youth group from Arkansas. You?"

"School trip from Texas." I pulled my phone out of my pocket. "Where are you staying?"

She took my phone before I offered and punched in her number. "You know. In case I don't see you."

I took my phone back.

She crinkled her nose. "See you tomorrow, Texas."

"Looking forward to it, Arkansas."
I turned to face Ivy's smug smile.
"Awww… You already have cute nicknames for each other. It's a ski trip romance."
"Not one more word."
I took another long look at Arkansas.
Things were looking up.

CHAPTER 35

Mary

Jacob skied my way and skidded sideways to my side, complete with a spray of fresh snow and a sparkling smile. With his matching high-end ski clothes and all his own accessories, he looked like he was there to shoot a tourism commercial for Colorado.

Meanwhile, all of us with our borrowed clothing and zero skill sets were about to star in the *don't let this happen to you* portion of the video.

Scout even forgot his goggles and was unsure as to whether to go back until Jacob convinced him he did not want icy pellets of snow blinding him on the course. *You need to keep your eyes open, dude* was probably Jacob's best quote of the day—along with *Deacon, your boots and skis should be pointing the same way...*

Jacob, Deacon, Ivy, Scout and I huddled together as we waited for the mandatory safety review to begin.

Erin's mom counted heads. "Everyone have their sunscreen and lip balm?"

"Yes, ma'am," we sang out as we'd been doing a lot of the last two days.

Gavin and Corey and some of their friends lingered on the outskirts of the group like they didn't really want to participate. His cool gaze met mine a time or two as if he wanted to pull me in. I chose to ignore him and focus instead on Jacob and my real friends.

Scout tapped Deacon on the shoulder. "Incoming."

Two girls I didn't know approached our group.

"Hey, Texas," she said.

Deacon smiled so big he could have melted snow. "Hey. Glad you made it." He turned toward the rest of us. "Everybody, this is Arkansas."

She laughed. "No. My name is Char, and this is Erica."

"They're gonna hang with us today if that's OK."

What? Deacon had snagged a girl and it wasn't Claire Cannon?

"Of course it's OK," I said. "It's going to be a blast, despite the fact only one of us can really ski. I'm Mary."

"Yeah," Scout said. "If you want to ski for real, you'll want to follow Jacob down whatever hill he takes. The people stay upright on his slope and remain like that all the way down. Us, not so much. There will be carnage."

Char laughed. "I'm not that advanced either. I'm fine to take my time."

"And I don't want to be embarrassingly pulled out of here in a litter behind a sled, so we're good," Erica said.

A short burst of a whistle caught our attention. We settled in for a lecture from the ski slope police. "OK, just a few reminders, and then I'm going to take those of you who have never skied to see an instructor for a brief lesson and practice run and you can ask questions. As for safety, a few things to remember. You are here on one of the busiest weeks of the year. It will be crowded and there will be lines. Ski Patrol is very active on the slopes. You'll know us by these red bibs with white crosses. We're up and down at regular intervals. We have radios, phones, sleds, and emergency supplies. When necessary, we even have dogs and helicopters. If you have any problem at all, don't hesitate to flag us down and ask for help. Use your common sense. Before you merge or start down a hill, look uphill to make sure no one is coming toward you. Don't stop on a narrow trail. If you come up behind someone, assume they can't hear you and call out *on your right*, or *on your left* to make them aware. Pay attention to *caution* or *slow skiing* signs. Above all, steer clear of any area that says off-limits, or any closed trails. Stay on the marked path and never go past the boundary. Never. You got me?"

A collective *yes* reverberated through the crowd.

"Good. Come with me."

"I don't know any more than I did," Scout said.

"They have dogs and helicopters," Ivy added.

"I don't think they want us to have to use those."

Deacon snapped the clasp on his helmet. "I guess we're doin' this."

Jacob cuffed him on the arm. "It won't be bad."

I struggled to keep up with Jacob. We'd all spent a half hour just trying to learn how to get our uncomfortable boots to clamp onto our skis. After that, it was another twenty to figure out how to use the poles to slide forward rather than backward.

At one point, Char was skis-up in a drift.

Deacon fished her out by extending a pole for her to grab hold of.

He shouldn't have done that with his limited experience and sore ribs. His aching muscles were going to prove it the next day.

"You should go," I told Jacob. "I mean, look at us. Go enjoy yourself on the big-boy course. Find you some black diamonds. You should have fun while you're here."

"I can ski any time with my family. I'm not leaving you."

"Really, Jacob, I'm going to spend the day on the bunniest of all the green bunny slopes. You'll get bored watching me fall over all day."

"Hey, if you have to fall, soft, fluffy snow is the best place to do it."

"I'm not sure I believe that."

Ivy tried to steady herself and look down her ski jacket. "Let's see. Base layer, mid layer…"

Scout slid to an awkward stop. "What are you doing?"

"I think I missed a layer."

"And?"

"I could get wet and freeze to death. Should I go find my missing layer? The checklist said I need layers."

"How about this? We're not going to get much done today because, well, we don't know crap about skiing. We'll probably have to stop early because of hunger and injuries, so let's learn what we can and remember all the layers tomorrow. Otherwise, you'll miss your lesson." He tried to restart his skis, but didn't have the correct hold on his poles and slid backward. "Besides," he huffed out as he straightened himself. "I'm pretty sure you have all your layers. You've already checked twice."

She shrugged. "As usual, your logic is sound."

"It's what I do," he said, and fell straight down on his butt.

During the lesson, we did everything but actually ski. By the time the instructor took us on a practice green run, our legs burned and our knees ached.

And nobody really knew yet how to stop their downhill slide when they needed to. Everyone just tried to fall gracefully to come to a complete stop.

It was only one o'clock, and we were already done.

Jacob took control. "I know it hurts. Let's get some lunch

and then try to all go back up and come down one more time before we call it a day. I promise tomorrow will be better."

Erica had already given up. "Lunch sounds good. Another run? Not so much."

Scout collapsed on a bench beside her. "I have news. I can now do the splits. In related news, I am not designed to do the splits. Anybody have ibuprofen?"

Ivy dug in her backpack. "You know what I heard we could do tonight?"

"What?"

"Ice skating. There's a rink at the bottom of the mountain in town. They've got a fire, hot chocolate—"

"And marshmallows?" Scout asked.

"I'm sure there are marshmallows. Anyway, how about we see if a chaperone will take us down there? Skate rental can't be that much."

"I'd go," Char said. "Sounds like fun."

"We can talk more about it over lunch."

I touched my lips. "Are anyone else's lips chapped beyond recognition?"

Erica pulled out her lip balm. "Yes. Low humidity. Cold air. Freezing bullets of water in your face. There's not enough lip balm in Colorado to fix this. I'm going to look in our stash for one of those things that covers your neck and mouth."

Great. I was getting less kissable by the second. I thought six layers of waxy lip stuff had been enough.

Jacob helped me with my skis. "How's the elbow?"

"It's not bad. I thought all the arm work with the poles would aggravate it, but I'm good. It's Deacon I'm worried about. I think his ribs are still sore."

"I don't know. He sure looks like he's feelin' no pain over there next to Char."

"Yeah. It's good to see him having that kind of fun. He's been in a weird mood since the fire, and if he's not going to get serious and go after Claire Cannon, I'm glad someone has taken an interest in him."

"I'd say she's interested."

Char discreetly took Deacon's hand as they headed for an extra-large circular booth in the corner.

"That's sweet."

Jacob pulled off my gloves. "Wait a second." He warmed my hands between his. "After we make that run, can we maybe head back to the lodge and talk?"

"Sure. As long as you're done skiing. Our inexperience can't be fun for you."

"I don't care, Mary, I really just want to spend some alone time with you. We haven't had any time together since Thanksgiving, and you know…"

Yeah, I knew. We'd had that revealing conversation about his history that led to an awkward Thanksgiving at his parents' house. Nothing was wrong, but his world was so different than mine. I knew he didn't enjoy spending time in his own home. He seemed to be more comfortable at Thanksgiving game night with my parents as a football game played out in the background much more than the over-the-top and stuffy meal at his place.

And while he was as romantic as ever with the hand-holding, gentlemanly behavior, and the awesomely special angel-wing charm he gave me for Christmas, we still hadn't gotten any further.

Between my trauma over Gavin's possessiveness and forcefulness, and his probable trauma over his uncle's abuse, I wondered if we'd ever get there.

Ivy slipped past us. "Are you coming?"

"Yes, I'm starved, but I don't know how my ankles are gonna feel about ice skating after another run."

I gave Jacob a tentative smile and he nodded. I swear the guy regularly read my mind.

"Don't worry, Mary Angel, everything is fine."

"It is?"

"Yes. I've had time to think, and I just want to talk. Alone. Away from all my issues at home and the craziness of football—and fires."

"OK."

"And then I'm going to collect that kiss I asked for weeks ago over smoothies."

I snaked one arm under his coat and around him and used my other hand to smooth a piece of hair away from his forehead. Leaning into him was the safest I ever felt.

I put my finger to his lips. "I never answered you about that kiss," I reminded him.

He pulled my hand away. "You just did."

CHAPTER 36

M^{ary}

I pulled on the fuzzy off-white sweater my mother gave me for Christmas and headed to the giant fireplace in the ski lodge. Pine garlands with red berries still draped every entrance, and large green wreaths with glistening red balls greeted everyone coming and going. The place smelled like cinnamon and orange and Christmas heaven while white twinkle lights graced each window, and lighted holly-berry nests held trios of tall flickering candles on every table.

I never wanted to go home.

Jacob stood from one of the couches to greet me.

He only added to the magical illusion in his red plaid flannel shirt, soft, worn jeans, and brown leather boots.

Char wandered by. "Where are your coats? Aren't you going to come skating?"

Jacob hooked his thumb in his pocket. "I think we're staying in a while."

"I wish I could stay, but I've been nicely threatened by Ivy that my attendance is required."

"Have fun," I said with a laugh.

"Wait. Give me your phone."

"Sure. Why?"

"Stand by the fire. You two look like a Christmas card. Let me take some pictures."

I tugged the wire bracelet from inside my sleeve to make sure my angel-wing charm showed.

Char gave direction and took more photos than we expected.

"Do we look so bad it took that many tries?" Jacob asked.

"OK, you got me. I love photography and I was trying to get the light of the fire the way I wanted it in the background."

I swiped through my phone. "You're forgiven. These look great."

"I'm going to bring my real camera out on the slopes tomorrow. Maybe I'll get some good candid shots of you."

Jacob snorted. "Or maybe Deacon will ski over your camera."

I jabbed him in the side. "Stop. Deacon's doing pretty good." I prepared to text one of the best pics to my mom. "But yeah. No, I don't think anyone needs more documentation of me sliding backward on my butt all the way down a hill."

"See you guys in a bit. Save me some hot chocolate."

Jacob pulled me onto the couch and passed me a latte from the end table.

"Thanks. You thought of everything."

"Only if I got it right."

I smiled and took a sip. He almost got it right. "Perfect." I curled my fingers around the warm cup. "What did you want to talk about?"

He blew out a long breath, leaned back, and put his arm across the back of the bear-print upholstered couch. "I'm not stupid, Mary."

"Of course you're not. Who said you're stupid?"

"Nobody, but I feel like I showed up in the middle of a school play and don't know what it's about. I keep trying to find my place and learn my lines and I just get more and more confused."

I set my cup aside. "OK, start from the beginning. What's this about?"

"It's about you and me and Stonehaven. The first day we met we ended up in an electrical fire. You said weird things afterward, and from there, it's been one long mystery. The pool party, the weird feeling when I carried you around Scout's house to the car... All the odd conversations and the near-catastrophes. All the feelings I have for you." He took my cold hand in his warm one. "We are not in an average place. We're just not. Other things are going on and I can't wrap my head around it. I'm one step from falling off the stage."

Guilt and sadness overwhelmed me. Deacon, Scout, Ivy, and I had found each other in the most awkward way possible. We'd floundered around together in the discovery of the supernatural realm and continued to uncover its secrets.

Jacob came out of nowhere and landed in our midst. He had no one to guide him, *if* he was one of us. Was it our place to tell him? Where were his Guardians and Protectors? Where was his Enforcer like Sebastian? Where was my assurance I could speak freely and tell him the truth? Sebastian never said I could or couldn't share anything. The Warriors I was connected to had voluntarily vowed to stay silent for our own sense of privacy and protection. I couldn't share unless everyone knew.

The risk was too great to confide in the wrong person.

I had to decide if Jacob was the right person—though everything in me already felt he was.

"Let's talk this through," I said, in hopes of easing his concern.

"Fine. We'll talk about it some more, but you should know I know you have secrets. Don't get me wrong. I don't care. I don't need to know everything about you today. I can learn something new about you every day if you want, but I do know there are things you aren't telling me. I feel it. I know there are secrets you have with others, but I trust you because I know what we have together."

I had no response. My heart melted into my shoes. All I wanted to do was give him the comfort of truth he so desperately needed.

"I remembered something," he said before I could think of what to say.

"What's that?"

"You know how you've asked me a couple times if I ever experienced anything strange like the thing I felt at Scout's?"

"Yes."

"Or if I ever had a group of friends who seemed different, or talked about the kind of things we've been through?"

"Yes."

"Turns out I was wrong when I said I had no experience with this stuff."

"How?"

"Telling you about my uncle brought back some memories I don't usually bother to dwell on. It was so long ago—"

"And so hard to think about…"

"Yes, hard to think about, especially with my cousins' wellbeing at stake. Anyway, I did have a connection with someone. Someone did take care of me and talk to me, and I often felt that person knew and saw things they couldn't have known. I felt like I was safe in a bubble as long as that person was with me and in my life. Do you get what I mean?"

"I get exactly what you mean, Jacob. Don't you know? That's exactly how I feel with you. You've been keeping me safe since we met. My entire idea of being all right is wrapped up in being with you. It's why I couldn't stand another minute of Gavin as soon as I saw what it was like to be truly protected by someone. We barely knew each other, but your concern for me was so powerful it was like I couldn't stay away."

"Right. I felt that way about the person in my life who did it for me, then I felt that way about protecting my cousins. Now I feel that way about you. It's like it's my job to make sure you're OK. And it goes beyond whatever feelings I have for you."

Heat rushed up my neck. My face burned as we sat there for the longest time just looking at each other.

"Do you know who that person was for me?" he asked.

"It was your nanny, wasn't it?"

"Yes. She protected me from my uncle, and when she was gone, it was like I lost my best friend. My parents took away my safety net, and they sure as heck weren't going to watch out for me. The bubble burst, and everything was…"

"Broken."

"Yes, broken. I never felt safe after that. I realized after we talked, I haven't felt really good about anything for years. Not until I met you. And the only thing wrong is that I'm still on that stage and I don't know all my lines."

I checked the time. "Um… Can you give me one minute?"

"Now?"

"Yeah, I promise I won't be long. Don't go anywhere."

He sagged into the couch and put his hands up as if annoyed. "I'm not going anywhere, Mary."

I rushed to the restroom and texted Ivy. *Do you have a quick sec to call?*

You OK?

Yes.

Hang on.

Within a minute, my phone buzzed.

"What's the matter?"

"Nothing," I said. "But I need you to concentrate. I'm going to ask you a question and I want your real gut-driven, Warrior answer. It's important."

"No pressure there, but OK. I'll try. I hope no one's life depends on this command supernatural performance."

"I need to do something. Nothing drastic, but we promised each other we'd keep Warrior business between us. I have to share something with someone and I want to be sure you all know. Depending on your answer to my question, I may need you to tell the others I've shared some information. Not everything, and not like Deacon outed us to Mr. Parrington, but I may talk."

"Sheesh. Ask the question. The seriousness of your voice, along with my freezing butt, may interrupt my signals."

"OK. What about Jacob?"

"Jacob is real."

"Thank you."

"Wait. What? That just came out of my mouth like I wasn't even thinking those words and they flew out. Wow."

"Yes. You have a gift. That's part of it. I gotta go."

I ended the call and rushed back to Jacob. "Listen. I'm going to tell you something I think is going to make you feel better."

"OK."

"Jacob... Something happened between me and Deacon and Ivy and Scout last year. We discovered things about ourselves and the universe we didn't expect. There are powers out there in the atmosphere and there's this realm..."

"Is this a joke to you? Are you seriously going to tell me a UFO story?"

"No. Forget that. Let me try something else. The reason you were so close to your nanny is she was sent by the Creator to protect you. You learned how to do that from her. Your bond was strong, and when she was taken from you, you were too little to understand or fight it. You took what she taught you and also became a Protector. You are your cousins' Protector, and you are my Protector."

He blinked twice. "You're gonna have to back up and start again."

CHAPTER 37

Mary

Jacob took another lap around the couch and then sat on the hearth for a minute to down the last of his water. "I think I do feel better. The more you talk and the crazier it sounds, the more it makes perfect sense." He got up and carried the bottle to the recycling barrel by the door and aimlessly wandered back. "I never thought we were alone in the universe or anything. I figured there had to be a higher power or a God or something, but earthly Warriors? I didn't see that coming. It's like you're superheroes."

I shrugged. "I don't look at it like that, but I feel we were chosen for something bigger than ourselves and to help others."

"But you all have unusual origin stories like superheroes. Batman had the murder of his parents. Spider-Man had the radioactive spider bite. You drowned in a pool and Scout lost his family... Origin stories. Superheroes."

"No. We're not superheroes. We're not even basic heroes.

We're people who listened and recognized a special assignment in our lives."

There was so much I hadn't said. I didn't explain Shanar—as if I even could—but I did admit we knew there was a darker side out there in direct contrast to the good and positive one we tried to stay aware of. And I didn't tell him about meeting Sebastian in the garden. I figured if Jacob ever needed him, he might make himself known. Jacob had already felt the good and bad forces that night he carried me around Scout's house and smelled the frankincense. He'd been there for the fire too. He'd witnessed Deacon's powerful and healing hands and knew the obvious destructive nature of the falling scoreboard. There was nothing typical about any of those things.

No wonder he felt so out of place. He *was* out of place because he didn't know where he belonged. He hadn't belonged since his parents took his intended guide away from him.

He gazed at me again as if he could read my mind. I felt exposed and comforted at the same time.

"Why do you think my parents got rid of my nanny?"

"Seems strange they would fire the person who helped you and was someone you were comfortable with."

"I thought it was about the money. They didn't want her to talk. I thought they paid her to walk away and not look back, and to forget about my uncle and what she knew and saw."

"Maybe that's it."

"Or maybe she didn't want to go. Maybe they forced her and threatened her not to come back and help me. But if she was my Protector and worked for who you call the Creator, why would she stay away?"

"The Destroyer has an army too. Maybe she couldn't overcome that."

"Or maybe my parents are nothing more than Agents for the Destroyer and didn't want me to know. It still could all come down to money."

"Hey, Jacob, this is all new to you. The information is fresh and will take a while to fully understand. Don't go looking for trouble. You may never understand everything. We certainly don't."

Jacob grabbed a blanket from a nearby chair. "C'mon. Let's go out on the upper deck. It's dark, but the view is incredible and still all lit up with Christmas lights. And I need some air."

Cold air hit my lungs and took my breath away.

"Watch your step," Jacob warned. "Icy boards."

We wandered past lingering couples of all ages who gazed at the romantic starlit sky and laughed softly to each other. How nice it must be to not have the weight of the evil side of the world weighing on their shoulders. How nice to not see things like Ivy saw or analyze things like Scout did and try to stay positive when the numbers could only ever add up to disaster.

How were teenaged Warriors, Protectors, and Guardians supposed to grow up, go to college, and have families when they literally always saw the dark side of what humans could be?

I didn't know how anyone kept hope alive.

Worse, I'd just put the burden on one of the best guys the universe had to offer. Did I do that for him?

Or for myself?

We stopped to look out across the mountain. Lights twinkled and smoke curled from chimneys. Laughter from far below drifted to our ears in the thin mountain air.

Jacob wrapped the blanket around me and used it to pull me close.

I snuggled against his massive chest. "I'm sorry I told you, Jacob. It wasn't fair to put it on you."

"How was it not fair? Do you know how long I've been waiting to find my place? I knew there was something, but I never could have found it without you. Yes, it's different and wild and unbelievable, but it fits. I totally get it."

"It might fit, but it takes some time to grow into it. You don't know how much discussion we've all had about how it all works, and we don't know anything."

"But I know more than I ever have and it makes me feel better. I'm relieved. I know my part now. Think of it as a disease or something. People can't fight cancer until they know where it is. Well, in my case, maybe I'm part of the cure. You definitely are. Like you said. One assignment at a time."

"Yes, and you have to remember that. Don't take on more than you've been assigned."

"I understand."

"And stick with us. Usually when something's up, we all know. We're a weird pack of basic teenagers who find ourselves in the most unusual of situations."

"There's nothing weird or basic about you, Mary Angel."

Jacob's lips were on mine before I processed what was happening. We'd gone from zero to ninety before the speedometer caught on. Between my healing lips and lingering lack of confidence after Gavin, I thought I might crash and burn when it actually happened, though I'd waited for it forever.

I'd hoped for perfection, and I got it.

Kissing Jacob was the most natural thing I'd ever done. As I relaxed in his arms, my body warmed and tingled.

He pulled away, but I still stood there out of my mind with my eyes closed. "What's the matter?"

"Wow."

My eyes flew open. "What wow? It's these stupid chapped lips, isn't it? Erica was right. There's not enough salve in The Rockies to fix this. I can do better."

Jacob pulled me back into a bear hug and laughed against my cheek. "Stop. It's nothing like that."

I pulled away. "What is it?"

"Nothing is wrong. Didn't you feel that?"

"Uh... I'm trying to be a lady here, Jacob, so I'm not exactly going to tell you all the acrobatics going on in my body over here on this side of the kissing equation."

He laughed harder. "OK. But nothing is wrong. Couldn't be better. It's us, Mary. It's just us. This is what we are. Always."

We kissed and talked and laughed and kissed some more until the alarm on my phone went off.

"Who's texting this late?"

"It's not a text. It's the curfew alarm. We have about fifteen minutes to at least be in our own hallways for room-check."

Jacob shivered for the first time since we'd tried to stay huddled together in our blanket. "That is horrible timing."

"School trip. What can we do? Don't want to be sent home."

"No, we do not."

He wrapped his arm around me and led me across the common area and to the elevator. He kissed me one last time before he pushed me inside with a smile. "You really need to go."

"Goodnight, Jacob."

"Goodnight, Mary Angel."

There were others all around me as I stepped on and off the elevator and into the hall. Teens from other trips scurried back and forth to get to their rooms on time, and adults carried supplies and made notes on their phones and clipboards as they marked each kid alive and present.

I stepped into the small room on my floor with vending machines to find a candy bar.

And that's when everything went cold and dark.

I didn't even need the warning of a cold puff of air on the back of my neck like I'd had in the beginning to know when something was off. Seemed that each new event heightened my instincts.

I leaned into the intuition and tried to think. A threat was near. Why?

Was it because Jacob knew what he was? I figured the Destroyer didn't like it when the Creator's best and brightest came into their destiny.

I tapped out a text to Deacon and Scout who roomed with him. *Jacob is a Protector. Keep your eyes open. Someone may not like it.*

Better safe than sorry.

I rummaged in my pocket for uncrumpled dollar bills as the door came unwedged and slammed shut.

Gavin.

"What are you doing here, Gavin? You're going to miss room-check."

"I need to talk to you."

"Since when? And why now? You could have talked to me any time we crossed paths today."

"Your goon's not with you now."

"Do you have a point? Because I need to get to my room."

He stepped in front of the door. "I want to talk."

"I don't have time to talk now, Gavin, and really, I don't have anything to say to you."

"I want to say I'm sorry for the way everything went down between us. It wasn't supposed to happen that way."

"You mean there was another way you had planned to grope me and then break my nose?"

"You know that's not what I mean. I love you, Mary. I always meant for us to be together. I still think we should be together. I want you back. I want to try again."

"Are you delusional? We haven't been together for months, and it was never about love. I don't know what it was, but it wasn't love. You made me feel bad about myself, you tried to force me into things… You hit me out of anger in front of everybody. That's not love."

"I was wrong about a lot of things. I've been talking to a counselor about my anger. I have more control. I can prove to you I've changed."

"Gavin, you are not listening to me. We are not supposed to be together. We are never going to be together. Yes, you need to get better about some things, but that won't change anything between us. Your behavior even broke up our parents' friendship. Do you know how awkward it's been for them? Do you think they'd even allow me to be alone with you again?"

"We're alone right now."

"What's that mean? Is that some kind of threat? Because it sounds like a threat."

His expression shifted. "No. I would never threaten you. I really do love you."

Tears pooled in his eyes and exposed a possible red-eyed explanation that a non-partier like myself easily missed. I was an idiot.

"Are you drunk? Or high? Or is it both?" I stormed toward him and tried to reach around to grab the door handle.

He caught my arm and spun me till my back was against the door. My elbow smacked the steel doorknob with a thud.

I refused to cry out as I shoved him far away.

I turned, but he sped back and used his body to pin me face-forward on the door.

"Did you really think I was going to let you go so easy?" he spat in my ear. "I've put my life on the line for you. I've made sacrifices so we could be together."

"There is no *we*, Gavin. And what do you mean sacrifice? Was it a sacrifice to have sex with Corey in hallways and make trouble for Jacob? How can you claim to love me? There is no love in you. Everything you've done has been to hurt or control me or others."

"You have no idea what I've done for you."

A terrible thought entered my mind. "Where is Corey? Is she OK?"

"This isn't about Corey. We're done. It's you I want."

"But I don't want you."

"Oh, Mary. Don't you realize we are destined to be together? It's going to happen."

I gathered enough energy to buck him off my back and grab for the door in the small space.

Someone had the handle on the other side. The door popped open with a whoosh and barely missed my face.

Char stood in the doorway. She pinned Gavin with an icy glare. "Step off, Agent."

Agent?

My gut twisted and plummeted into my shoes. Physical pain gripped my chest as the word continued to ring in my head. Deacon had been right. He knew someone was an Agent.

It'd always been Gavin.

"Mind your own business," Gavin snapped.

"Not gonna happen. I'll tell you one more time." Char stepped sideways to expose the door. "Step off. You have no power here."

Gavin passed between us in a swirl of dark energy and disappeared down the hall.

I regained my composure. "I have to go find Mr. Parrington. The girl he's been seeing is not safe. He's been drinking or something. And I should check on the others."

"Everything is fine," Char said.

"How do you know?"

"He was already out of control at the skating rink. Your people were on top of it. Mr. Parrington is aware."

"My people?"

"C'mon, Warrior, keep it together. Don't let that Agent keep you rattled. Focus."

"All right. I'll text everybody as soon as I get to my room and ask my chaperone if I can see Mr. Parrington." I paced a short line in front of the candy machine. "Am I your assignment? Are you here because of what just happened?"

"No. You can take care of yourself."

"How do you know that?"

Char smiled. "Every Warrior knows that. You're the special one. I could see it as soon as I looked at you."

"Then why are you…? Wait. You're here for Deacon. Is he OK?"

"He'll be fine. I'm only here for backup."

"Does he know?"

"Not yet. You guys are all new to this. You'll get stronger and stronger at reading the signs and identifying your allies. One step at a time."

"But Deacon's really in to you. Do you like him at all, or is he just a job? Don't lead him on like that."

She dropped her gaze as a touch of red hit her dark-brown cheeks. "I do like him. We're havin' a blast, but this is a ski trip. We may not ever see each other again. Get some sleep, Warrior."

"Wait! Has the threat passed?"

Char put the wedge back under the door. "I don't know. You know how these things work. Sometimes you don't know you're on assignment until you're right in the middle of it. I would tell you if I knew."

"Have you talked to Deacon about this?"

"You mean have I revealed myself? No. And he hasn't said anything either. All I know is he's coming back from an injury and something about a fire at your school. My guess is I was drawn to him because of that. He has power abilities, but he can't use them if he's hurt. And hurt Warriors are sometimes doubting Warriors."

That's exactly what was going on. Deacon had been out of sorts since the fire.

"C'mon, Mary. Everyone is safe right now, and remember, we're the good guys. We're not the ones who live in fear."

She gave me a friendly hug. Warmth and energy coursed between us. She passed strength and confidence to me through her embrace. I called out for Sebastian in my head. *Help me... Show me...*

The scent of frankincense wafted from somewhere in her puffy jacket. Either that, or Sebastian was literally in our presence—in the midst of our embrace.

My mind was in a complete whirl, but I knew the truth when I saw it—and smelled it.

Char was one of us.

"Let's rest so we can kick that mountain's butt tomorrow," she said.

I turned to leave. "'Night, Warrior."

She smiled over her shoulder. "Back at ya, Warrior."

CHAPTER 38

Ivy

I got dressed to ski and left my room before the others were ready, and found Corey's door.

After several sharp knocks, she answered. "What do you want?"

"Good morning to you too." I shoved my way in. "Are you OK?"

"Yes."

"Why aren't you dressed? Everyone is going down for a quick breakfast before we ski."

"I'm not going."

"Are you sick?"

"No. I'm not allowed.

I shed my jacket and made sure my goggles and mitts didn't escape my pockets. "Why not?"

Corey unplugged her curling iron and crammed it into the side of her bag, then yelped when she accidentally touched it.

She yanked her hand back and almost cried. "I'm being sent home, that's why! Happy now? I know you and the others didn't want me here anyway."

"What do you mean we didn't want you? You didn't want us! You've refused to talk to me since you came back to school."

She rolled up her thermals and punched them into one of the lodge's plastic laundry bags. "I know, all right? I've been a jerk. A stupid, stupid jerk. Why did I think I could be in charge of anything? Why did I think Gavin was serious about me?"

"You were struggling to find your place, Corey. You wanted to get back to school and feel better. Gavin made you think you were a part of something with him."

"What a nice warm fuzzy way of saying he used me. Well, thanks for reminding me of that."

"I'm not trying to hurt you, Corey. That's the last thing I want, but I'm angry. I almost lost you to suicide. Do you know what it was like to think I might have to attend your funeral? And then you came back to school and *poof*! Not only were we no longer friends, but you'd become the very thing that sent you over the edge."

She dropped on the bed to pull on her boots. "OK, stop. I'm sorry for the way I acted when I came back. Gavin and some others started visiting me while I was away, and I got things turned around for a while. I forgot who my real friends are, and after Gavin and Mary broke up and he showed an interest in me… Well, I was a first-class idiot."

"You're not the first girl to fall for a guy like Gavin."

"I'm, by far, the dumbest."

"Don't say that about yourself, Corey. Gavin can be persuasive and controlling."

"And I walked right into it." She stood and straightened her pants. "But I can tell you this, no one will ever make me feel that way again. I am not a weak person. I am nobody's doormat."

Pure joy sailed through my heart. "I'm glad to hear that."

"And I know you want to ask, so go ahead. Do your duty. I know you. You won't feel right unless it's all out there."

She was right.

"Are you having suicidal thoughts right now?"

"No. I am not. I know I need to keep seeing my counselor, but I also know dying is not the answer. Now listen, I may or may not be back at school next semester, but I'm going to be OK."

"Wait. Why would you not come back to school?"

"You have to ask that after last year and this? I'm being sent home in disgrace from a school ski trip. Sometimes you can't stay well in the same environment that helped keep you sick, Ivy. That's a simple fact. I need to start over."

"Oh. Here." I handed her a mascara that rolled out of her makeup bag. "Don't forget this."

"Thanks."

"What exactly is the reason you're going home? I obviously missed something."

"You saw the fiasco at the skating rink last night. Gavin had alcohol. I was with Gavin."

"Were you drunk?"

"I had a drink or two—something else I'm not interested in doing anymore—and I had to admit to bringing several of those little bottles of vodka from my house. My mom had a bunch from divorce party gift bags she made for her friend. They weren't even bachelorette bottles of vodka. They were to celebrate a divorced woman's freedom. Who celebrates that?"

"Sorry, girl. Wish you could stay and try to ski with us today."

"I'm not sorry. It's a fitting end to a ridiculously stupid infatuation."

"What happens now?"

"Erin's mom is going to drive me and Gavin down the mountain and into the next town by the nearest highway to meet our ride. We're under house arrest until we leave. Gavin's mom and my dad drove all night to get us."

"*Ooof*. That is going to be one long awkward drive home."

"You have no idea. But anyway, you should go. I'm on restriction and the warden should be bringing breakfast any second. And then I wait."

I gave her my best friendly and supportive hug. "Good to be your friend again, Corey."

"Thanks for taking me back."

"Always. Text me if you need moral support on the ride home."

She rolled her eyes. "There must be a thousand funny gifs for situations like this."

"I'll find them all."

As I clicked the door closed behind me, Mr. Parrington stood in the hall with a tray of food from the cafeteria-like restaurant downstairs.

"I only wanted to check on her, sir. I didn't know she was on restriction."

"How is she?"

His question surprised me. I would have betted on a *move along* any day of the week.

"She seems OK with the situation and the consequences."

"Any other concerns?" He pounded on the door. "Breakfast!"

I stepped away as Corey opened it and contritely took her tray and said thanks.

He motioned me farther away. "Other concerns?"

"No, sir. I came right out and asked her if she was having suicidal thoughts. She said no and I believe her, but I'm not a doctor, and I can't read her mind."

"But you often know more than you say."

"Sometimes. It helps when I can get people to listen to me."

"Noted."

We stood there and looked at each other. I wasn't sure how I was supposed to respond to his sudden newfound interest in my opinion. Perhaps Deacon's unusual info dump in his office had struck a chord, but if he wanted more information from me that day, I had no idea what was about to happen.

There'd been no visions, no words in my ear, no warning bells in my head.

I saw movement at the end of the quiet hall, beyond Mr. Parrington's right bicep. I stepped to the side and caught a glimpse of a man I recognized. He stood at the fire exit on his phone. He hadn't seen me.

I stepped back in front of Mr. Parrington.

"What's wrong, Ivy? You just turned whiter than that fresh powder out there."

"There's a man at the end of the hall and…"

I snuck another peek

He caught me looking.

I took off running toward him. "Wait right there!"

Mr. Parrington spun in my wake and followed. "Ivy, stop! You can't just chase strange men down the hall."

I could and I did. Especially when I knew the guy was a threat.

He bolted through the fire exit doors and onto the stairs.

He had a big head start and took the levels much faster than I could keep up. Mr. Parrington huffed and puffed behind me. I scrambled for my phone, but there was no way to watch my step and get a picture at the same time. At one point I shocked myself by doing a movie-type thing as I sailed over the end of the rail and onto the next set of stairs without hitting the landing. I think it was the padding of the ski jacket and pants that upped my confidence.

Both things also rapidly slowed me down, and the other problem was, the guy ahead of me hit that move every time.

I lost my goggles in the chase.

At the bottom floor, he crashed against the door. It stopped him when it wouldn't open. He appeared to do his best not to turn around and look at us. He jammed at the bar on one side then the other until it finally broke loose and he disappeared into the massive crowd of skiers on the ground floor.

Mr. Parrington gasped beside me and bent to catch his breath. "Do you know who that was?" He kept his gaze on his phone.

"Yes. That's why I chased him."

"Don't do that kind of thing. It's dangerous."

"Who are you calling?"

"The police, I guess. I don't know who to call about spotting a guy here who the authorities are looking for in Texas."

"Maybe call your Texas contact and they'll get in touch with Colorado?"

"Maybe."

I trekked up a level to retrieve my goggles. "I couldn't get my phone out to snap a pic."

Mr. Parrington smiled. "You didn't think I was that out of shape, did you?" He turned his phone my way. "I was slower because I filmed the whole chase."

I took a closer look. "I was right. That's him."

Mr. Parrington got serious. "Why did the electrician from the Stonehaven Gym Fire follow us to Colorado?"

CHAPTER 39

D eacon

Char took my hand after I managed another ugly stop. "I think that was our best one yet. What do you think?"

"I didn't fall as much that time, but I think it's because I'm not going very fast."

I wasn't about to tell her the practice the day before and the skating had rendered me unable to move from the moment I'd gotten back to my room. I honestly didn't know how many more runs I could make.

She wrapped her arms around me and I prayed she both would and wouldn't hold me as close as she could. "This mountain might make a skier out of you yet."

"I'm not holding my breath."

I was totally holding my breath—because it hurt to breathe. I may not have been as honest as I should have about my injuries. I was feeling bad I wasn't truthful with the others. The doctor warned me I could easily aggravate breaks that hadn't completely healed. Rolling end to end or being impaled by a ski pole couldn't help.

"C'mon," she said. "The others are waiting at the chalet. Ivy and Scout got delayed. They missed us at the top and will be down soon. They have news and need to talk to us."

I was grateful for the break, but it wasn't always good news when both Ivy and Scout needed to talk.

"Where's Erica today?"

"She stayed with our youth group. They're going to try snowboarding."

"Aww, that sounds fun. You should have gone. I mean, you didn't have to stay with me... You know. If you didn't want to..."

"I wanted to."

"Good. And I would have invited myself along anyway if you'd tried to get away."

I hated myself as soon as the lame words came out of my mouth. There was no way to fix that level of goofiness.

Char smiled and pulled off her helmet and goggles. She wiped drops of water off her face from the biting snow and gave me a quick kiss. "We're all good, Texas."

Hottest. Woman. Ever.

"OK, but just so you know, I would have been as horrible at snowboarding as I am at skiing, but I would have tried."

"You don't have to impress me, Texas. I know you're hurting. It's probably time to rest those ribs." She put her arm around me. "C'mon. Let's stow our gear."

Inside, Mary pulled chairs up to a big table while Jacob stood in line for coffee.

By the time Ivy and Scout fought their way to the end of the run, we were halfway through a hot drink.

We spotted Scout through the large glass windows as he tossed his poles, helmet, gloves, and goggles aside and wrestled out of his skis.

Ivy stood near and laughed.

"I guess it's not going well," Jacob said.

"Apparently not," Mary added.

Jacob waved them over when they finally made it inside. "I got you something to drink."

I pulled out the chair beside me. "What's the matter? Did the Olympic ski team turn you down?"

"Yes. Yes, they did, Deacon, because this is a horrifying and ridiculous sport that is definitely not for me."

Mary helped Ivy as she shrugged out of her jacket and sprayed fresh snow everywhere. "You look like you were doing pretty good."

"Not as good as you. You rocked that last run. Are you going to try something harder next time?"

Mary glanced at Jacob. "I think we might."

"She's a natural," Jacob said.

"I know I won't be doing anything harder. I have to tell you guys, my ribs might be done."

It was easier to admit that after Char was aware, but I didn't miss the glance of understanding that passed between Char and Mary. What was that about?

"I thought we were talking about me," Scout said and shed his jacket. "First of all, that pizza or snowplow thing does not work to slow you down."

"It worked for me," I said and took a drink. "Not well, but I did manage to stop."

"Second, this place is dangerous. Even the beginner slopes have steep drop-offs. You think you're doin' good, then suddenly you're going too fast and can't stop." He ran a hand through his half-wet shaggy hair. "And don't get me started on the snowboarders, or the jerks who don't follow the rules."

"My problem isn't the actual skiing so much as it's the chair-lift," Char said. "I haven't gotten out of one yet without sliding off course and into a drift. I lose a ski every time."

"They're the worst," Scout said. "I've been violated more than once today by someone else's ski or pole when I couldn't get out of the way in time. True, I was usually on the ground in front of them, but still. There's no respect for beginners. And those snowboarders..."

Jacob laughed. "I can work with you a while if you want. Show you some tricks. You'll be carving and edging in no time."

"I don't even know what those words are, so no. I didn't get that far in all the YouTube videos I watched, which by the way, didn't help me with anything."

I was shocked by that. Usually Scout could figure out anything given enough time to research it.

"No help necessary," Ivy said and gave Scout a sarcastic motherly pat on the arm. "Grandpa here has informed me we are going into town with the next group to do something safe like shopping for souvenirs and antiques." She dropped her gaze to hide a certain eyeroll. "And there's a bookstore and a little museum of Rocky Mountain history, followed by hot apple cider."

Scout sent her a withering stare, but he couldn't hold it. "All right, *Grandma*, you don't have to go."

"I'll go," she said. "Not sending you into town for that kind of raucous adventure alone."

Mary moved her cup aside. "You said you had news?"

"Yeah..." Ivy looked around the table.

We all knew Mary had brought Jacob into our world, but we didn't know how far. Char was a complete outsider as far as I knew.

"Go ahead," Mary said.

It was likely she knew none of us Warriors were going to spill anything private. We'd gotten good at speaking in code.

"OK," Ivy said. "First, Gavin and Corey."

Mary bristled. "What's the latest?"

"I talked to Corey this morning. The good news is, she seems back to her old self. She's through with Gavin and even apologized to me. I think she's gonna be OK."

"What's the bad news?" I asked.

"Well, it's bad news for them. Probably good news for us. They're both on house arrest in their rooms until Erin's mom takes them to meet their parents. They were caught drinking." Ivy crumpled up a napkin and raised a brow to Mary. "And... I think Gavin may have been up to some other stuff? Last night?"

Mary sat back with a sigh. "Don't worry. Everybody knows everything about that, from what Gavin did, to Char coming by as it happened."

Every muscle and vein Jacob had seemed to twitch through his gray, merino wool shirt—which I didn't know existed until Ivy explained merino wool to me.

"Are you sure he's gone?" he asked.

"Should be by now. I saw Corey early, and I know Mr. Parrington wanted them out of his custody and into their parents'."

The red in Jacob's cheeks continued to grow.

Mary touched his arm. "It's fine."

"No, it's not fine."

"All right. It's fine for now. Is that good enough? He's gone."

Jacob nodded.

I wouldn't have wanted to be in Gavin's shoes if Jacob had been the one to walk in on Gavin's assault of Mary instead of Char. My only experience with a Protector was hearing it from Sebastian. I didn't know any until Jacob, and apparently Jacob just learned of it himself. We hadn't even had time to discuss it alone. If Warriors were the last line of defense with power abilities, it would stand to reason a Protector would be equally strong but serve a different purpose. Jacob had stepped in to help from the beginning.

It all made sense.

Scout nudged Ivy. "Tell them the second thing. I know they don't know the second thing."

"Right. Uh… The electrician from the fire is in Colorado."

"What?"

My hands pulsed heat at the mention of him. I'd learned some reactions were simply remnants from a dangerous time. Other, more persistent heat and feelings, were about actual active events where I was needed to act and react.

My heating hands that day were only a memory of the day I busted down doors, helped Jacob's head injury—and hurt myself.

"How do you know?" I asked.

"I saw him," Ivy said. "I was in the hall and he was at the end. Mr. Parrington was there. We chased him out the doors and down to the ground floor."

"Holy crap, girl, why didn't you text for help?"

"No time. Mr. Parrington has him on video. It happened too fast to text for uh…backup." She paused. "Mr. Parrington wanted to gather the whole group and talk, but everyone had already scattered for the day. He's getting the police involved and is going to send out a text. I think if he had it his way, he'd pack everyone up and head home. He still might."

I glanced at my phone. "Nothing yet."

Mary's gaze darted around as she considered it. "Why would he be here? Is he looking for us? Is it a coincidence?"

"There are no coincidences," Jacob, Scout, and I all replied in unison. Then we looked at each other like *that* was the weird part of the conversation.

"If it were innocent, he wouldn't have run from us," Ivy said. "He didn't want to be spotted."

"I don't like it," Jacob said.

"None of us like it," I said. "But what do we do about it?"

"All we can do is keep our eyes open. We don't know who he is or what part he has in anything."

Char hadn't said much. "What's this about?"

"Long story. I'll fill you in later. I have a picture." I scrolled and showed it to her. She had no reaction one way or the other. "If you see this person, tell ski patrol you need the police. This guy is wanted for questioning."

"For something in Texas involving you guys?"

"Yes."

"And now he's in Colorado?"

"Yes."

"That can't be good."

The news of the electrician went over like a turd in a punch bowl. Air visibly left the bodies around the table as everybody sagged with disappointment and concern. I hated that fear had entered our circle.

I tried to be logical like Scout. "Look, you guys, there's nothing we can do but watch for that guy. Now that he knows he's been spotted, he's probably long gone. Would you hang around once you knew the cops were looking for you? And he was in the lodge, not on the slopes. He's probably not here to ski."

"But we're in Colorado, Deac. Why is he here?"

"He's right," Jacob said. "We can't let that guy ruin our trip. We go home tomorrow—or any minute—and it's a great day to ski."

"Yeah, look," Ivy said and pointed outside. "It's snowing again."

Big flakes tumbled out of the sky and swirled through the pines that lined the wide, green-level slope. "It's what we came for," I said.

"Yep," she continued. "A snow globe is why we're here." She frowned. "Wait. Is it safe for you all to ski in the snow? I know that sounds like a dumb question, but—"

"Not a dumb question at all," Jacob said. "As long as it's light snow and the visibility is good, we'll be fine. It's not advisable to ski in a whiteout, or when fog socks you in, but that's not predicted today. We're good."

Char smiled at me and then sent another wary glance toward Mary. I was gonna have to figure that out. She pulled her camera out of her bag.

Everyone groaned.

"Oh, stop. We need a good group photo in the snow. It won't take long."

Jacob cleared his throat as he stood to follow Char's orders. "Ivy, Scout, be careful in town. You guys the same, Deacon. Stay in contact and watch your backs. Maybe we can get some more info out of Mr. Parrington later."

I was beginning to like the Protector.

CHAPTER 40

Mary

Jacob pulled a ski slope map out of his pocket after the others had gone.

He wiggled his eyebrows and all I could do was laugh.

"Let's see." He rubbed his hands together. "What combination of trails can we navigate to show off your natural skiing ability?"

"First of all, don't overestimate my ability. I had a couple of good moves. I also face-planted and skidded sideways out of control. My skis were pointed up the hill, and I didn't even know I was going the wrong way. That's pretty bad, considering it's a ski *slope*. Don't give me too much credit."

"We were in a flat area. Anyone could have gotten turned around."

"Uh... The people skiing right for me should have been my first clue."

"Stop." He turned the map. "Look. There's a green slope that has a spot where it branches off to a blue area. It'll be busier and narrower with more trees, but it looks pretty tame."

"Can you imagine how pretty that will be in the snow?"

He brushed a mass of hair away from my face. "Yes. I can imagine how pretty you are in the snow."

A snowflake dropped on his eyelash and I couldn't stop staring at him. "I don't think that was the answer to my question."

"Same difference." He stuffed the map in his inside pocket and pulled on his gloves. "Less talking, more skiing, and later, more kissing."

"Deal."

And I didn't say a word as we rode the chairlift to the top.

But I did take a lot of selfies.

"Zip that in your pack before you drop it. I promise it's gone if you do."

"I'm not going to drop it." But I did what he said anyway because, duh, we were on a chairlift. "I don't think I've gotten off one of these successfully since I've been here."

"You can do it, Mary Angel. I got you."

He lunged first, and with a couple of graceful swipes of his skis, he was clear. He stopped, and I bobbled and wobbled as close as I could without getting tangled up in his or anyone else's poles.

"Hey," he said. "You stayed upright."

"There's that…"

"This way."

Blue sky gave way to light gray as gentle snow continued to fall. The fresh white fluff, kicked up and sparkled in the fading sun. The glare left the top of the vast white slope, and snowy peaks formed like puffy clouds on every branch.

People were everywhere, and I scanned them as they slid by for the face of the electrician. If he was there, I would never see him under the gear.

And that was exactly why I didn't believe the electrician was there to ski. It made no sense. He had to have been there for something else.

But I was really only concerned about one person.

My Protector.

"Ready?" he asked.

I checked all my equipment and made sure my hands were in the right position through the straps and on the grips of my ski poles.

I looked over my shoulder one last time. "Yes."

CHAPTER 41

Mary

I'd just found my rhythm on the mountain as Jacob skied by me on the right. I slowed. Well, my version of slowing, and slid farther his way.

He motioned toward a group of signs.

I nodded and knew to follow him toward where we could merge onto the blue slope.

I remembered to glance uphill and make sure I didn't ski right in front of someone, but the skier to my left didn't offer me the same consideration as I tried to maintain speed. He sped past me too close and I lost my balance. Jacob again swooped by me on the right in case I started tumbling.

I didn't.

Skiers on the intermediate slope moved faster. It was more crowded and there was more noise. I thought I heard a female voice call my name, but I couldn't look. I assumed it was someone from my group who'd caught up to and recognized me, but I never saw. When I heard it again, I tried, but couldn't spot her in the mass of moving heads.

I worked my way to the middle-right because I was slow and that seemed logical. It's what I did in a car, so it felt right on the busy, snowy road equivalent of a freeway. I continued to lose sight of Jacob, and couldn't really search for him while I tried to stay safe and focused. Once, when I paused to wipe snow from my goggles, my vision cleared to reveal I was too close to the trees.

Still, Jacob always showed back up when I'd halfway decided to hug the edge and make as many pizza slices as it took to make it slowly to the bottom. He seemed to carve out space around me on the left and help me keep my bearings. I fell more than once, but I managed to get the feel of my first next-level-above-the-children's-slope long enough to stay upright most of the time.

Yellow tape flapped ahead.

Several signs had been covered with *closed trail* markers, so I planned only to focus on my path and get down safe. I passed one wooden barricade marked *danger*.

Orange plastic patches of ski netting came closer and closer together, and more and more yellow tape caught my eye. Jacob swooped by me again and had to veer left to avoid someone who'd stopped directly in my path. I figured he expected me to go to my right, but the skier who'd stopped stood their ground as I approached. Not only that, he appeared to be looking right at me through a pair of extra-large goggles. Between those and the neck gaiter, I couldn't see his face, though I never expected to recognize him.

He stayed there, fixed in his spot, as other skiers dodged him. Jacob made a quick horizontal line back across my way and glanced up at me as I prepared to go around.

From there, everything was wrong and too late and out of place.

I tried to go right. The frozen-in-place skier moved, but only to block my way. I went farther right—and straight onto a barricaded trail.

Jacob yelled for me as yellow tape wrapped around my middle and then snapped free as I slid over a big enough dip in the path to pick up speed.

I thought I would just fall. I tried to fall. I made a plan to fall into the next available pile of fresh snow. But the trees grew closer and closer together, and others were behind me.

Others?

I knew Jacob would come, but it wasn't Jacob who plowed by me too fast, clipped my left pole, and made an obvious attempt to knock me down. I braced to fall, or possibly ski into a wooded area and somehow stop or catch myself on a tree. There was a risk of injury, but at least I could get off of a closed, heavily wooded trail that hadn't been recently checked. I could only guess what branches and even rocks were hidden under the beautiful, deceiving mounds.

"Mary, stop!"

Char? Was she the one who'd called to me before?

"I'm trying," I yelled.

Jacob flew by me. "Stop, and stay here!"

"Don't! It's not worth it!" I yelled back. "I'm fine!"

Silence fell as both skiers disappeared down the closed hill.

I grabbed a branch and made sure all my things were in the right place.

Char made a clumsy stop. "Are you all right?"

"Yes, but Jacob chased that idiot! What are you doing here?"

"What do you think I'm doing here, Warrior? Who's the threat? Is that guy who steered you off course the electrician?"

"No."

"All right. You're not safe. I'm going after them."

"No, Char, I'm going. That's Jacob down there." I pushed ahead. "Do you know who the other guy is?"

"It's Gavin."

"How could it be Gavin? He's been sent home, and he can't ski like that."

"Wake up, Warrior! You can't possibly believe Agents are always where they're supposed to be."

"No, but they can't suddenly ski like experts."

"Really? Haven't you and your Warriors done things you shouldn't have been able to do?" Char charged ahead. "Whatever. I gotta go. See if you can get signal to alert someone we're on a closed trail."

"No time. I'm right behind you."

If only my confidence and determination translated to actual skill.

We started slow and picked up speed. My mind reeled with the possibility that Gavin had again put me in danger. Supernatural abilities aside, could he have hidden skiing from me our whole lives? Or was I just not aware? Then again, his family had taken a winter vacation every year up until high school—to Utah.

I had to get better with the details, and I had to take care of Jacob as he tried to take care of me.

Sebastian... I need your help! Please! Sebastian!

We went faster. The only good thing about being on a closed course was that we were alone. Given enough room, we could possibly navigate a total unknown. I remembered all the reasons the brochure said a run or a catwalk might be closed. Not enough personnel to *groom the area*—whatever that meant. Uncleared hazards, threat of avalanche...which reminded me of all the fresh snow.

The run opened up a bit. Char and I were able to pick up the pace on a short, flat area that had widened. We crested what seemed like a small ledge. Char sailed over it and was able to land.

I was not.

I plopped into new snow in the cleft and sank. In less than a minute I was up, but Char had forged ahead.

In the distance, Jacob and Gavin traversed the course, trying to outmaneuver each other.

What was the point?

I screamed for Jacob, knowing full well he wouldn't hear or may not respond.

The wide area gave way to a more narrow, wooded trail. The left side of the slope seemed to evaporate before my eyes in a haze of light but blowing snow. When I spotted the orange netting and the tops of trees to my left, I knew we'd reached an even more dangerous area.

I hugged the right side.

Jacob and Gavin slowed. Gavin tried to jab Jacob with a ski pole, but lost his balance. He wiped out, which gave Char and I enough time to almost catch up.

Jacob twisted and spun as he appeared to try and orient himself and keep eyes on Gavin. He regained control and scrambled to close the distance and stop Gavin from getting up.

"Leave it alone, Jacob!" I screamed. "He's not worth it! We'll get help at the bottom!"

My noise only alerted Gavin to our approach. He tried again to get in my path. I didn't understand. He knew I was a beginner, and a collision would only hurt us both. What was it he wanted?

Once again, I prepared to head off into the wooded area and hope for the best as Jacob tried to get closer to him. By that point, I knew if he got his hands on him, he was going to beat him half to death where he stood.

Without much control, I couldn't make a clean turn between the two orange sections of fence. Deep, new snow covered my skis to the point I couldn't see them.

I slid right by Gavin.

And he let me.

Jacob yelled, but I couldn't make out what he said.

The path narrowed again as it took us toward a series of frightening curves I could see below. In several places, there didn't appear to be any ground on at least one side.

The mountain just peeled away from view and into fogginess.

Large pines with snow-laden branches hid everything from deep snow wells to pointy rocks.

I tried to come to a stop.

It made perfect sense. I was a novice at best. We were on a slope we weren't supposed to be on. All we had to do was...*stop*.

It was me Gavin wanted. If I stopped, he would either come straight for me, or he'd ski away. It was three against one. If he caught me, what could he do? Defeat two Warriors and a Protector?

He couldn't do that.

Sebastian would show up. We'd all stick together and send Gavin down the mountain like the coward he was.

Eventually, we'd get to the bottom, or get a few bars, or someone would realize we were gone.

I dug my poles into the ground, wedged left, and tried to stop my forward motion.

I stood precariously near an edge. Deceptive snow disguised boundaries and threats I couldn't imagine. How deep was it? Where did it end?

I set my skis sideways to inch my way toward the middle and back up to a wider, and hopefully safer, spot.

Char skied past and slowed to do the same. "Good thinking," she called out.

"Logic. Scout would be proud of me."

Behind us, Jacob and Gavin still struggled to get up to speed and race down the trail.

Char and I stood our ground as Jacob got his bearings and flew toward us.

Gavin flanked him on the right and tackled him.

"That's it." Char leaned back and released her boots.

"What are you doing? You can't walk in those things."

"Well, I'm not gonna stand here on my skis and watch those two hit each other."

I fought with my own bindings. "I'll help you."

"No! This is my assignment, Warrior. I'm going to knock that Agent off this hill so we can get down and get help. This one is not your fight."

"How is it not my fight?"

Char dug her boots toe-first into the snow and stalked toward them, using her poles to steady herself.

Ripples of energy emanated from her body as she shook loose the shin-deep fresh snow in her path and caused it to rush away from her body. Bursts of icy white pellets twinkled in the air around her in the thin rays of sun that poked through the early afternoon winter sky.

"Step off, Agent," she commanded. "One chance."

Gavin stood to face her. He didn't relent. He came right for her.

Char stopped him with a wall of pure, white light, mingled with the snow. "Are you kidding me?"

Gavin countered with dark energy of his own that didn't match Char's abilities. His pathetic show of force, while inexplicable and supernatural, was not effective. Especially against Char.

"You won't win this one, Agent. Mary does not die today."

Jacob skied around the showdown.

"Get her out of here," Char yelled.

Jacob tugged on me. "C'mon."

"I can't let Char fight alone!"

"Looks like she's got this."

"I can't leave her. It's me Gavin wants."

"Seriously, Mary, I have no idea what's happening here, but

Char looks more than capable, and my instinct is to protect you, so we're going on down this mountain."

"He's right," Char called over her shoulder. "This one's mine. I got it."

I should have gone.

I didn't.

Was it my pride? Probably.

I'd been fighting the Destroyer my whole life. I battled his wicked minion, Shanar, on a regular basis.

It was my fight—I thought.

With one ski on and one off, I made an ugly charge toward them. Jacob was at my heels and tried to stop me.

Char's surprise weakened her defense.

It didn't take supernatural strength for Gavin to see his opportunity and pounce. He barreled toward us with nothing more than skillful, human agility.

We were caught off guard as he attempted to mow us down.

It was a four-person tangle of skis, poles, and bodies.

Until three of us tumbled over the side of the mountain in a massive cascade of snow.

CHAPTER 42

Jacob

Everything gets quiet when you die.

Sounds don't mean a thing when you can't react, and energy is wasted when you try to hear what doesn't matter.

And nothing mattered.

Nothing but Mary's safety.

I opened my eyes for a moment.

Char dangled from a large pine branch as snow continued to slide past her. It tumbled in sheets down the side of the hill with each move she made to try and free herself and climb to safety.

I didn't want to use my last breaths to call out to her. Somehow, I knew that was more wasted energy—like hearing things.

You can do it, Char... Grab that other branch...

I sensed Mary beside me. She crawled toward me on her belly as blood dripped from her nose. Funny how I'd seen that before. I didn't hear the snow give way beneath her body, or the crunch of the icy surface as she tossed away her gloves and clawed at the ground to reach me.

"Hey, Mary Angel."

"Don't talk, Jacob. Save your energy. Char will get help. *I'll* get help."

I closed my eyes to rest. Mary had one hand on my forehead and the other touching my chest. Her eyes had been wide with shock, but I was fine.

"Chaaarrrr!" she screamed.

Char responded, but I didn't hear it.

"Hang on, Jacob."

"I can't. I landed on a rock, Mary. This is it, but it's all right. We're all right."

"You have internal injuries. We'll get you help. It's good you're talking. That means your brain is probably OK."

"You see that kid over there?"

Mary sobbed and scanned the mountainside. "No, Jacob. There's no kid."

She tried to take off her jacket and keep me warm, but there was no use. She was tired and injured and couldn't do it.

"There's a kid. He looks just like me when I was about four. I'm going to go with him."

"You're not going anywhere but to a helicopter to get out of here."

"It's OK, Mary. I really need to go with him."

"I'd like you to stay, Jacob. I need you to stay. So, we'll rest here and wait for help because I'm afraid to move you. You need to stay warm and save your energy."

Love, shock, and terror glazed her eyes. I had to go. It wasn't fair to let her try any more, and it was a done deal.

"Hey, Mary Angel, promise me you won't ever let any Agent get the best of you."

"Of course, Jacob, but you can help me with that yourself. You're my Protector. I know I got in your way today…"

Sobs choked off her words. I'd been afraid of that. She was going to blame herself forever.

"Not your fault, Mary. All Destroyer. Remember your enemy."

"I should have listened."

"I really have to go, Mary. The kid's waiting."

"No. Hang on."

"I love you, Mary Angel, and I think I just might see you again someday."

I got up and met the kid on the hill. We didn't talk, and it was all OK.

I was fine.

Mary screamed and screamed and didn't stop.

I saw it for a brief moment, but I couldn't hear her.

Everything was quiet.

CHAPTER 43

Sebastian

I cradled Mary in my arms.

I could barely contain the energy of her wrath and pain as it shook the mountains.

"Where were you?" she screamed through the space we shared in the supernatural realm.

"I was here, but choices had been made."

"Bring him back," she wailed.

"I cannot change what has happened here."

My answer was never going to help.

She thrashed in my presence until her determination tore through the realm and ripped my being.

"Mary, stop! I cannot contain you this way because we are similar. I cannot fight myself, so do not fight me. I am not the enemy. It will not change this."

"If you cannot change it, I will. I will take more and more of you until I have the power to bring him back."

"You are not three years old, Mary. You are not near death. Do not fight me."

"I am near death. My body is there and doesn't move, and if you think for one minute I can live with this mistake you are wrong."

She lunged for me and further disrupted the protective bubble of light we existed in. Pure tenacity and the hidden power she bore from her previous brush with death enabled her to take more than I could—or should—share.

She was never meant to capture so much of the essence the Creator gifted me.

"Mary, I cannot help you with anything if you do not stop your violence toward me. I will have to leave this place."

"If you cannot bring him back, I don't want you here."

"Let me help you understand. The Destroyer is strong—"

"But the Creator is stronger. Isn't that what you said? There were three of us on that mountain! Three against one. How did the Destroyer win?"

"There were choices, Mary."

"You mean *choice*. One choice. My choice to not listen to Jacob and Char and leave the slope."

"The Destroyer is tricky. We have lost a battle today. We have not lost the war."

"This is not a battle! This is a person. *My* person. *My* Protector." She wilted in my swirling embrace. "*My love.*"

"I know this is painful, Mary, but this is not the end for you. Jacob is well in this other realm. There may even be work he can do here. Take comfort in that."

"There is no comfort."

"I'm sorry Jacob is gone from your world, Mary."

"That means nothing to me! Don't you understand? What is the point of all this if we lose one of our own? Jacob is dead!"

"But you are alive, Mary."

Rage vibrated in her chest and rippled through our space.

"*But Jacob is dead!*" she screamed, and shook with such force she propelled herself out of the safety of my embrace and outside of my presence. As I reached for her, she burst through my calm atmosphere and straight through my being. She drew power from me as she split my energy field and pulled pieces of my being into her—just as she had as a child.

"Oh Mary…"

My pain for her loss was great and unbridled, but she could not hear me.

I had to leave her there.

CHAPTER 44

Mary

I awoke to the soft, mumbling voices of my parents.

My mother rushed to my side. "Thank God. She's awake. Get the doctor."

Everything ached.

I blinked a few times.

Jacob.

Char. Gavin. Jacob.

My body jerked. I couldn't focus. A scream lay buried in my throat and tried to claw its way to the surface.

Bright light filled my eyes as panic strangled me.

Jacob!

"Looks good," a white-coated guy said. "But we have to keep her calm."

Sebastian was there, but I could not rest in him. The scent of his presence wafted to my nose, but nothing eased what my mind already knew and my heart, body, mind, and soul couldn't handle.

I wasn't ready to wake up.

I didn't want to.

They tell me it was days.

Broken pelvis, internal injuries, lacerations…and more.

I heard things I didn't understand.

There's nothing neurologically wrong.

It takes time for the body to heal from this type of trauma.

No, her eye wasn't like that.

I can get an ophthalmological consult, but there's nothing to be concerned about.

She'll wake up when she's ready.

It was a terrible accident with severe injuries.

Wait. What?

"It wasn't an accident," I blurted, and tried to sit up. "Not an accident."

My parents darted to my bedside and hovered in my face. A wash of emotion flooded my eyes and caused sharp pain in my chest and legs. My dry mouth cracked with each word I tried to form.

"No accident."

My mother gently raised the bed and rubbed my arm and held my hand. Tears welled in her eyes. She pushed the call button.

"Jacob is dead," I said.

"Yes," she whispered.

"Char?"

"Banged up, but not as bad as you. She's been released."

"Gavin?"

"He's home, honey. He went home the morning of the accident."

"No, he didn't. Didn't Char tell you?"

My dad kissed my cheek and forehead and then fussed around to fluff pillows and move blankets. "You need to rest."

"No. I've been resting for… How long have I been resting?"

"Three days." My dad gave my mom a weird look. "The doctor said you should take your time."

"I don't want to take my time. Jacob is dead because Gavin tried to kill me."

"There she is," a nurse said as she bustled into the room and around the bed and checked plastic tubing. "Take it easy. First, the pain. Between one and ten, where are you?"

"Twelve, but who's counting? Don't knock me out again."

My mom smiled. "She has a high tolerance for pain, but let's keep it under control."

"I'll check with the doctor and then we'll talk about some water or a popsicle or a cracker."

I searched my dad's face. "I don't want food. Please tell me Gavin is locked up somewhere."

"The doctor said you need to take your time and let your mind process what you remember."

"Don't do this, Dad. I know what I'm saying. I need the truth. What has been happening? Didn't Char tell you?"

"I'll tell you what I know if you'll try and relax."

I attempted to move my legs without much success. "I'm so stiff."

"Stop moving. You need to wait for the nurse or the physical therapist. They're going to work with you."

"Gavin, Dad."

"All right. What do you remember?"

"Gavin knocked me off course and down a closed trail. He tried to hurt me. We went off the side in the fight." The pain of the memory jarred my head and heart as if I'd crashed into a wall of rough, snow-covered terrain all over again. "Jacob is dead." Terror rose in my chest.

"OK, OK, OK... Breathe."

"Stop," my mom said. "She needs to take her time."

"No! No time. I want to know what has happened."

My dad dropped the rail on the bed and slid as close as he could. "Listen, Mary. Char told the same story. She was in much better shape than you when she was rescued. She told us everything, even how she found you and Gavin at the vending machines." He paused. I knew my dad. He was trying not to explode. "But here's the thing. The investigators can't make the timeline fit. Gavin and Corey left with Erin's mom not long after you would have seen Gavin on the slope. Between the conditions and the lift's wait times, it's almost impossible to see how Gavin would have been on the slope with you and then in the van with Corey a short time later."

My world tilted and swirled in front of my eyes.

"Mary?"

"I'm all right."

"No one knows what to make of it, especially since Gavin was not easily identifiable in his gear. No witness can positively confirm who drove you off course."

"It was Gavin."

"We believe that. We just don't know how we can prove it."

"The way he moved... It was Gavin." My mind wandered to Jacob but refused to picture him on the ground with snow blowing around his powerful dying body. I pictured him the night on the deck. "The electrician. What about the electrician?"

"It wasn't the electrician," Mom said.

"I know. It was Gavin. But what about the electrician?"

She moved closer. "Arrested on his way back to Texas. He couldn't have possibly been on the slopes."

"I know. It was Gavin." Agitation twisted in my gut.

Gavin had tried to kill me. Gavin had tried to kill Char. Gavin had killed Jacob.

I fought back that same scream and squeezed the blanket in my fingers until my arm burned where the IV poked my vein. "Jacob. His parents. Where are they?"

"Jacob's parents chartered a plane and brought us all here together as soon as we heard of the accident. They've already taken Jacob's body back to Texas. I know they're in contact with the investigators, and they've hired their own private detective, but they're very private people, Mary. They're not saying much."

I took that information and plastered it behind a wall in my head. I simply could not imagine their faces, their grief, their agony. I bit back the sorrow and put another stone in the wall until I could deal with it.

"Are Deacon, Ivy, and Scout OK?"

My mother managed a pinched smile. "Yes. They refused to leave Colorado until you woke up. Scout's grandma and Deacon's mom came up and they're in a hotel nearby. Mr. Parrington stayed too." She couldn't hold her tears anymore and cried into her gray flannel shirt until my dad stuck tissues in her hand. "I'm just so glad you're alive."

Dad touched my cheek. "Your eyes are different."

"My eyes?" I felt for my arm. "Where's my bracelet?"

"Right here." Mom dug in her purse. "It's here, don't worry."

She secured it around my wrist and I held the angel-wing charm.

I closed my eyes. "I need to see my friends. *Now*, please."

CHAPTER 45

Deacon

I buried my head under the covers in the hotel room and answered Char's early-morning call.

I said hello and then we listened to each other breathe a while.

"Did you sleep?" she asked.

"Not really."

"Me either. I don't know if I'll ever sleep again."

"You get home OK?"

"Yeah. We had to stop on the way out one more time and talk to the police, but yeah. I'm home."

"How's the shoulder? And the knee?"

She sighed and things rustled. I imagined her as she stretched and tested her limbs.

"I'm sore, and this sling is getting old, but I'll be fine. I see the ortho tomorrow to be sure. How are things there?"

"Still waiting to see Mary. Everyone says there's no reason

she's not awake, then they turn around and say her body is processing the trauma and she should rest and will wake up when she's ready."

"Sorry, Deacon. I hoped by this morning you'd know more."

"They said they might let us try and talk to her today if nothing new happens."

"That's good. She'll wake up for you guys."

"Why, Char? Why would she wake up to remember Jacob is gone?"

"I'm sorry. It's my fault."

"No. We've been over this. If anything, it's my fault. If I hadn't gotten myself hurt on another assignment, I would have been there to help you with yours."

"But if you hadn't given everything you had on the day of the fire, many lives would have been lost."

"Why do *any* lives have to be lost? No matter how we look at this, it's a tragic circle. Someone is dead. Our existence as Warriors means nothing."

"I know how you feel now, but all I can say is, I've been doing this a lot longer than you, and sometimes things go wrong. Sometimes the Destroyer gets the edge. We can't save them all."

"Do you hear yourself right now? *We can't save them all?* Screw it. I'm out. Why would I do this if I can't make a difference?"

"Wait, Deacon, I didn't mean to sound so cold about it. I'm only trying to say there's only so much we can do. Everyone has to use their abilities and work together. And the reason you have to do it is because you're the one the Creator called to do it. No one else can do your work."

"What good is work that doesn't work?"

"But that's the thing. It usually does work. This was just one of the very few times it didn't." Her voice thickened and she sniffed. "It should have worked. I had it... I don't know what else to say…"

"Well thank you for not saying Mary should have listened to her Protector, at least. My friend is injured and won't wake up. Kicking her when she's down does not help me."

"Oh Deacon, I promise I have no bad feelings toward Mary. I'm only in pain for all of us, and I'm concerned about Gavin still being out there."

"Whatever." The tone of my own voice irritated me. "Look, I'm not trying to be mean either. I'm tired and I'm upset."

"I know. I'll let you try to get back to sleep. It's still early."

"No point in that, but you can answer one question."

"Anything."

"When you walked up to me that first day, was it because you already knew something was going down? Were we already your assignment? And, if so, why didn't you warn us? We would have listened."

"No. I walked up to you because I was interested. I've never done that before—just walk up to a total stranger and ask for a phone and force my number into it. Sheesh. I can't believe I did that."

"I couldn't believe it either."

"I told you I didn't even suspect the threat until after the vending machine incident. Then it became clear that next day when we were headed back to the lodge."

"And you didn't tell me you were headed to a fight."

"It wasn't your fight, Deacon. It was my assignment."

"My friend, my fight."

Tension mounted across the line. As much as I wanted to go back to the epic two days we had together, I knew it wasn't going to happen.

Maybe if she wasn't in Arkansas.

More likely never after what had happened.

"All right, Arkansas. Thanks for answering my question," I said. "I'll keep you posted on Mary."

"And I'll let you know what I hear about the investigation, Texas."

We listened to each other breathe again.

"Hey, Deacon, we both know who's really responsible for Jacob."

"Yeah. And we're gonna get him."

Scout's voice interrupted a nightmare.

I didn't know whether to be upset about the dream, grateful for the sleep—even though it was restless—or aggravated it was already over.

"Sorry," he said. "I know you haven't slept much, but there's news."

"I fell back asleep after talking to Char."

"Mary's awake. We need to get downstairs for breakfast and then we're all going to the hospital. I'm jumping in the shower."

In less than ninety minutes we were on our way. My legs felt like tree trunks as we walked toward her room. Hospital smells crept up my nose and choked me. Everyone smiled and tried to be nice, but all I saw was a sea of scrubs and sick people. I wanted my friend to run toward me down the hall.

I wanted to hear Jacob wasn't dead and that he was somewhere nearby in a bed and about to wake up any minute.

"Deacon? You OK?"

If Ivy was asking, I must have looked pretty messed up. I put my arm around her. "Yeah. Just need to see Mary."

"Me too." She stopped and slumped against the wall near a waiting area.

My mom and Scout's grandma went ahead. "We'll check it out," my mom said. "Take your time. We're going to see if we can get Mary's parents to get some food or something. They haven't left her side for days, but they might now since you're here to stay with her a while. I understand she's doing well."

I nodded.

Ivy didn't budge from the wall. "I don't know if I can do this. Her Protector is dead. His parents are somewhere reeling with grief." She clutched at her heart as if the pain were truly hers. "I can't imagine."

Poor Ivy. She took everything on herself like a heavy quilt of other people's patchwork pain. She wore it until she collapsed under the load. My mom had said she and Scout's grandma took turns sitting with her and holding her in the hotel room as she cried for seven hours straight.

"Ivy, I know this is hard, but Mary needs us."

She slashed a tear from under her eye. "I know."

Scout stepped to her side and didn't say a word. He just moved a chunk of wet hair from her cheek.

"I should have known about this," she said. "But I heard nothing. I saw a freakin' black cloud before a fire, but I got nothing to prevent *this* from happening? Was I not listening? Did I ignore something?"

"Not possible," Scout said. "Your intuition is spot-on. If you didn't know, you weren't meant to."

"Then what is the point of all this Warrior crap?"

"I've been asking myself the same thing," I said. "Char and I talked this morning, and she tries to make sense of it, but there's no making sense of this. She's done this a long time and she says sometimes we don't win the battle."

Scout scoffed. "In other words, we can't win em' all."

"Yeah, but I know she's not cold or unsympathetic, and she's kinda right. We didn't win. We also didn't help anyone here."

"We can still help Mary," Scout said. "You guys know I understand being the one left behind. She needs our support."

"Of course we're going to support her," Ivy said. "It's the

whole reason we have to support her that's the problem. How did this happen? We're the good guys, and Gavin is a murderer. An actual *murderer*, and no one can prove it. Our classmate caused another classmate's death. What do we do with that?"

"You wait. You watch. You listen." Mr. Parrington stepped around the wall that separated the coffee machine from bathrooms—and us. "You do your job... *Warriors*."

My mouth dried up like a thousand cotton balls were stuffed inside. "Mr. P... You heard everything."

Scout's shoulders sagged as he stuffed his hands in his pockets. "But you already knew everything."

"Yes."

Ivy launched from the wall and slammed into his chest with both fists. "Then why didn't you do something?" she screamed.

Mr. Parrington wrapped her in his arms as she wept. Scout peeled her away, and together, they put her in a chair.

People who'd paused to stare chalked it up to a dying patient and returned to their own problems.

"Listen carefully," Mr. Parrington said and crouched in front of Ivy.

We all gathered around.

"I did not know this was going to happen. I am not a Warrior. I don't have gifts like yours. Not even close. But I do work for the Creator, and I became aware very quickly that you four had been brought together at Stonehaven Academy for a reason. I believe that reason is to support Mary. She carries strong abilities that are important—and will be—far into the future."

"And yet, she almost died," Ivy snapped. "On our watch."

"Hear what I'm saying. The Creator loves you and will sustain you in this time of grief."

"I don't feel very sustained," Ivy said. "Our help didn't show up. And where is this great Creator we work for? Why can't we see him or her and ask for ourselves what the heck is up? All we have is your word that some supreme being loves us. How is anything that happened here love?"

"I don't have all the answers, Ivy, but Mary will get well."

"And a murderer goes free," I said.

"No murderer really gets to be free," Mr. P said.

Ivy looked like she could jump straight up out of the chair. "Really? Is that some kind of religious or exi…exist…"

"Existential," Scout said and rubbed his temples.

"Yeah. That. Is that some kind of philosophical thing that's supposed to help us? *The murderer isn't really free…* Well, he is free. He's at home in his own bed getting a good night's sleep. And Jacob's parents are…"

She couldn't even finish in a puddle of new tears.

Mr. Parrington took the chair beside her as Scout grabbed a wad of napkins.

"All right," Mr. P said. "We can't do any more of this here. I'm going to say a couple more things and then I'm going to tell you all what to do, and you're going to have to trust me."

We didn't acknowledge him either way.

"There is a Creator and there is a Destroyer. In my personal life and belief, the Creator is like my God. He loves me and he chose me to help people like you guys get your work done. You are special and you have abilities. Now. Again, in my world, the Destroyer is an evil being. One can't exist without the other. For every good thing, there is a bad one, and there is always a choice. For whatever reason, you four have extraordinary and powerful gifts, and you get to use them on Earth and in a realm I can't begin to understand. Mary is exceptionally gifted—you all are—and you were brought together to form a team with her. The Destroyer would like nothing more than to stop Mary, and he won't give up."

"We. Lost. Jacob." Ivy emphasized every word with a painful punch.

"And you know what? Nothing like that will ever happen

again *because* you lost Jacob. This is a lesson for you. Char is right. Not everyone can be saved. Bad things are going to happen, but you guys need to keep going and I guarantee a murderer will not go free."

He stood. "I know this is hard, but you guys are going to go see your friend, and you're going to comfort each other and get through this tragedy. And then you're going to fight again because that's your job. You're the only ones who can do what the Creator called you to do." He turned to leave. "Go see your friend, and then we're going to get you home."

I stepped toward him. "You said you're not a Warrior."

"I'm not."

Ivy wiped her nose. "Are you a Protector like Jacob?"

"No. I'm a Guardian."

CHAPTER 46

Ivy

Guardian.

I stood in a haze and dried my eyes.

"Mr. Parrington is right. I have to stop all this bawling for my sake, and Mary's, and do my job."

Scout handed me a fresh napkin. "He didn't say not to cry. Grieve however you need to, Ivy."

"I will. But right now, I want to take care of Mary."

"We all do."

I headed down the hall with Scout and Deacon at my heels. "I think I get it now. Mr. Parrington being a Guardian makes sense. Trinity was a Guardian for me, remember? She had the big picture in mind. She stepped in when she needed to. She warned me and helped me, but she was able to fly under the radar in the realm—like between the two sides. Mr. Parrington does that. He watches everything and guards things. Like he runs interference for us."

"Yes," Scout said. "So, where a Protector seems to have a defending or shielding-type job for a specific person, a Guardian watches over all and looks for trouble. Like a watchman on a wall."

"Or an early-warning system," Deacon said.

I stopped at Mary's door. "And then there are Warriors. Like tough-as-nails Char, Mary, and Deacon."

Deacon shook his head as if he'd learned something new and it was too much. "And psychologically, emotionally, analytically, and logically gifted like you two. Honestly, how do you two contain the knowledge that constantly floats around in your brains? Especially you, Ivy, with all the visions and psychic stuff?"

I turned to him. "How do you bust down doors and heal people with your hands?"

"OK, I get it. Can we go in now?"

I pushed Mary's door open with a light tap. She sat up, but barely opened her eyes as she spoke. "I'm glad you all are here."

I rushed to her side. "Of course we're here. We came as soon as they'd let us." I tried to get close to her. "Umm... How can I hug you?"

She smiled. A little. "Here." She raised her arms and we all took turns.

And I wish I could say we were calm and strong... We weren't.

We all ugly-cried for a minute as we pulled chairs as close as we could. The guys tried to be cool about it, but everyone passed around the box of scratchy tissues before we could stop.

Mary just sat there and stared ahead. Her eyes looked so different. I thought maybe it was the light sneaking in from the partially-open blinds that played tricks on my mind. Or maybe it was the way a bandage covered something on her forehead and blocked the light and my view. I glanced at Deacon and Scout and we exchanged odd looks.

Before I could ask, she jerked and scratched one arm and then the other.

"Can I get you something?" I asked.

"No. It's the stupid pain medication. The itching is driving me crazy. I told them I didn't want anymore."

Deacon leaned forward. "How are you sitting up straight with a broken pelvis?"

"They made me move a lot this morning when they got me cleaned up. Later this afternoon I have my first full evaluation with the physical therapist. The break didn't require surgery, so it sounds like I'm supposed to be able to use crutches or a walker or something until it heals. I don't know."

Scout nodded. "And the internal injuries?"

"More CT scans and ultrasounds tomorrow to check on everything."

She rearranged her IV tube and used the bedrail to pull herself into a slightly different position. She seemed agitated.

I tried to take her hand. "Mary, what can we do?"

"No one can do anything, Ivy. Jacob is dead and it's my fault."

"No, no, no. Gavin is the one who knocked you off the side of that slope."

"And that happened because I didn't do what I was supposed to do. I made it about me, and Jacob is dead."

"It was about you, Mary," Scout said. "You weren't supposed to die. It wasn't your time."

"It wasn't Jacob's either, but he's as dead as he'll ever be." A sharp gasp left her mouth. She had a white-knuckle grip on the rail.

Deacon tried to peel her fingers away and comfort her. "Take it easy."

She jerked her hand away. "I cannot take it easy. Don't you understand what happened? The Creator had a plan for all our safety. I got in the way."

"Gavin got in the way. The Destroyer did this."

"Everyone has a choice, Deacon. My choice killed Jacob."

"You did not deliberately choose for Jacob to get hurt."

"I might as well have."

"Stop." Scout left his chair and watched the monitor as if he understood all its information. "Breathe," he said and touched her back.

My heart fluttered at both the intense sadness and comfort in his gesture.

Tears welled in Mary's very different eyes and splashed on her chest.

"Tell me about Sebastian," he said. "Didn't he show up? He promised he'd show up."

Mary let out a long, uncomfortable-looking breath. "He came too late."

"Were you conscious? Were you able to talk?"

"He was there after Jacob died. He claimed there was nothing he could do at that time."

"I don't understand," Scout said. "We had no idea what was about to happen. No warning like we got for the fire."

"I told you," Mary said. "The Creator had a plan for our safety. I messed it up." She gasped again. "I fought with Sebastian in the aftermath. I screamed at him and demanded he bring Jacob back. I asked him why he didn't warn us. He said there was no reason to warn us because everything was under control. Everyone was there to do their part. It was me who busted up the plan. I didn't listen to Char and Jacob."

"Wait," Scout said. "Sebastian said it was you who did something wrong?"

"No, but it's the truth."

"I get what you're saying," Deacon said. "But if the Creator is our good force and the Destroyer is the bad force, Jacob's death could still be an accident, right? The dark side was after you. It didn't get you. Char said Gavin charged the three of you on the mountain. He made choices too. Gavin is the one who pushed Jacob over the side."

"But no one can prove it," I said.

"You're splitting hairs," Mary said. "The whole thing ended the way it did because Gavin is an Agent for the Destroyer. He was going to kill someone that day. If it wasn't me, he did the only thing that would hurt me worse. He took Jacob from me."

Scout shuffled back to his chair. "Can we give this a rest a minute? We're giving our enemy way too much credit. You're still alive, Mary. You're going to fight again as a Warrior. Gavin will not get by with this."

Mary got super quiet.

"OK, I'm just going to get this out there," I said after a few long moments. "Mary, have you seen your eyes? What's going on there?"

"I don't know what you're talking about."

"Really? Your parents haven't talked about this?"

"What?"

I carefully sat on the edge of the bed and studied her face. "Mary. As long as I've known you, you've had green eyes. Like really pretty little emeralds."

"And?"

"Now you have a green eye. Like one eye is green. Your parents really haven't talked to you about this change?"

Deacon got closer. "And you haven't seen yourself in the mirror?"

"No, Deac, I can't walk. There are tubes everywhere—and I mean everywhere—and I haven't been allowed out of the bed. I brushed my teeth this morning and spit in a plastic cup..." She paused and took a breath. "Wait a minute. I do remember hearing people talk, and my mom was kinda protective of her compact this morning." She smacked the bed. "I need a mirror."

I pulled a vintage lipstick holder out of my bag and flipped up the little rectangular mirror.

She paled. She blinked. She tried to speak, and nothing came out.

Deacon looked to Scout. "Dude. Does she need a doctor?"

"No, she's just taking it in."

"I don't understand," she whispered. "Where did my other green eye go? Why is it blue? And it's like really blue. Not even blue-green. It's like Jacob's dark, crystal-blue color. Like the sky met a blueberry." She dropped the mirror. "Look this up, Scout. What happened to me?"

"I can look, but I don't know. Heterochromia—two different colored eyes—usually doesn't happen when you're almost grown or later in life. It's something you're born with."

"That's what the talk was about," she said. "My parents were asking if something was wrong. Everyone thought it was just the way I was. I remember my parents asking someone... They didn't want me to see this yet. They were worried about how I'd react."

"But they didn't tell us not to say anything," Deacon said. "We didn't even see them when they left with my mom and Scout's grandma."

Scout scrolled through his phone. "I don't know. There's no immediate discussion coming up about it. I don't think it's a medical trauma thing."

"What else would it be?"

Ivy moved her bag. "What exactly happened up there when you met Sebastian? If it's not medical, maybe it's supernatural."

"I don't follow."

"You're already part angel, Mary, remember? It doesn't show. At least it *didn't* show."

"But why this eye color like Jacob's? To torture me? To punish me? Why not orange hair or an extra toe or a brown eye or something?"

"In time it may comfort you," Scout offered. "And she's right. You were fighting for your life again. Jacob and Char's too. Do you recall if it was like before when you were little? Was Shanar there?"

"Shanar didn't even bother to show up. The damage was already done. Sebastian came to comfort me. I fought with him."

Deacon grimaced. "You fought with your own guardian angel?" Then he realized how that sounded. "I'm sorry. Ignore me. I don't know what I'm saying. You have enough on your mind."

Mary dropped her head into her hands. "I did fight with my own guardian angel. I was so angry. He said he couldn't bring Jacob back. I lost my mind." She looked up again. "I was so out of control I think he had to leave me. I chased him away when I needed him most. Not only that, I tried to take power from him so I could help Jacob."

Nobody knew what to do with that confession.

Scout finally shrugged. "Well, you are a Warrior. You have supernatural gifts. I imagine that power under such distress and duress would cause you to lose control. You don't know what all you're capable of."

"I wasn't capable of saving Jacob."

"Oh Mary." I tried to hold her. "We're still only human—even when we're working with supernatural forces."

"Powers, forces, abilities, gifts…supernatural. I'm so sick of all those words. I didn't ask for this, and now Jacob's dead because of it."

"No," Deacon said. "Jacob is dead because the Destroyer is evil."

"What's the difference? He's still gone. And the word *supernatural* doesn't ease the pain. It's not the fairytale word it sounds like. Death is death. Final is final. There's nothing glorifying in an untimely death. There's no comfort in it. Do you think his title of Protector for the Creator does his parents any good now? They don't even know, and they never will because he wasn't brought up to serve a Creator. He was introduced to the

Creator's world through adversity—just like us. He survived and earned the job and died because of it."

Scout studied the monitor again. "Breathe." He scooted his chair closer. "Listen, Mary, I totally hear you. We all hear you. But you can't give up. You have important abilities, and yes, untimely deaths make no sense. Believe me, I know. You have to remember Jacob embraced his role as Protector and he fulfilled his purpose, even though he didn't last on this earth. You have to heal and grieve. And then you have to fight for all the others who are going to need you."

Her brilliant blue and green eyes glittered with tears. "I'm going to fight, all right. I'm going to do everything I was called to do in honor of Jacob. I refuse to allow his death to be associated with failure."

Scout nodded. "Right. That's good. And we'll be right there with you."

"But first." She caught her breath on an obvious stab of pain.

I offered her a sip of water from the stand by the bed. "But first?"

"First I'm going to kill Gavin."

CHAPTER 47

Ivy

Scout picked up my bag and put it in the back of the SUV.

I hated to see his shoulders slumped beneath the heavy pain of reliving his own grief journey as he took on the pain of losing Jacob—and the pain of everyone else feeling the loss.

"C'mon." I took his hand. "Let's get one more look before we go."

"What's there to look at? We're in a hotel parking lot."

"I know, but this is Colorado in the winter time. Between the mountains and the snow, you can always find a beautiful view somewhere."

I led him to the closed, snow-covered patio off the restaurant's side entrance. "See? Mountains and snow."

"Yes, it's beautiful, but I don't know if I can ever take another ski trip."

I shook my head. "Me either, but I want you to know something."

"What's that?"

"As bad as this is, I'm choosing to not let the worst of it overshadow the best of it."

"What was the best of it?"

I snuggled closer to him. "You and me on the skating rink in the snow…kissing and holding hands. I'm tucking that away in a memory snow globe to keep to myself. When I think of Jacob and this horrible tragedy, I'm also going to think of our special time together here. And I'm going to remind myself this is not our last memory together. We'll make more."

He turned to look at me. "Thank you."

"For what?"

"For reminding me there is something good here."

"There's always going to be something good when you and I stick together, Scout. I'm here for you."

"And I'm here for you."

"All right you two, get in the car." Deacon stomped around in the fresh snow on the deck. "And by the way, I'm here for you," he taunted. "Don't ever forget that."

"Good to know," Scout said.

Deacon slowed as he kicked slush across the lot. "I don't want to leave Mary behind."

"I know," I said. "Feels like we're going home without all our stuff or something. I don't want us alone in Texas facing all the questions and the memorial or whatever, and I don't want her here without us."

Scout opened the door for me. "The longer she stays away, the harder it's going to be to face everything at home."

I knew that was true, and everything about her that seemed so normal was outweighed by the burden of her grief, her strange new eye color, her pain level, and her staggering comment about Gavin.

I blamed the meds and hoped the best for her.

"And what are we supposed to do about Gavin?" I asked. "We're bound to see him. We have to go back to school."

Deacon's clenched teeth caused his jaw to tighten before my eyes. "If he has any decency at all, he won't come back to school."

"He's too arrogant to go somewhere else," Scout said. "Besides, we're the only ones who really believe he killed Jacob. Everyone else seems ready to let that go."

"There isn't enough evidence to make it stick." Deacon tossed me my blanket. "We need sleep. Maybe we can just sleep on the road and deal with it all when we're home and rested."

But five hours later, after a pit stop and a couple of hours of sleep, I was jarred into another dip in the roller coaster that had become our trip.

Scout's grandma and Deacon's mom carried on a rapid-fire discussion as Scout and Deacon studied their phones.

Scout shook me awake and pulled my phone out of the seat-back pocket. "Here. Find one of the local Houston news stations. We're looking for a live feed."

"A live feed of what?"

"Stonehaven Academy has gone up in flames."

I said my thank-yous to Scout's grandma in front of my apartment building and hooked my backpack over my shoulder.

Scout picked up my bag. "I'll walk you to the door."

"No," I said. "It's late. I texted my mom. She's watching for me, and I'm fine behind the gate and with all the lights. We've been over this."

"Which is exactly why you know I'm going to walk you to your door. What kind of guy do you think I am?"

"The good kind."

A door opened along the path. "Ivy! I didn't know you were coming home tonight."

"Hey, Mrs. Terrell."

Her dog, Tootsie, pulled her forward on the patio. "Umm... Do you think...?"

I took the dog's leash. "Sure. We'll take a little walk to my apartment and unload, then I'll bring her back after she's visited the tree."

"You're such a dear."

Scout rolled his eyes. "Really?"

"I have clients now, Scout. They've missed me." The tubby sheltie pulled me along. "You should go. Your grandma is tired too. It's been a long drive, and Tootsie here has an attitude like you wouldn't believe. She growled at an extra-large magnolia blossom once. She's not going to let anyone bother me. Really. I have protection. Get your grandma home."

He glanced at my apartment door two stories up and then at the well-lit area where other late-night walkers let their pets take care of business. "All right, but I'm going to run your bags up."

"Deal."

He kissed me on the cheek. "Get that dog to its tree and get some rest."

"I will."

"Text me when you get in."

"I will. Now go, and tomorrow we'll go by the school and see what we can find out."

"Are you sure—?"

"Me and Tootsie are walking away now."

I headed for the patch of grass as he ran upstairs with my bags and then came down and walked backward away from the building to keep an eye on me. It was the only thing that had truly made me smile for days.

He waved and almost tripped.

"C'mon, Tootsie. Get the job done."

I walked her back to Mrs. Terrell's patio and knocked on the glass doors.

"Thanks, sweetie. Put it on my tab."

"This one's on me," I said. "She was fast and it wasn't a real walk."

I dragged my tired self up the first flight of stairs and paused at the top when I heard something behind me. The hard steel rail and concrete steps didn't typically budge, so what was all the sound?

In the middle of the second set, someone spoke.

"Ivy, wait."

I didn't recognize the male voice.

I grabbed my phone and prepared to bolt.

"I'm not going to hurt you. I only want to talk."

I took the next steps two at a time on shaky legs and tried to put distance between us.

A light flashed behind me. "Please stop and listen, Ivy Lynette Van Camp. I won't come any closer. Just stop and listen. Here. I'll put the light on my face, and I'm stepping backward."

No one knew my middle name. No one. My mother didn't ever mention it. She called me *Ivy L* and said we could have it changed to just an initial if I wanted.

Why would she offer that?

I didn't hear another step, and couldn't stop the beat of curiosity in my thumping heart. I put my thumbs on 911. "You have thirty seconds. Explain yourself. I'll call the police."

"Don't bother. They've already arrested me once, and they had to let me go because I haven't done anything."

His phone light shone on his face.

"You're the electrician who caused the gym fire and ran from me in Colorado." I stumbled upward and tried to hit the buttons, but even I calmed down when I realized he was nowhere near me and didn't appear to be trying to gain ground.

283

"I didn't cause the gym fire," he called up the stairs.

My gut did a flip. The way he dropped his gaze warned me that was probably a lie.

"I'm not even an electrician," he continued. "I mean, I was, I'm certified, but that's not my job. Not now. And I ran for a reason in Colorado."

"Stonehaven Academy is on fire. Did you do that too?"

He looked straight at me. "What? No! Please. I only want to tell you something and then I'll go."

Rays of light bounced off his phone and mine as we maneuvered to see each other in the dim stairwell. The dogwalkers wandered by beneath us, and I felt no immediate threat from the stranger on the steps.

That in itself should have scared me more.

I didn't get any closer, but didn't continue to run either.

"Say what you need to say and go away. My mother will be looking for me, and I'm calling 911."

"I'm not who or what villain you think I am, Ivy. That scoreboard fire looks like an electrical malfunction, and I sure haven't tried to burn down your whole school. I didn't even know about that."

"How could you miss it?"

"I told you, the authorities just let me go." He looked genuinely distraught through the bars of the rail below me. "Ivy Lynette Van Camp," he called out. "Lynette is your grandmother's name, by the way. That's why it's your middle name."

"How would you know that?"

Especially when I didn't even know that.

"You were born December seventh at two-thirty-eight in the morning," he continued. "And you are my daughter."

WANT MORE WARRIOR SAINTS?

Will Mary, Deacon, Scout, & Ivy survive the ultimate battle between good and evil?
CLICK HERE
Warrior Saints - Victor:
Stonehaven Academy Saints Book 3

WANT MORE WARRIOR SAINTS?

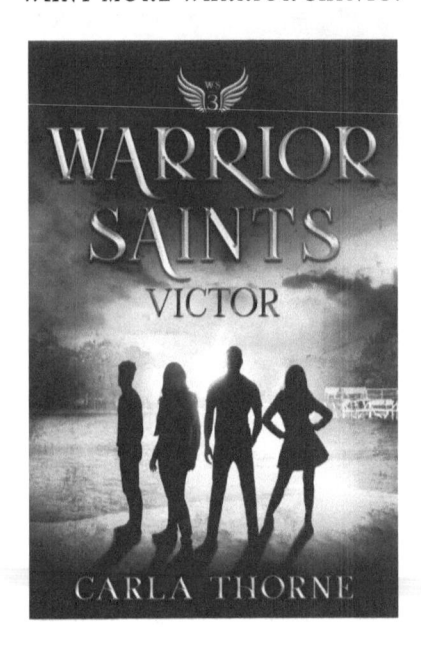

ABOUT THE AUTHOR

Carla Thorne has been writing YA fiction since 2013. She is a multi-published, award-winning author as well as an editor, cancer survivor, life-long musician, speaker, and writing teacher.

Sign up for Carla Thorne's newsletter for the latest news, giveaways, and special offers.

For sweet contemporary romance and inspirational romance, visit carlarossi.com

Connect with Carla
https://www.carlathorne.com

Made in United States
Troutdale, OR
06/10/2025